# CONTENTS

# JILLIAN HART

## Countdown to First Night

HARLEQUIN®

entertain, enrich, inspire™

ISBN-13: 978-0-373-83779-3

COUNTDOWN TO FIRST NIGHT

Copyright © 2013 by Harlequin Books S.A.

The publisher acknowledges the copyright holders of the individual works as follows:

WINTER'S HEART
Copyright © 2013 by Jill Strickler

SNOWBOUND AT NEW YEAR
Copyright © 2013 by Margaret Daley

A KISS AT MIDNIGHT
Copyright © 2013 by Brenda Minton

Recycling programs for this product may not exist in your area.

www.Harlequin.com

**Printed in U.S.A.**

# CHAPTER ONE

THE OLD CHEVY GAVE a cough as it idled at the intersection of Second and Cascade avenues. Which way did she go? Shelby squinted at the signpost barely visible in the night. Cascade Avenue? Huh. No idea where that was.

She'd been absolutely sure that the moment she rolled into Snow Falls everything would come back to her. Memories of summers walking along Main Street slurping a dripping chocolate ice-cream cone. Pedaling rattling bikes from one end of town to the other with the sun hot on her back. Once, she'd known every street like the back of her hand.

Sure, twenty years ago. It may as well have been a century. She was no longer that carefree girl. The heater puffed lukewarm air over her face—*please, don't let the heater conk out next,* she thought and tightened her hands on the steering wheel. A lot had changed in twenty years. The Bavarian-styled town was bigger these days, spruced up with cheerful awnings and carefully designed storefronts. Designer street signs marked every corner and old-fashioned street lamps spilled light onto sidewalks. Sidewalks. What had once been a humble little mountain stop was now a ski-resort town drawing from nearby Denver. Snazzy.

*Not like me,* she thought, hitting her right-turn signal. *As they say, it wasn't the years but the mileage that got you.*

"Mama?" Caleb sounded groggy, more asleep than awake in the backseat.

"Yes, baby?" She glanced in the mirror to check on him—a big yawn, fists rubbing his eyes, half sitting up—and her heart lurched with a mother's love. When did her boy get so big? At eight years old, she'd better stop calling him baby soon. But not just yet.

"Are we there?" he asked.

"No. Go on back to sleep and I'll wake you when we're at Granny's." She tried to banish the worry from her voice. "You lie back down before you wake Riley. Tell me what you were dreamin' about."

"I had a horse that was a cloud and I was ridin' him and I was flyin'." Sleepy, those words.

"Bet you were sailin' fast through the sky."

"Yes, ma'am." Sleepier.

"Could you reach up and touch all the stars?"

No answer. He'd gone back to sleep, back to his dreams of wonder and light.

While she was lost in the dark. She shivered. The temperature was dropping, so she nudged the heater to high and hoped it would oblige. *Hold together, car,* she willed, and shifted into First. The drive up from Texas had taken a lot of oomph out of the handed-down Chevy, so she checked her rearview—the road was empty behind her—before giving it a little gas.

She'd learned to ignore the sputtering engine and the cough as the four-door sedan lurched forward, but the backfire was new. *That* couldn't be a good sign. If she'd had more than three figures in her checking account,

# WINTER'S HEART

## Jillian Hart

she'd steer right into that gas station on the corner first thing tomorrow morning. As it was, she'd have to put the repairs off. Again.

Funny, she absolutely did not recognize where she was. Wait—that Colonial set back from the sidewalk looked familiar, a stately old house that was now a bed-and-breakfast. Okay, that meant she was headed in the right direction. Except what was that thunking sound? She turned down the heater to get a better listen. No, it wasn't a *thunk,* more like a *whap-whap.* Okay, now that she thought about it, the car was listing to the right.

She hit the brakes, which squealed slightly as she came to a stop. "Daisy, what am I gonna do with you? We're seven blocks away. Don't let me down now."

The idling engine misfired as if in answer. Shelby rested her forehead against the top edge of the steering wheel. Okay, fine, so it wasn't the engine that was the biggest problem here, it was the—

Knuckles rapped on her window. She would have jumped three feet, but her shoulder belt seized up, strapping her to the seat. Heart knocking, she peered up at the tall, uniformed man looming out of the night. A badge glinted on his chest, thanks to a not-too-distant street lamp and the ambient light from his flashlight.

Great. A cop. Just what she needed. She didn't want to roll down her window, but she did. "I can explain about the—"

"License and registration," he interrupted her with a low bark, perhaps aware of the sleeping children. Dark eyes, chiseled high cheekbones and a granite jaw gave him an intimidating appearance. And by the hard slash of his mouth, it looked as if he never smiled.

"Yes, sir." She kept her voice to a whisper, hoping Caleb and Riley would stay asleep. She rummaged through her purse. "I put that license somewhere. Oh, here it is. Are you having a nice evening, Officer?"

"Other than freezing my toes off?" His tone had a bite to it. He took the paperwork from her and shone his flashlight over her license. Reading all about her— Shelby Craig. Newton, Texas. Five foot four, one hundred and five pounds. Twenty-nine years old. Probably wondering what she was doing so far from home. He arched one brow as he studied her registration. "Why haven't you renewed your tabs?"

Good question. One she didn't want to answer, but the truth was always best. "At the time, I had to choose between food for my little ones or buying a sticker for my license plate."

Sure, she was ashamed, but this mess she'd gotten herself into was only temporary, so she looked him straight in the eye. Nice eyes, too. It was too dark to see their color, but they made him seem wise and soulful. And they had pleasant crinkles at the corners. Not even the shadows could hide the cut of his cheekbones or the straight blade of his nose. That strong jaw lent him a sort of honor and integrity. A handsome man, he looked like a good guy. She knew he was just doing his job.

Was it her imagination, or was there something vaguely familiar about him? She blew out a sigh. "How much is the ticket?"

"Expensive. Very expensive." His gaze cut to the back of the car at the sleeping children. A muscle ticked along his square jaw. "More than it's worth. Are you here visiting family?"

"Yes, and no. My granny lives here, so I'm staying with her for a short spell, but mostly I've come for a job. Then I can afford your ticket."

"You're a single mother?" He arched one eyebrow.

"Since my husband died on a routine patrol. Drunk driver. He was a cop, too."

"I'm sorry to hear that, ma'am." Compassion softened his hard tone. "I'm Deputy Winters. You've come a long way for a job. I hear there isn't much available, mostly a few temporary positions with the city."

"Sure, for the First Night celebration, but I'm not after those. I already have a job lined up, although it's temporary, too."

"Temporary?"

"Hey, it's better than a poke in the eye." She grinned up at him with determined cheer, and that said something about her.

"You're right. I've had a poke in the eye. Can't say I recommend it."

"Exactly." She was a beautiful woman. Long blond hair, wide blue eyes and a smile that made it hard to notice the strain in her expression. Exhaustion bruised the delicate skin beneath her eyes.

It wasn't hard to put the pieces together. Ronan spotted the jar of peanut butter and loaf of bread in a small sack of groceries on the floor, the boxes and suitcases and the little kids covered with homemade afghans. The family might not be living out of their car, but it was a near thing.

"Okay, so I *think* I know where I'm going." She peered up at him, ensnaring him with her earnestness. Something caught in his chest. He forgot about the frigid north wind battering the back of his neck. She swept her hair away from her cheek. "Since I've got you, Deputy, I'd better ask directions so I'm not wandering the streets this time of night. I'm looking for Snowy Peak Lane."

"You're almost there. Take a right at the end of this street. One block over." Awareness of her cut through him like the winter cold. It's as if he knew her somehow, or someone like her a long time ago.

"I have a problem with directions," she went on breezily. "My husband used to say, 'Shelby, you are sorely navigationally impaired.'"

"How long has he been gone?"

"Since before my youngest was born. Almost seven years now."

He did the math. She would have been twenty-two when she lost her husband. He handed over her license and registration. Normally he'd at least run a check on an out-of-date license, it was policy, but he knew trouble when he saw it. Trouble was not Shelby Craig.

"Thank you, Deputy Winters." Her chin went up. She was pretty in a delicate way, just a bit of a thing. "Thanks for letting me off."

"No problem." It wasn't why he'd stopped. "You have a flat."

"Tire?" She blew out a sigh. "Yep, I was afraid of that. How flat is it?"

"Flat enough you shouldn't be driving, not even a few blocks." He swiped a snowflake off his cheek. A few stray flakes were coming down from the ever-darkening sky. "Pop the trunk. I'll change it for you."

"If only it were that easy." Her forehead drew up

into little furrows. "There's a big problem. My trunk is full of boxes."

"Let me guess. The jack and spare are *beneath* the boxes?"

"Of course. You can't go to all that trouble."

"Watch me, Shelby Craig." Then it hit him like a brick. Shelby *Danners*. The memory popped into his brain of a girl with blond hair in a ponytail, honest blue eyes and a singsong laugh. He remembered how she'd pedaled away from him on her hand-me-down bike, the chain rattling as she rode off the curb and into the street, taking his ten-year-old heart with him.

He stepped away from her window. "You stay here where it's warm. Sit tight, and I'll get you fixed up in no time."

"Deputy Winters, you are the best thing that's happened to me all day."

"Sorry to hear that, ma'am. If my changing your tire is the best thing, I hate to think what was the worst."

"Let's just say things are looking up."

Her smile of thanks lit up her whole heart-shaped face. She'd grown into a beauty, but he could see the traces of the girl he'd known. Same indomitable pluck. Same tug on his heart.

Funny, nothing had touched him there in a long time. He was a different man these days, since his last tour. He passed the sleeping children, catching a glimpse of a dark-haired boy and a blonde girl.

He carefully opened the trunk. Boy, she hadn't been kidding. He eyed the boxes, blew out a sigh and got to work unloading. It didn't take long, as she didn't have much. Boxes labeled Clothing, necessary items like bedding and towels and another of toys. That was it. He couldn't help wondering what her life had been like. If she had recognized him yet.

He got down to the uncomfortable task of changing the rear tire. He jacked up the car and stretched out in the snow. Cold seeped through his jacket and trousers. Well, it wasn't the first tire he'd changed on a winter night. Although he *was* missing the warmth of the station and a fresh cup of coffee about now.

"Mama?" The tiny voice sounded muffled inside the car, not far from his right ear as he wrestled the tire off the axel. Sounded as if the little girl was awake. "Mama?"

"I'm right here, honeybee." Shelby's voice was everything a mother's tone should be—gentle, soothing, loving. "Did you have any good dreams?"

"Uh-huh. Where are we? I don't like the dark."

"Okay, then, why don't you climb up here with me. Don't wake Caleb, now."

"I'm bringin' Chewy, too."

"There's just enough room for all three of us in this seat." Shelby's dulcet Texas twang could probably tempt just about any man into feelings for her. But not him.

As he fit the spare in place and tightened the lug nuts, the ratchet drowned out the rise and fall of Shelby's voice, much to his relief.

He repacked the trunk, wiped the falling snow off his face and circled around to her. She must have seen him coming because her window rolled down when he came into range. A little girl sat snuggled on her lap, her face buried in her mama's shoulder.

"I don't know how to thank you, Deputy. You must

be frozen clean through." She blinked her long lashes. Hard to miss her concern. Concern for him.

A steel band tightened around his chest. "Don't worry. I'm tough."

"Yes, you men always are. I know." She rolled her eyes, and recognition flared through him again. Little Shelby Danners. She tilted her head to one side, peering up at him through the window frame. "Thank you for everything."

"All part of the job." He thought of the years between them, the different paths their lives had taken. The innocence of youth felt a world away, and yet the night didn't seem as dark as she smiled up at him.

"Sure, part of the job. But be warned, I'll get back at you for this. When you least expect it."

"You owe me nothing." He added, "For old time's sake."

"Old times?" Her forehead crinkled, her rosebud mouth puckered up as she thought. "What does that mean? Hey, do I know you?"

"Sorry, that's classified information, ma'am." Boy, he thought, did those big baby blues of hers reach into a guy. He'd never felt anything as powerful since the navy SEALs broke into his makeshift prison and rescued him. He tipped his hat and stepped back into the darkness. "You have a good night, now."

"But, wait, I—"

"Remember, go right, one block over." He backed off, boots crunching in the snow. "Your grandma's house is on the corner." He tossed her a smile and opened his car door. He didn't smile often and it felt good. Very good. "See you around, Shelby."

He kept an eye on his rearview, making sure she pulled away from the curb all right. Just to be sure, he made a pass through the neighborhood an hour later. Her bright yellow four-door sat parked and dark in Mrs. Danners's driveway.

At least one of them had found their way home.

## CHAPTER TWO

"CALEB IS OUT LIKE A LIGHT." Shelby eased the bedroom door closed in the narrow hallway, wincing when the floor squeaked under her weight. "Riley finally went down, but she may be up later to climb into bed with me."

"That's why I put you right here." Her grandmother opened the door across the hall and flipped on the light. "Your old room."

"It looks the same." Like stepping back in time. The drawn, ruffled yellow curtains had been here when Shelby was a child, matching the quilted bedspread on the four-poster bed.

"I didn't have the heart to change anything." Georgia Danners patted at her curlers, pink against her silver hair. "Those summers having you here were some of my best. Besides, no one's needed this room until now. So glad to have you here, honey, for however long you want to stay."

"You have no idea what that means to me." Her granny had buried a husband over twenty years ago and her only child was Shelby's dad. She ran a hand over the carving on the bedpost. "Being here is a sanctuary. We had nowhere else to go. Just when I thought

I would have to lower my pride and accept assistance, you stepped in."

"Oh, I didn't do much." Georgia knelt to click the electric-blanket control on high. "I made a call or two. You're the one came all this way and brought those two beautiful children with you. My great-grandchildren. I haven't seen them since my trip down in July. They've gotten big."

"Bigger every day. I swear those two grow like weeds." And she wanted them to grow up happy. That's all she wanted. Times had got tough, but her father raised her to take the good with the bad and when the bad hit, to battle it down. "Just so we're clear, Granny. I owe you, big-time. Where would I be right now if it wasn't for you?"

"Not in Colorado, that's for sure." Georgia plumped a pillow, ducking to hide what looked like a tear in her eye. "Now, settle in, get comfortable. I sure hope you'll be staying awhile. I want lots of time to spend with my great-grandkids."

"That would be nice." It must get lonely rattling around alone in this big old house, living with memories of people long gone. "Stop, you don't need to turn down my bed. No fussing over me, got it?"

"Can't help myself, I guess."

She hugged her grandmother, thinking of the summers she'd spent here before her mother died and they'd moved from Denver to Houston. "Every memory I have in this house is a good one. Being here with you feels like a turn in the road, Granny. Like my luck just has to change."

"I know it, sweet pea." Georgia pinched her cheek

gently. "Now, let me fix some tea. You must be wound up after that long drive. A cup of chamomile will be just the thing to help you relax and fall asleep."

"Sounds good."

"Holler if you need anything."

Life was a cycle of good times and bad. Shelby had to believe better times were coming.

She set her cell phone on the nightstand so she'd remember to charge it. It was six years old and the battery was on its last leg. The framed photo next to the clock radio caught her attention. Her picture.

She recognized herself as that nine-year-old. Blond pigtails trailed over her skinny shoulders, her nose and cheeks had freckled from the sun. She straddled that old red bike Granny kept in the garage. Two other kids near the same age grinned with her at the camera. Talia from down the street and the boy who'd lived next door with his grandmother.

She remembered that boy. She studied his dark blue eyes. His dark shock of hair sure looked familiar. She took a closer look.

It couldn't be. What were the chances? Pulling herself away from the photo, she padded quietly past the closed bedroom door where her kids slept. That handsome deputy and his rumbling, smoky voice. She should have recognized his smile. Who would have thought he'd still be living in this small mountain town, the first boy who'd ever stolen her heart?

"Shelby, I'm just puttin' on the kettle now," Georgia called down the hallway from the kitchen. "Should be ready by the time you're done."

"I'll be quick." She plucked her winter coat off the

coat tree by the front door and shrugged into it. "You wouldn't happen to have any oatmeal cookies?"

"I made 'em just for you."

"Lucky me." She burst out into the icy night. The air burned her lungs as she hurried down the snow-covered porch steps. She'd just bring in a few vital suitcases—things they would need for morning—and leave the rest for tomorrow. In the silence, she heard a footstep on concrete.

Uh, what was that? And why hadn't she noticed exactly how dark it was out here? Something moved just out of sight of the porch light. The falling snow made it even harder to see. She caught a glimpse of a man's shoulder, his arm, and took a step back. Exactly how much crime did Snow Falls have these days? Not that she felt in peril. No, that wasn't the reason her heart jammed up in her throat.

"Didn't mean to startle you." Officer Handsome lingered at the edge of the light's glow. "Just on my way home."

"Deputy Winters. Your shift is done for the night?"

"Yep. Work two to ten. Not a bad shift."

"And you live nearby?" She tugged gloves out of her coat pocket, fitting her hands into them. "Or do you usually wander around in other people's yards at night?"

"That's my cruiser right there." He nodded behind him to the open detached garage of an old-fashioned two-story. Her grandmother's neighbor. "I was heading in when I spotted you. Didn't think to tell you that spare won't take you far."

"Don't I know it. It's as bald as an egg." She squinted

through the darkness at him. "Guess I'll need a new tire."

"No kidding." He hesitated, not coming closer. "If you get over to Gleason's Service and Tires, mention my name and he'll give you a good price."

"Thank you, Ronan." Saying his name felt good. He'd been the new boy to town, a quiet but steadfast companion one summer long ago. "Didn't think I'd remember, did you? But it came to me."

"Surprising. I'm not the boy I used to be." He quirked one eyebrow, smiling. "It's too bad, too. Didn't live up to my potential."

"You still have a self-deprecating sense of humor, I see. What else is the same, Deputy?" She leaned against the hood of her car. "Still living with your grandmother?"

His smile faded. "She passed away."

She felt like an idiot. "Oh, Ronan, I'm sorry. I just didn't know. Granny didn't say a word."

"She wouldn't. She and my gran were close. Hard to talk about."

Still, Granny should have said something. "Your grandmother raised you. That had to have been a hard loss."

"It was," he admitted. "She'd been sick for a long while, so I know she's in a better place. Out of pain. With my grandfather."

Ronan might think he was hiding his feelings, but she felt them as if they were her own. Strange how twenty years evaporated as if they'd never came between them.

Maybe once kindred spirits, always kindred spirits.

How about that. Shelby laid her hand on his arm. "How long has she been gone?"

"Three years." In the half light she saw him wince. "She fought it for a year, then she was gone. She left me her house, likely because of all my cousins, I was the one she felt sorry for."

"Felt sorry for you? Maybe it's because you were the one she raised herself. Maybe she did it because she loved you."

"Maybe." His lips curved upward.

"The house is dark." She pointed in the direction of his windows instead of looking a second longer at his mouth. She removed her other hand from his sleeve and took a step back. "It must mean no wife and kids. No one waiting at home for you."

"A bachelor at thirty. Only one girl ever got close to my heart, and she was you."

"Right. I forgot how funny you could be."

"I try." Not that he'd been kidding. "Let me help you unload your car. That is why you're out here, right?"

"And why you came over. To help." Realization crossed her face, and her hand landed on his sleeve again. A squeeze of gentle appreciation.

If only she knew what that did to him. His chest ached with emotions he didn't want to feel, emotions he never thought he could feel again.

"Might as well make myself useful." He broke the connection as fast as he could. "You've had a long drive, you've got to be tired."

"And you just finished working. You must be tired, too." Her chin went up defiantly. "I can do it myself."

"What was I thinking?" He held out his hand for

her keys. "That you would have outgrown your stubbornness?"

"Sorry to disappoint you, Deputy." She unlocked the back passenger door. The light on her slender shoulders accentuated her graceful movements. "I've honed my stubbornness over the years. I'm afraid it's become gargantuan."

"Is that so?" He opened the car door before she could. This close, he could see the faint freckles across her dainty nose and the threads of vibrant blue in her irises. Summery eyes, he used to think of them. He swiped a snowflake off her satin cheek, holding his feelings still. "I'm sorry you've had to do so much on your own. Let me get this for you."

"Tempting." Exhaustion lined her face. She blinked up at him. "I have a no-leaning policy."

"A what?" Leave it to Shelby to confuse him. She'd dazzled, intrigued and puzzled him as a ten-year-old. No surprise she could do the same to him as a grown man.

"I don't lean on anyone. It's easier that way." She plucked a small suitcase off the floor behind the driver's seat. "I do what needs to be done and I get through it. It's worked so far."

"Seems like you've come on some hard times." He gentled his voice. "Things might be easier if you let someone help you every now and then."

She hid a lot behind her pride as she raised her chin. "Last year we lost our home. A little house Paul and I bought right after our honeymoon."

"That had to be rough." He covered her hand, the one

gripping the suitcase. The news didn't surprise him. "You're here because you have nowhere else to go."

She nodded, her hair bobbing, catching snowflakes. "We couldn't pay our January rent, so here we are. It's hardest on the kids. I'm trying to turn it into an adventure. A trip to see Granny, and where we go after that is a surprise. An adventure."

"You're not staying?" Thank God. This woman was like a punch to the gut. He'd taken enough hits.

"No way can I impose on Granny a second longer than I have to. I've been applying for jobs like a madwoman. Not that receptionists are in great demand, but I'm good at what I do. In the meantime, I take whatever I can get. Minimum wage, but it adds up." She didn't seem to realize he'd finessed the suitcase out of her tight grip as she leaned in to grab a little pink suitcase from the backseat. "Why am I telling you all this? You have an effect on me, Ronan Winters. You always have. I open up to you like to no one."

All sorts of questions filled his head, questions he wasn't sure he wanted answers to. She knelt to grab a backpack off the car floor. "It's going to be nice having you for a neighbor again, Ronan."

"Likewise." He stole the keys from her. "Now, what do you want from the trunk?"

"Just the big navy suitcase with the broken handle."

She closed the car door absently, hardly aware of the cold wind driving through her coat. He paced out of the porch light, a shadowed figure with mile-wide shoulders. Yes, the boy she'd loved as a child had grown up to be a fine man. "Now I owe you twice."

He hiked up the trunk lid, disappearing from view.

"This isn't the first time you've owed me big-time. Remember how you used to make it up to me?"

"Sure, but isn't it a little cold for that?"

"It's never too cold for *that*." He snapped the trunk shut and moved through the shadows, a shadow himself—a dark curve of face, the faint line of his arm and the blur of his boots in the snow. "Believe me, I'm going to expect payback."

"Some things never change." She met him at the foot of the stairs where the light wrapped them in a golden glow. "Guess I'll see you around?"

"Be hard not to." He lifted the heavy suitcase easily, setting it at the top of the steps as if it weighed nothing. "So, where is this temporary job of yours?"

"At your aunt's bakery. They needed extra hands for the New Year's Eve celebration."

"For First Night?"

"Yes, and Granny talked them into hiring me."

"I'm guessing she didn't have to talk too hard. I'll put in a good word for you, too. Make sure Aunt Jules goes easy on you."

"Don't kid me, Deputy. I know what you're up to. You want me to owe you one more time."

"Yep, that's it. Three times now. Your debt to me is piling up. You know what that means."

"I do, and I'll come looking for you tomorrow. Consider it fair warning." She glanced toward the light in the window and thought of the children she needed to check on and Granny waiting to share a pot of tea. She didn't know why she went up on tiptoe to kiss Ronan's cheek. Slightly rough from his day's growth, he smelled like snow and warm man and shampoo. Nice. Her palms were damp as she stepped away.

"What was that for?" His dark fathomless eyes met hers.

"For old times' sake." She tightened her hold on the backpack and small suitcase so she wouldn't drop them on her way up the steps. "Nostalgia. Auld lang syne. All that."

"And back at ya." She heard what sounded like tenderness in his gruff voice. The wind rose just enough to hide anything else he might say. Two steps took him out of the fall of light and he was only a shadow, then darkness, then nothing at all.

Yet her heart continued to feel his presence after she'd hauled in the suitcases and closed the door.

Granny peeked into the hallway in her fuzzy yellow robe and matching slippers. "The tea is ready. Come warm up. You look like an icicle."

"I feel like one." She shook her head, as if that would scatter her thoughts enough to get Ronan Winters out of them. No such luck.

After all the hardship of the past few years, it heartened her to be reminded of that simpler time.

She shrugged out of her coat, hopeful in a way she hadn't been in a long while.

## CHAPTER THREE

"I GOT A TEXT FROM Ronan this morning," Jules Barker commented from behind the counter of Sweet Delights. The bakery smelled like fresh cinnamon from the rolls Shelby was icing and chocolate from the cupcakes Jules rescued from the oven. "He told me you two went way back. I didn't know you hung out with him."

"One summer when I was nine. Ancient times." Shelby dipped the pastry brush into the sugar icing and painted it across the still-warm rolls. "I thought you knew."

"No, that was about the time I was finishing my master's at the University of Washington." Jules eased the pans onto the prep table to cool. "Business management. I worked in Seattle for a while managing an ad agency. That all changed when I came home one Christmas and ran into someone I used to go to school with."

"Ah, so the love bug bit?"

"One big love bug. The biggest." Jules closed the oven door with her slender hip. Her dark hair was swept back in a tight, high ponytail, the blue bandanna she wore accentuated her dark blue eyes—the exact shade of Ronan's.

Ronan. Her heart skipped a beat. Probably from mortification. She really had kissed him. A blush warmed her face. What must he be thinking of her?

"Dan used to be this quiet, serious kid in high school. You'd hardly notice him." Jules tossed the oven mitts on the counter and paused to peer out the door to the shop area. Faint sounds of shoppers, the *ka-ching* of the cash registers and the whir of the espresso machine filtered through to the kitchen. Jules nodded to herself. "He came in to pick up his mom's Christmas-cookie order. She'd been too busy with his sick dad to do her holiday baking. The first moment I set eyes on him, it was like being struck by a meteor. *Ka-boom*."

"Been there. Done that." Wasn't looking to do it again. "That's how it was for Paul and me. Love at first sight. It's too strong to fight."

"Exactly. I thought, who was this incredibly handsome man and why did he have a hold of my heart?" Her eyes sparkled as she leaned against the counter. "When he introduced himself, only then did I realize who he was. I hadn't seen him in years. He proposed on New Year's Eve, and no way could I go back to Seattle after that. I wound up staying here and taking over my mom's business."

"You don't seem unhappy living here."

"I love this town. It's small, it's friendly, the mountains are beautiful. Couldn't imagine a nicer place to raise my kids."

"Exactly. How long have you been married?"

"Fifteen years." Jules smiled her happiness. "How about you?"

"It was three years for me. Paul was my high school sweetheart."

"It doesn't get better than that." Jules beamed. "You were happy together. I can see it in your eyes."

"Happy?" Absolutely. "Paul and I disagreed on everything. He drove me crazy half the time always doing everything the opposite way I would have done it. We laughed together almost constantly, and when he was gone there was a hole in my life that could never be filled."

"No, nothing can ever be the same after that." Jules tilted her head to one side, nodding slowly in understanding. "Love can't be replaced. But I'm glad you're here. I just wish I could offer you a permanent job, but in this economy—"

"I'm grateful for a few days. Believe me." Every little bit counted, especially if she found a job somewhere else and had to move on. She'd need deposit and rent money. "There. The cinnamon rolls are done. Anything else you need me to ice?"

"You are an excellent froster." Jules studied Shelby's work. "Couldn't have done better myself. A nice, generous layer, too."

"What's a cinnamon roll without lots of thick, gooey frosting? That's what I want to know."

"I like your outlook." Jules winked, glancing again toward the door. "Okay, the noon rush is mostly over. Why don't you go on your break. When you come back, I'll train you for the counter. That's where you'll be primarily for the First Night celebration. Hi, Ronan. I wondered if that was you."

"She has supersonic hearing," the man explained as he ambled into sight.

Ronan Winters in the night had been impressive,

but in full daylight he was breathtaking. Hard muscles, solid strength and steely masculinity. He moved with the easy athleticism of a man confident in his own skin. Add to that his dark hair a rich shade of molasses, freshly shaven face, showing off lean cheeks and strong jaw, and her heart stammered frantically. Oops, maybe it was because he made her forget to breathe.

"Ronan." His name caught in her throat. Likely because she still wasn't breathing. Heat scorched her face as she met his gaze. They were practically strangers. Except it didn't feel that way. Not at all.

"I had to drop by and see how you were doing. Call me curious." His dark winter jacket was partly unzipped, revealing a navy Henley beneath it. Worn jeans hugged his lean, long legs. Definitely not the boy he'd been. Nope, not at all.

"She's doing great," Jules piped up. "Just sending her off for lunch. Maybe you ought to show her around. Acquaint her with a few of the nearby shops. I heard a rumor the Ludwigs are hoping to hire a new soda-fountain clerk."

"I'll take her by." His cheek faintly tingled where she'd kissed it. She stood there in a pink-and-green ruffled apron, her luxurious hair tied into a ponytail. Cute. "Ready for lunch?"

"Sure, but I brought mine." She reached around to untie her apron. "I'm brown bagging it. Granny made me a roast-turkey sandwich. Leftovers from Christmas. Come to think of it, those sandwiches are huge, much too much for little old me to eat. Why don't you join me. You'd keep all that food from going to waste."

"Can't say no to that. I've had your grandma's roast-turkey sandwiches. I was laid up with a busted leg for a while, and she took it on herself to feed me."

"Look at him, being modest." Jules took Shelby's apron and hung it on a wall hook. "A busted leg, my foot. Don't believe him for a minute."

"What else shouldn't I believe about this man?" She ducked into the break room and emerged with the bagged lunch.

"He broke more than a leg, but I'll let him tell you that story." Jules handed her her coat and hand-knit scarf. "Stay warm, now. A Texas girl like you isn't used to this cold."

"No kidding. I nearly froze my nose off coming to work. It was going to take me at least ten minutes to scrape the ice off my car, so I hoofed it. This town might be a winter wonderland, but the scraping-snow thing wasn't in the brochure."

"We keep that under wraps." He took Shelby's coat and held it for her. "Think of it as—"

"Deceptive advertising?" She slid her arm into the sleeves.

"More like accentuating the positive." Her hair brushed his chin as he helped her into her coat. "Looking on the bright side."

"That is my exact philosophy." She moved away before he could help settle the garment on her shoulders. "Right now, for instance, I *could* be seeing your dropping by as an inconvenient thing."

"Inconvenient? Great." He held open the back door for her. "That makes me feel better. Glad I stopped by."

"Hey, I said *could*." She breezed past him, and he

followed in her wake. "But clearly this is my chance to pay my debt to you. See? The bright side."

"Don't think I've forgotten what you owe me." He fell in stride beside her in the alley. "That kiss you planted on me last night isn't going to do it."

"What kiss? I don't remember any kiss." She looked up at him, blinking innocently.

"I must have misspoken. I do that sometimes." He'd thought of little else but that kiss. Its innocence stuck with him like a sunbeam on a winter's day. "All I seem to remember is your promise."

"Well, let me make good on it." She stopped in the alley, framed by tall brick buildings on either side. The busy street behind her teemed with activity, but all he could see was her.

He pulled open a steel door next to an empty garbage bin. "You can pay me back in a bit. Right now, I have plans for you."

"That's what I'm afraid of. What kind of plans exactly?" She feigned suspicion as she waltzed past him into the dark bowels of the building. Bare bulbs lit the way down a narrow hallway.

"You'll see. Trust me."

"I wound up marrying the last man who said that to me." She shook her head. "I've been leery of the phrase ever since."

"Well, I overheard what you said to Jules. You were happily married." He held another door for her, leading to a big common area full of shoppers. An indoor mall, she realized as he led the way up a set of wide iron stairs.

"Guilty as charged." She caught sight of a food court

up ahead. White plastic tables and chairs sat beneath an awning of twinkle lights, all set up for the upcoming New Year's celebration. "I was truly happy in my marriage. Every day was better than the last. Because of Paul, I know what true love is."

"That had to be hard to lose."

"Yes. There's a saying my daddy taught me. Don't cry because it ended, smile because it happened." She didn't want to talk about the grief, giving birth without Paul by her side, knowing he would never see their daughter. "It hasn't been easy, but it got me through."

"You haven't changed all that much." He took the brown bag from her and handed it across the counter at a hot-dog stand. "Heat this up for me, Mel, would ya?"

"Sure thing." A plump man with a goatee took the sack and headed to a microwave on the counter behind him. He quirked one heavy black eyebrow. "Your usual?"

"Make it two." Ronan's large hand landed on the curve of her shoulder. "Turn around and take a look at the view."

She tried to ignore the searing heat from his touch and the comfort of it. The instant she gazed through the floor-to-ceiling windows at the cloud-shrouded mountains she was hooked. Thick white cotton-candy clouds broke apart to reveal hints of the powder-blue sky behind. The sun's rays pierced the clouds like a sign of hope. After every storm, the sun shone again.

"It's breathtaking." The mountain peaks dominated the horizon, so close she felt as if she could reach out and touch the thick snow clouds. It looked as if it was storming in the mountains. Fresh snow textured the evergreens blanketing the mountainside, and the white town spread out before her. Light posts, old-fashioned and charming, lined the streets below, where workers put up banners advertising the coming festivities. Everything looked too cozy to be real. If she blinked, the scene might disappear. "Granny always traveled to see us for Christmas. I've never been here in winter."

"It's really something, isn't it? Whenever I was away from home and things got tough, this is where I would go in my head."

"I can see why. Those mountains, that sky, it's like you can just breathe them in, all that beauty." Okay, that didn't exactly make sense, but it was hard to think with his hand on her shoulder. It was hard to make sense of anything when he stood so near. His hand on her shoulder was a connection that eased the ache of loneliness in her. She felt his body's heat, reminding her he was a man. An attractive, solid man.

An old friend. "No wonder you've never left this place."

"Now, I didn't say that." He broke away to draw out a chair for her at a nearby table. "I've spent my time away from Snow Falls, but there's nothing like coming back. Coming home."

"No kidding. This town *does* feel like home, or close to it. That's good enough for me." She slipped into the chair he held for her, doing her best not to meet his eyes. No way did she want him to know everything she'd been through. "When you left town, where did you go?"

"I got a notion to join the marines. See the world. Make a difference." He dipped his chiseled chin. Mel called him and he bounded over to the counter.

So that explained the man's steely, quiet confidence. His do-anything aura. The discipline that radiated from him.

"These are the best fries in town." Ronan set two red baskets on the table, lined with red-checked paper. Half the turkey, stuffing and gravy sandwich steamed alongside a generous heap of seasoned steak fries. "Hope your favorite drink is still the same."

"Absolutely. Why change a good thing?"

"My philosophy, too." He dropped into the chair across from her. Definitely hard not to like a man who shared her love of cherry lemonade. He leaned in. "Is Georgia watching your kids?"

"Watching them? Oh, no, she's spoiling them." She unwrapped her straw and poked it through the plastic lid. "When I left the house this morning, she was making them snowman pancakes. I caught her decorating those snowmen with candies. Hate to think of how fast they'll buzz around her house with all that sugar."

"Georgia's got a lot of energy. She can keep up with them."

"Right, 'cause she ate the pancakes, too." Shelby took a sip of lemonade. Sweet, tangy. "Poor Granny. She's campaigning hard to find me a permanent job here."

He uncapped the ketchup bottle and upended it over his fries.

She freed a couple paper napkins from the dispenser in the middle of the table.

"How long have you been between jobs?" He tackled the sandwich with a plastic knife and fork. He'd learned that from prior experience with Georgia's sandwiches. "Don't try to make light of things, either. You're driving a twenty-six-year-old car and everything you own was in the trunk."

"You don't want to hear about my problems, Ronan. They're a downer and I'm trying to stay positive."

Her sunny outlook was one thing he'd always been drawn to. "Sometimes it's healthy to talk about things. Share the load. It's got to be hard carrying everything around on those skinny shoulders of yours."

"Skinny?" She arched an eyebrow at him. "That word used to insult me back in the day. Remember how angry I'd get at you when you called me that?"

"I do, but it was the truth."

"After having two kids, you just won my heart, Ronan Winters. Then again, you've either seen me sitting behind the wheel, with my coat on, or wearing that apron."

"What about now?"

"I'm hiding behind the table. You just keep on calling me skinny." She flashed a smile at him.

He was the one who'd lost his heart.

"Two years. That's when I lost my job answering phones at a law firm." She tackled her half sandwich with a knife and fork. "We were all right for a while. I still had some of Paul's life insurance money, so I wasn't panicking yet. I found a job in Beaumont. It was an hour drive, but it was a job. Eight months later, that law firm cut back on employees and I was out."

"I'm seeing a pattern here."

"I've worked fast food, made lattes, scrubbed floors and delivered pizza. None of it was enough to keep up with the mortgage. I couldn't sell the house before the bank seized it. Look at that worry on your face. Hope it's not for me."

"Not at all. I was worrying about Mel over there. He's battling a case of gout."

"That's good." Her ponytail bounced over one shoulder. She made a pretty picture sitting there, sipping from her straw with the mountains behind her through the windows. Life had given her a hard run lately, but she hadn't let it harden her. When his eyes met hers, he saw the innocent, gentle girl he'd known as a child.

"It's all going to work out," she declared. "I've filled out one thousandish applications."

"Anyone would be a fool not to hire you." He looked away. Before she'd driven into Snow Falls, he'd been afraid he might never truly feel again. That somewhere in the dark underground tunnels of the Afghanistan mountains, he'd lost the gentler places in him.

He took another bite of roast turkey. "Sounds like Georgia is doing her best to keep you here. Maybe I'll help the cause."

"I won't turn down help." She nibbled on a fry, studying him thoughtfully. "I'm glad we crossed paths again, Ronan."

"Me, too." He swallowed hard against the affection welling up and threatening to overtake him. What surprised him most was he wanted to let it.

## CHAPTER FOUR

"YOU KNOW ME—NOSY. So I have to ask." Shelby tapped the display glass above the chocolate razzle-dazzle-flavor ice cream, on special for the New Year's celebration. The gal behind the counter nodded and grabbed her scoop. "Why hasn't some woman snatched you up and put a ring on your finger?"

"Uh, I'm a fast runner? I'm hard to catch?" His dangerous dimples ought to be illegal. "I see a woman with marriage on her mind and I flee the country?"

"Ah, mystery solved. You're one of those men. Commitment shy. Afraid to grow up." She winked as the woman behind the counter handed over the cone. "You know the type, don't you?"

"Do I. Men like that? A dime a dozen." Ashley, according to her name tag, gave Ronan an appreciative assessment. Proof that if he'd wanted to be caught, he would have been.

"I prefer real men."

"Hey, I'm a bona fide man. Aside from the commitment issue," he defended lightly. "That cone looks good. I'll take one, too."

"Reach for your wallet, and you and I are gonna have problems." Shelby pulled a ten-dollar bill from her pocket. "He'll take three scoops."

"Proof you know me." He eased in behind her at the counter, tall man, unmistakable presence. "So, you're paying up on that debt all at once?"

"No need to drag it out." *Breathe, Shelby,* she thought, suspecting she knew exactly why it felt as if all the oxygen molecules had been sucked out of the atmosphere. "I'm not one to let an ice-cream debt slide."

"The last time a pretty girl bought me ice cream I was ten."

"An unlikely story I don't believe. How about you, Ashley?" She slid the greenback on the counter.

"Not one bit. With a line like that, he looks like a player to me." She handed over the triple cone.

"A player? Yep, you called it." Shelby bit the side of her mouth to keep from laughing. "Slick, smooth, thinks he's charming."

This was fun. The glint of humor in his eyes wasn't half-bad, either. "So that's why you've never settled down. You just play one female after another."

"I have a way with the ladies, what can I say? It's a gift." Mr. Slick accidentally stumbled over his own boot on the way to the door. The look of surprise on his face? Priceless. "Well, maybe not a gift, but real close."

"Right." She stepped out into the wintry air to join the madness on the sidewalk. People were arriving to fill the cobbled streets for the First Night celebration tomorrow. Bright banners snapped in the wind overhead and festive light displays topped the old-fashioned street lamps. She could just make out the closed-off street up ahead and the giant walls of ice, where workers were putting the finishing touches on the snow maze. Now, *that* looked like fun. Something the kids would definitely want to do. She'd make sure to tell them all about it when she got home.

"What about you?" His baritone's rich cadence did something amazing to her stomach. It was really hard to ignore all those tingles.

"What about me?" she asked, a little dazed—no, not dazed, she corrected. Confused. All this commotion on the street, everything going on, it was muddling her, making it hard to concentrate.

"You've been widowed six years. That's a long time." She sighed as he fell into stride beside her. Her senses felt hyperaware, noticing everything.

"A long time to be on your own. To raise a family on your own," he added. He spotted a bench in the sunshine and gestured toward it. "You haven't looked for someone else?"

"It never crossed my mind." She eased onto the bench—yep, cold as the day, but the sun felt good on her face. Reassuring. "Guess I've been too busy to think about it."

*Way to go, Shelby.* She'd dodged the painful truth. She took a swipe of her ice-cream cone, letting the chocolate sit on her tongue.

"I can see that. Raising two kids would keep you busy." He settled beside her, all six-feet-plus of him, so substantial he took up most of the bench and all the available oxygen.

Funny how she kept having trouble breathing around him. She licked her cone, resolute. She was a Texas girl. She knew how to make a stand. "Who was she?"

He turned his cone, licking it, focusing his attention there. "Maybe the player story is true."

"Like I believe that. It's your turn. Fess up, buddy."

"She was my ex-fiancée." The wind gusted, blowing a shock of dark hair across his high forehead. "Met her in a parking lot when I was stationed in California. She was in the process of being mugged."

"And you stopped it."

"Roger that." A muscle bunched along his jawline as he gazed out at the street. A uniformed cop was writing tickets to the few cars still parked along the curb in defiance of the posted signs.

"I'd dated on and off for years," he confessed. "But nothing seemed to be right, you know, as if I'd found The One."

"You know it when you feel it." She turned her cone. The best part about ice cream in this weather was that it didn't drip. The worst? She was shivering. "The first time I saw Paul, he held a door for me on my way to chem lab and it was like getting hit by a truck. A life-changing moment. Very hard to miss."

"Yes, that's what I was looking for. A hit-and-run." He crooked a smile, leaning back against the bench. "I didn't feel that when I met Karen, but I was hoping it would turn into something bigger."

"Did it?"

"I hung in there, hoping. It might've in time. I loved her." He swallowed hard, surprised it had just popped out. It no longer hurt, but the scar remained. "She didn't wait for me. Maybe I rushed the proposal, we got on well, we liked the same movies—"

"Not those action-adventure ones?"

"Of course. What else?"

"Give me a romantic comedy any day."

"We wanted the same things." Security, home, family. "She promised to wait for me, but when my deployment was over I came home to her planning a wedding with someone else."

Shelby touch his arm. "I'm sorry." Nothing could be lovelier than the concern for him on her heart-shaped face. "That had to devastate you. She didn't at least let you know? All it takes is a stamp and a piece of paper. Well, and an envelope."

"I was a little hard to reach." He didn't like to remember when his Humvee had tangled with an IED and the gunfight they might have won if they hadn't run out of ammo. "Plus, I was gone longer than expected. She wrote, but the letter found me too late."

"How long ago was this?"

"Three years." He had to look away from her gaze, so full of caring. He stared at the booth going up across the street, listened to the hammer and tried not to feel. "I'm over it. No harm, no foul."

"I don't believe that for a second." She squeezed his arm. Her touch was killing him. "She hurt you."

"Well, now, I'm grateful to her. She saved me from what was sure to turn out to be an unhappy marriage." His hand crept up to catch hers. He couldn't help entwining his fingers through Shelby's. Her fingers so dainty and delicate.

"I suppose that's an optimistic way to see it." She peered up at him. "I'm just glad you didn't wind up with an unhappy marriage, too. Love is too important for that."

"Yes, it is." He wished he could stop aching for this woman beside him. "So I've just hung out by myself."

"And you're still waiting for the truck to hit?" she asked. Wisps of blond hair tangled around her face. He wanted to smooth them back.

"Not sure that will happen at this point," he admitted. Because it already had struck. He felt closer to her than to anyone. Ever. He felt vulnerable to her, without defenses, without a single barrier.

Maybe this could be a new beginning for them, he thought. A new year, a new start, a new chance to win her heart.

"Oh, I don't know about that." Shelby's hand remained in his, her warm palm against his, her slim fingers tucked trustingly between his. "You don't deserve to always be alone, Ronan."

"I could say the same for you." His voice sounded thick to his ears. All he needed was a hint from her that she could feel more than friendship for him. Just a hint, that's all. "Maybe you'll fall in love again."

"Me? Oh, I can't see that happening." She shook her head, sweeping her ponytail from side to side. "Nothing could be more unlikely."

"Really? Why?" His future hinged on her answer.

"I'm certain true love only comes once into a person's life. Like a rare gift. One singular chance." She had a soft faraway look in her eyes. "I already got that. I've already had my fairy tale. I can't see it happening again."

"Didn't you just say to stay optimistic? To keep the hope?" But inside he was dying a little.

"I can't see myself loving someone again. It's just not an option."

"Oh." The mortal blow. "Why's that?"

"Since Paul's passing, I've never given another man a thought. First I was grieving and now... I have the kids, providing for them all by myself, figuring out exactly how I'm going to get us back on our feet again."

"Right." At least he knew the truth. He released his hold on her. His hand felt empty without hers, his skin cold.

Not a beginning after all, he thought. At least not for him.

SHELBY CAUGHT HERSELF going over her conversation with Ronan throughout the afternoon and now, five minutes to the end of her shift, was no exception. She balanced the tray, blinked against the lazy snowflakes, crossed the cobblestone street toward the volunteers doing the setup for First Night and tried to drive his memory from her brain. If only it were that easy. No matter how she tried, he stuck like glue.

"We were hopin' you wouldn't forget us." A friendly middle-age man with round cheeks, his large nose red from the cold, gladly plucked a paper cup off her tray. "Nothing like the cocoa Jules whips up. Hits the spot."

"Give me coffee any day." The second volunteer, gray-haired and spry, chose a latte. "Tell Jules thanks, little lady. It was thoughtful of you to find us."

"Just doing my job." Was it her imagination, or was the building across the street the local cop shop? She couldn't read the sign in the fading twilight, but the string of parked police cruisers out front had to mean it was. And yes, that meant her mind arrowed straight to Ronan.

After she'd paid off her ice-cream debt, he'd walked

her back to the bakery. On the way he'd taken her into two different shops and introduced her to the owners. First, they went to the Ludwigs' hoping they would keep her in mind if they should choose to hire more employees and gave her a glowing recommendation. Really nice of him. It had teared her up a bit.

"Missy?" The elder man's voice pierced her thoughts. "Rumor has it that you're Georgia's granddaughter."

"Yes, that's me." She couldn't help noticing the way the man's brown eyes lit up. Yep, call her interested. "So, you know my granny?"

"Oh, I've known her for years. Fixed her car more than a time or two back before I retired. Used to own a garage." Those brown eyes didn't just light up, they twinkled with something far more telling.

Well, how about that. Was he sweet on her grandmother? She had to know more. "I'm Shelby Craig. And you are…?"

"Robert Gleason. In town for our First Night celebration."

"Jules gave me a few days' work because of the event, but my kids will be able to enjoy it. I see all kinds of things for them—inner tubing, the snow maze, face painting—"

"Jolie Godwin does the face painting—she's one of ours. An artist. And don't forget the reading at the library." Robert gestured to the sedate brick building behind him. "Renowned children's author Ellie Summers will be telling stories. Your kids might like that."

"Absolutely. I'll tell Granny to put it on their agenda. She'll be taking them."

Robert nodded. "So, how long will you be staying with Georgia?"

"I'm on the hunt for work, so however long that takes."

"You and a lot of folks. I hope you find what you're looking for, young lady."

"I'm a fighter, so I have no doubt. I won't stop until I find it."

"Just like Georgia, eh?" The elderly man sipped his coffee. No wedding ring on his left hand. Now that she noticed, he was a handsome man in, what, his early seventies. Well dressed, well groomed. He'd be a good match for her grandmother.

"Yep, that's me, just like Granny." She passed her tray to the third worker, who put down his hammer and joined them. A younger guy, probably just out of high school, he opted for a cup of cocoa.

"What are y'all doing here?" she asked Robert.

"Putting up the chamber of commerce booth." Robert was really quite amiable. "We're behind schedule, too. Should be quitting for the night, but—"

That's as far as he got. He saw something beyond her right shoulder, a smile crossed his distinguished face and he got a dreamy look in his eyes. She knew who was coming up the street behind her.

"Mom!" Caleb's boots thumped with each step. "We came to get ya."

"Hi, honey." Granny looked adorable bundled up in an ivory winter coat. The angora scarf she'd knitted brought out the blue in her eyes and her rosy cheeks. She held Riley's hand. "We were at the bakery, but Jules sent us here to look for you."

"I'm handing out freebies to the volunteers. I've got two extra cocoas right here. Do you happen to know any kids who'd be interested in drinking these for me so they don't go to waste?"

"Me," Caleb called out.

"Me, too." Riley broke free, running in her pink boots, her blond pigtails bouncing.

She knelt so the tray was within easy reach. Her kids had clearly spent a happy day with their doting great-granny, that was for sure. And that was perfect. Exactly what she'd wanted. She wanted so much for them.

That's when she saw him out of the corner of her eye—Ronan Winters just across the street.

## CHAPTER FIVE

HE OUGHT TO JUST KEEP on walking, Ronan thought. Get in his truck, drive home and forget about his feelings for her. But it wasn't that easy.

"Howdy, neighbor. What are you doing working?" Georgia raised a hand, motioning him over. "I thought you had the day off."

"I do. I just dropped by the office to check my schedule for tomorrow." His voice carried across the street, devoid of cars but filled with people. Tourists strolled through town looking for restaurants or browsing through shops. Volunteers finished up their First Night preparations for the day. Townsfolk were just getting off work.

There must be something going on at Wildwood Lodge, judging by the stream of foot traffic heading up that way. All the commotion ought to diffuse his hurt, but when Shelby turned toward him, it was as sharp and as keen as a grenade hit. *I can't see myself loving someone again. It's just not an option.* Shelby's announcement had hammered him all afternoon, each word a blow.

"We're heading to the lodge." Georgia didn't mind hollering over the crowd. She appeared to be enjoying it, if the wide grin on her face was anything to go by. "I've decided. You're coming, too, so get on over here."

"This is news to me." His gaze swiveled to Shelby, who stood with an empty tray at her side and shot him a smile that made his kneecaps melt.

"Great idea, Granny. Get over here, Ronan. You've got nothing and no one waiting for you in that big old house of yours. Besides, I want you to come."

How could he say no to that?

"Are you sure about wanting my company?" he called out.

"Absolutely. You're a shady sort, but I'll look right past that."

Funny. "What are you up to, anyway?"

"We have a rip-roaring good time planned, that's what." She planted one hand on her hip, looking as pretty as a cover model with her wind-kissed girl-next-door looks. "Are you opposed to rip-roaring good times?"

"No, but I am immune to them. I'm dour. I frown at the idea of a good time. It goes along with my job." And he had to bite his lip to keep from smiling.

"I can handle any frowning you throw my way." She lifted her chin, apparently not afraid of his supposed dourness. "Maybe I can change your opinion on fun. Don't underestimate my powers of persuasion. I'll make a party man out of you yet."

"*That* I have to see." Why his feet carried him forward, behind the barriers up to block traffic, he couldn't say. What he felt for Shelby was a force stronger than disappointment, greater than impossibilities. So, she would never fall in love with him, he never had the chance to win her. That didn't seem to matter as much compared with what she needed from him.

"Why don't you come along, too, Robert." She tossed her megawatt smile at the elderly gentleman. "The more the merrier."

"Oh, well, you're headed to Wildwood Lodge, you say? As it happens, I'm an excellent inner tuber. Can't turn down an invitation like that. Do you kids know what the secret to a good inner tube run is?"

"What?" Caleb asked, bounding forward. His little sister trailed after him, eyes wide.

It wasn't chance that he and Shelby were left behind as the group headed away from the half-built booth near the library. Ronan nodded hellos to the other workers, clicking their toolboxes closed, done with their day's work. Robert Gleason offered to return Shelby's tray to the bakery.

"That's right nice of you." She beamed at him. "Do you all want to come along, too?"

The young man shook his head, clearly overwhelmed by her. Ronan knew just how the kid felt. Tommy Gleason declined Shelby's offer, having other plans.

At first the two of them walked in silence behind the others, listening to Caleb chatter about the few times it had snowed in their Texas hometown. The crisp night air felt invigorating, and the tiny, flawless snowflakes fell from the darkening sky.

"Sorry my granny roped you into coming along. But not really." Shelby trudged alongside him. "It feels right having you with us. We've got to be better company than your television."

"I don't know about that. Recorded a great game I missed last weekend. Riveting."

"Not sure we can compete with that."

"You're a close second." He watched her in the street-light.

"Look at everyone! It's a crowd," Georgia called out, walking backward. "I guess we aren't the only ones with the same idea. Glad I brought a few extra cans."

"That's right, it's Wildwood's food drive tonight. A ticket for a can of food." The lodge's First Night activities dissipated from his mind as he breathed in the scent of honeysuckle and frosting.

"Look at it all lit up," Shelby breathed, gesturing with a gloved hand toward the wood-and-stone lodge hugging the base of the mountainside, picture windows golden against the dark. "It's like something out of a fairy tale."

"It's a castle." The little girl spun around looking like a fairy herself in her pink coat, purple hand-knit scarf, her honey-blond curls framing her button face. "Mama, it's where the princess lives."

"Is that right, honeybee?" Shelby's voice dipped low. "What princess is that?"

"Princess Sugarplum." The girl—Riley—tilted her head to one side, clearly as fanciful as her mother. "She's defending her people from the evil dinosaur people. But right now she's having a party, so everyone isn't fighting and the dinosaur people aren't trying to eat the regular people."

"So everyone is just going to have a fun time to-night?" Shelby asked, gently cupping her hand over her daughter's head.

"What are dinosaur people?" Caleb asked practically. "Dinosaurs can't be people."

"I guess that's for me to figure out," Shelby answered amiably, her shoulder lightly bumping Ronan's arm on purpose, a friendly gesture. Friendly. She was completely unaware he felt more than friendship for her.

Just went to show how well he was hiding his feelings. He excelled at it. Might even be why he'd survived those six long months underground, kept in the dark, not knowing what would happen next. When his family hadn't known if he'd been dead or alive. He breathed in the icy air, tinged with the smell of evergreen, snow and the faint hint of wood smoke. There was a bonfire at Wildwood, he remembered, something fun for the guests, and later a marshmallow roast for the kids.

"It's a game of ours," she told him, bringing him back to the moment, back to her. "The kids come up with an idea and I tell a story about it. It's our bedtime routine. I tuck them in, turn out all the lights and pick up the story where I left off. I love to tell a good yarn."

"Some things never change." He remembered the girl she'd been and the boy he'd been, standing beneath the stars with their bikes parked in the gravel behind them, staring up. "What was that story you made up? Something about lost stars?"

"Like I could remember? Boy, that was a lot of stories ago." Her laugh touched him. Unaware, she talked on. "Let me think. I've made up a lot of tales about stars over the years. Was it about a Martian?"

"No."

"The moon?"

"No." Wildwood towered above them ablaze with light and filled with people. The kids trotted ahead on the shoveled sidewalk, with Georgia and Robert close behind.

"The rings of Saturn?" She shook her head, stepping into the light. "Well, then I don't have the foggiest idea. It'll come to me, though. In the middle of the night, or six months from now when who knows where we'll be, but it'll come to me. I never forget a thing."

"Is that so?" He laughed, relaxing, no longer feeling separate from the world surrounding him. He nodded to folks he recognized, neighbors and townspeople, as he protected Shelby from the crowd near the building's entrance. A doorman opened the door for them. "You might remember just fine, but your recall is faulty."

"Wish I could argue, but I can't. They say memory is the first to go. Thanks for pointing that out. I sure appreciate it."

"Anytime. That's what friends are for." His chest hitched painfully, but he hid it well.

"Friends. You have no idea how great that sounds to me." Her hand fluttered to rest on his chest. Surely she could feel the crazy pounding of his heart, but if she did she didn't react to it.

She tilted her head up and nailed him with her infectious grin. The world silenced, and he shut out Georgia digging cans of food out of her gigantic handbag, the opulent surroundings and the fire roaring in the massive floor-to-ceiling stone fireplace. Shelby gazed at him as if he were the only man on planet Earth.

"I've been battling life on my own for too long,"

she said. "First, it was Paul's loss and getting the kids through their grief. Then it was providing for them, and all the bumps life puts in the road took up all my time and attention. I hadn't realized how much I needed a real friend."

"Well, I'm always here. Got that?" He resisted the urge to touch her, to press the heel of his hand against the curve of her cheek and cradle her dear, dear face. He had to resist, because she wasn't his to hold.

"I'm glad our paths crossed again, Ronan. You do my heart good, and I thank you for it. See, that's got to be a sign, too. Things are already looking up." She patted his chest, a friendly caring tap. Before he could figure out what to say, Caleb rushed up to her, talking away, taking her attention.

Ronan gladly stepped back to catch his breath. Even if he did not have a chance with her, his affection remained, growing stronger with each passing minute.

Likely it always would.

"I DON'T KNOW ABOUT Y'ALL, but I'm ready to call it quits." Shelby knelt at the top of the bunny hill, where the groomed inner-tube run tracked downward like a glazed runway. "I'm frozen clear through. And did I just hear a stomach growl?"

"It was mine!" Riley tried to hug the gigantic inner tube Robert carried for her, the gentleman that he was. "It's growlin' like a big brown bear."

"Mine's like a polar bear." Caleb looked lost beneath the enormous black rubber tube he insisted on hauling. "No, like a grizzly. It's ginormous."

"Not bigger than mine!" Riley chimed in with glee as Robert set the inner tube on the ground and held it firm. She hopped aboard, her blond hair peeping from beneath her protective helmet. "I'm faster, too."

"Nuh-uh." Caleb plopped his tube down; it shot across the snow and watchful Ronan caught it before it could sail down the track on its own.

Ronan. He looked fine in the snowy night—real fine. He was all man, strong, iron hard on the outside, but on the inside tender as could be. She remembered the ten-year-old boy who'd knocked on Granny's front door the first day she'd been in town, when she'd been worrying about her sick mother, and offered her a Dixie Cup.

"Hold tight now." Ronan's words carried on the wind like silk, gliding over her, making her shiver. "I don't mean to brag, but this time I'm beating you, kid. You're fast, but I'm the master."

"So, then why did you lose the last eight times?" Caleb wanted to know.

"Oh, I was just learning the course, finding your weaknesses."

"Sounds like loser talk to me." Caleb adjusted his helmet.

"That may be, but you'll see I'm right. I'm the master." Ronan's inner tube shot out beneath him the moment he tried to sit on it, intentionally, Shelby realized as he landed on the ground with easy laughter and the kids roared. "Well, I'm still the master."

"Right. That's what you say." Caleb, pink with delight, fine-tuned his position on his inner tube. "But I've still got my tube."

"A minor setback, but nothing I can't handle." Ronan scoped the group of them standing at the top of the hill, his gaze settling on her. Amazing the power his eyes had to hold her riveted in place. "Adapt, improvise, overcome."

"You're not getting my tube." She tightened her hold on it, refusing to set it down. "Don't even think it—"

"Oh, I'm thinking it." He stalked toward her, a powerful predator hunting his prey. "And I am getting your tube."

"Do you really think you can fight me and win?" Hilarious because he was clearly twice as big as her, maybe almost three, counting all those muscles of his, which were bulging quite nicely beneath his winter coat. She strengthened her stance. "I'm a toughie."

"A toughie, huh? Well, they make the best opponents." He wrapped one steely arm around her waist. His body heat drove the chill away as he hefted her from the ground like a sack of potatoes.

"Hey, there, wait one minute." She could have protested better if she hadn't been laughing so hard. "Put me down. We're clogging up the bunny hill."

"Not for long." With one quick twist of his free hand he stole her inner tube, dropped it to the ground, steadied it with his boot and, the next thing she knew, they were going down.

The rubber tube bounced beneath their combined weights. Vaguely she heard someone shout, "Go!" Caleb, she realized way too late, probably because she wasn't breathing. Her brain had shut down, as if it had given up all hope of cognitive function due to the overwhelming male holding her tight. Bits of icy spray brushed her face as down they went, bouncing over bumps, whizzing along the sloping white, dizzying and breathless. He held her safe against his chest, against his body, as they zoomed along.

"I can't believe you…did this." Laughing this hard made it tough to speak. "I thought…you were going to steal the tube, not take me with you."

"A man's got to do what a man's got to do." His deep tones resonated in her ear.

"Where can I lodge a complaint?" she asked, gazing up at the sky, at the endless snow and deep night, and felt Ronan's chuckle move through her.

"No idea, but inner-tube hijacking isn't against any law I know of."

"Just the answer I'd expect from a guy I'm suspecting is a crooked cop."

"Only when it comes to inner tubes," he quipped as they reached the bottom of the run.

"Yes! I did it!" Caleb danced in victory at the bottom of the run. "See? First, again."

"You're the master." Ronan lifted his fist as the inner tube slowed and managed a fist bump with the boy. "You have skills, my friend."

"We can be the master together," Caleb decided. "We can share it because you lost your inner tube."

"Thanks." He planted his boots, stopping their slow glide. He had no idea where his had gone, but he'd hunt it down. "Do you know what this means?"

"What?"

"A rematch." He felt Shelby stir from where she was still tucked against him. He helped her onto her feet, hating to end the moment. She shot upward, small and slender, the snowflakes clinging to her hair like a tiara.

It was frustrating knowing she couldn't love him, that nothing would change between them. But he stayed the course, gathering up Caleb's tube along with Shelby's, waiting for Riley to slide to a stop with Georgia and Robert right behind her.

"One more time, Mom, please. *Pleeease?*" Caleb begged.

"Hmm, let's see. Didn't I agree to that last time, and look where it got us." She poked him gently in his growling stomach. "I hear that grizzly-bear hunger. That simply cannot be a good thing. Let's head home—"

"No way." Time to put his foot down. Ronan scooped up Riley's inner tube. "We're here at Wildwood. We'll eat at the lodge. My treat. Robert, you and Georgia, too."

The older folks brushed off snow, cheeks pink and smiling from their trip down the hillside.

"That's too generous of you." Shelby's touch felt supercharged. "Plus, you haven't seen that kid eat."

"Like a grizzly," Caleb agreed.

"Me, too." Riley clung to her mother's hand. "I'm a grizzly, too."

"A very pretty grizzly," Shelby agreed, kneeling to straighten the little girl's scarf.

"I happen to like grizzlies." Ronan thought he saw something different in her gaze when she turned toward him. For one nanosecond. "The lodge has great food. I don't know about the grizzlies here, but I've heard bears love cheeseburgers."

"With pickles," Caleb added.

"And ketchup," Riley chimed in.

"And lots of fries." Shelby smiled quietly. The look she gave him was very serious. It gave a man hope.

# CHAPTER SIX

MUTED MORNING SUN GLARED on Shelby's laptop screen as she pulled a shirt over her head. With toothbrush in hand, she squinted at her inbox hoping, wishing, pleading for an email from one of the tons of applications she'd applied for in person and online. All she needed was one of them to grant her an interview. Just one. Once she got her foot in the door, she had a chance of charming them into hiring her. And if charm didn't work, her tenacity and work ethic might do it.

But no, she thought as she scanned the spam mail, spotting a message from her former landlord. Looked as if he'd refunded the damage-and-cleaning deposit on her apartment. The check was in the mail. Good, that ought to tide her over a little further.

She plunged her toothbrush into her mouth, used both hands to log off and shut down, and returned to brushing. Time was ticking by, she'd best get a move on if she wanted to be extra early. She caught sight of Ronan's house as she rushed past the window.

Ronan. Wasn't he a surprise? She did not know what to think about last night. Being tucked against his chest, feeling his arms around her, his laughter moving through her as they raced down the slope...well, maybe she'd be smart *not* to think about it. Yes, that's exactly what she'd do. Not another thought of Ronan Winters. That was that.

She spit and rinsed, catching her reflection in the bathroom mirror. Her eyes glimmered like sapphires. Rosy cheeks, a smile nearly ear to ear. She hardly recognized herself. How long had it been since she'd looked this happy?

*It's because we're here with Granny,* she told herself, dashing down the stairs. She heard voices in the kitchen as she sped by to grab her coat from the rack.

"Shelby, aren't you eating breakfast?" Granny stood in the kitchen archway wearing her checked red apron that read, Kiss the Cook. "You can't expect to get through the long day you've got when you're running on empty."

"I'll get something at the bakery. Croissants, muffins, scones, pastries." She stabbed one arm into her coat sleeve. "No worries. I'll be fueled by carbs."

"And sugar." Granny waggled her spatula. "I've made a nice omelet. You have time to sit down to a decent meal."

"I had time, but Jules liked how hard I worked and tacked on a few hours before my shift. Can't turn that down." No way. She was grateful for the paycheck. "I've got work for today and tomorrow, and that's all I have for sure. So I've got to make hay while the sun shines."

"It's looking a little cloudy out there. They're forecasting more snow."

"Then I have no time to waste." She kissed Granny on her appled cheek. "You're especially glowing this morning. Could it have to do with a certain gentleman who was in your company last night?"

"Certainly not!" A blush accompanied Granny's swift denial. "I'm just glad to have you here with me, is all."

"Sure. Like I buy that." She'd seen how attentive Robert had been last night, getting Granny's chair, listening carefully to everything she said.

"Hey, you two." Her kids must have heard her and came running. She brushed back the flyaway hair from Caleb's eyes and cradled Riley's cheek.

"Can we go tubing again today?" Caleb wanted to know.

"Yeah, can we go?" Riley tossed her ponytail over her shoulder.

"I have no idea, as I have to work." She buttoned her coat as fast as she could. "You'll have to take that up with Granny."

"I'm the master." Caleb punched his fist in the air. "Do you think Ronan can come?"

"I think Ronan has to work. Just like me." She grabbed her purse, wishing she didn't have to run. "I'll see you guys later." She touched noses with them. "Be good for Granny."

Riley wrapped her arms around Granny's hips.

"Thank you, sir," she said as she swept out the door Caleb opened for her. The wind's bite promised the weatherman's predictions would ring true as she clomped down the steps.

"Bye, now," Granny called from the doorway with Riley at one hip, Caleb at the other. "We'll swing by the bakery later to check on you."

"Try the bakery's booth. That's where I'll be most likely." She walked backward to keep them in sight as long as she could until her grandmother closed the door against the building cold. The sky tried to swallow the last of the sun as she tromped down the walk. She breathed in the scent of coming snow as she hiked past her car parked in the driveway.

"Shelby." Ronan ambled into sight. Look at him—sculpted face, that thick dark hair with a hint of a cowlick in back and that tough-guy aura she knew hid a gentle heart.

Last night, the way he'd treated her kids, made them laugh—bought them enormous cheeseburgers with fries—had charmed her thoroughly. So thoroughly not one single word popped into her mind as she skidded to a stop in front of him. She was a talker, always had been, always would be, and he rendered her wordless. Breathless, too.

"Figured you'd be walking to work again today." He circled her car, rolling a tire.

A tire? No. Her chin hiked up, indignation fueling her. "Exactly what do you think you're doing with that thing?"

"I happened to find it—"

"You mean, bought it," she interrupted.

"*Bought* it," he corrected amiably, "at the local garage. Thought I might bring it over here and change out that sorry excuse you have for a spare."

"Oh, you did? You just got this idea all by yourself and didn't even think about running it by me?"

"No, didn't occur to me." He leaned the tire against the bumper. "I've got nothing else to do this morning before my shift, so this will help keep me busy and out of trouble."

"I think you've just landed in more trouble than you realize." And so had she, apparently, because she wanted to run up and hug him. She hiked her chin up another notch and planted her feet. She'd gone this long without leaning on someone and she didn't need to start now. "I'm perfectly capable of getting my own tire."

"Sure, I know that, but you've got your hands full working for my aunt, so I figured I'd be a good neighbor." He kept coming her way on those long legs of his, towering over her in his masculine way. "Besides, I want to do this for you. Especially after last night. Getting to spend time with your family, you don't know what you gave me."

"I thought it was what you gave us." She faltered. "The kids had a great time."

"What about you?" His shadow fell across her, blocking the sun and sky until he was all she could see. "Did you have a good time?"

"I sure did." Was that really her voice? It sounded strained, as if she was choking.

"Good. You work hard, Shelby. Something tells me you haven't had a whole lot of fun in a long while."

"I can't remember the last time I played like that." The wind whipped her, pinkening her cheeks. "There's something else I owe you for."

"That's the whole idea."

"You're building up favors on purpose?"

"Sure. I'm partial to ice cream." He leaned against her car's fender, crossed his arms over his chest.

"I need to reimburse you for the tire, of course, with real money." She rolled her eyes, gazing up at him so sincerely. Her hair, in a ponytail, hung over her shoulder. He could count the freckles on her nose. No one, anywhere, had ever looked as beautiful.

He could not look away. "Sorry, but I'm not taking your money, gorgeous. You'll just have to live with it."

"I'm used to doing things on my own. It's the way I like it."

"I know." It was the little things he saw, the small changes that hadn't been there the day before. How she turned toward him when they talked, how she seemed more open, as if her walls were coming down, too.

"I was racing to work when I spotted you. It's your fault if I'm late."

"I'll text Jules. She'll understand."

"Sure she will, as she knows you and the trouble you cause." Her soft mouth curved upward. She winked at him, at the edge of the driveway now, walking backward fast. Her boots crunched in the compact ice and snow on the street. "You're not so much, Ronan Winters."

But she said it in a way that said she thought he was. Her words were warm, resonant with caring. For one magical moment, her smile became his, her gentleness filled his heart and he stood staring after her as the first snowflakes fell, spiraling all around her.

And all around him.

"SORRY I'M LATE!" Shelby skidded through the bakery's kitchen door and glanced at the nearby wall clock. "Whoops, almost late."

"Five minutes early isn't almost late." Jules looked up from the worktable where she measured flour into an industrial-size mixer. "Ronan texted. He said he held you up."

"Yes, yes, he did." She shrugged out of her coat. "It was all his fault. I was entirely innocent. When a man that good-looking talks to a woman, she is powerless to walk away."

"Ronan does have that effect, I've noticed." Jules leveled off her measuring cup, flour tumbling onto the table. "Then again, I'm biased. As his aunt, I think he's amazing."

Shelby hung her things in the closet, moving fast. "Right now he's putting a new tire on my car. It went flat the night I came to town."

"And Ronan came to your rescue?"

"He does that a lot, I bet." Her hands trembled as she washed up at the sink.

"Ronan does like to make a difference for everyone he comes across." Jules traded her measuring cup for a teaspoon.

Make a difference? That was exactly what Ronan had done for her. His kindness, his friendship, his closeness... She gulped, turned off the water and dried her hands. She'd always felt comfortable with him, at home. Maybe true friendship was always like that.

Or maybe this wasn't friendship she felt.

"I figured," she answered Jules, wondering just how many women Ronan helped. "Likely that man comes to every female's aid, young and old. Half the town is probably in love with him."

"Probably." Jules glanced around at the kitchen full of workers whipping up frosting, making fondant, rolling pastry with care. "The thing about Ronan is that he's never been interested in anyone."

"Since his broken engagement." Shelby took a place at the worktable.

"Oh, no. That isn't the reason, not really. Karen calling off their wedding was hurtful, it couldn't be anything but. He was missing in action for thirteen months—"

"He was *what?*" Shelby went to lean against the table but missed somehow. She caught her balance, but she felt as if she went right on falling. "Missing in action? When he was—"

"Enlisted. Right. An IED in the road, an ambush, we thought we'd lost him for sure." Jules grabbed the vanilla extract. "Go ahead and pour the batter in the cupcake tins for me, would you, dear? No telling what he endured hidden in a mountain cave for so long. He didn't tell you any of this, did he?"

"Not this." Her hand felt wooden as she gripped the bowl of batter on the table. The whole of her went numb. "Why didn't he tell me? Wait, scratch that. It would be hard to talk about something like that to anyone."

"Honey, I'm glad you came back to stay with your granny, and I'm hoping you can stay on for a while. Being around you has been good for Ronan." Jules checked the mixer setting. "It was as if he left a piece of himself behind. At least that's what I thought until I spotted him up at the lodge last night."

"You were at Wildwood?"

"Had to take in the art exhibit there and the crafts in Aspen Hall while we could, since today and tonight will be all about working." Jules turned on the mixer, talking over the noise. "I caught a peek at Ronan with you and your little ones. There was the man, whole and healed, the one I'd never thought we'd see again. Laughing and smiling, the way he used to. You're good for him, Shelby. And I'd say he's good for you."

"Oh, it's not like that." Heat flamed across her face. Her hand trembled and she spilled a droplet of batter on the table. "I mean, we're just friends."

"Go ahead and keep telling yourself that." Jules stopped the mixer and grabbed her spatula. "Sometimes your heart decides for you, and you have no say in the matter."

"Luckily that's not me." She set the bowl down, the tins full of thick, chocolate batter, almost sure that statement was true—and more afraid that it wasn't.

## CHAPTER SEVEN

"THERE. HUBCAP ON." Ronan dusted the snow from the driveway off his jeans. It had stopped snowing, but the clouds hung low, as if it would start again soon. "I think we did a good job."

"Me, too." Caleb nodded in agreement, crossing his hands over his chest like a little man, considering their morning work. A smudge of oil stained his cheek. "You're a good mechanic, Ronan."

"My granddad taught me." He hauled a purple rag out of his back pocket and swiped at the oil streak. He felt warm inside, paternal and surprising. Hard not to like this kid, so like Shelby.

"My granddads are dead." Caleb squinted thoughtfully. "I'm glad you know stuff, Ronan."

"Me, too, buddy." He tossed the rag into his toolbox. "Looks like we're done here. Just in time, too. There's your great-grandma."

"I couldn't help noticing you were done," Georgia called from the doorway. "It's nearly noon. I packed up a lunch for you."

"A lunch? You didn't have to go to that kind of trouble." He clicked the lid shut on his toolbox and moved it off the driveway. "I have to head out. I promised the mayor I'd help with the final check. I'm pulling double duty tonight."

"Fine, that works right into my plan." Georgia stopped to admire the snow angel Riley had made in the front lawn before returning her attention to him. "Shelby forgot to take anything to eat, so I packed up a picnic. Figured you might want to bring it to her."

"You are all kinds of mischief, aren't you?"

"I sure try to be." Georgia produced a wicker basket. It looked a little heavy, so he climbed the steps to take it from her.

"It smells good. What do you have in here?"

"You'll just have to wait and see." Definitely trouble, that woman, who saw right through him. "I couldn't help noticing, you seem to get along with the kids pretty well."

"I like kids." He'd always figured on having a family of his own, but it had never worked out. As he gazed at the boy stooping to make a snowball and the little girl lying in the snow, he wondered if he ever would have a family. He felt his phone vibrate, tucked in his coat pocket. He hated to think what the text would say.

"I hope you're coming with me." He gripped the basket, breathing in the smell of chicken and gravy. "I'd like to be surrounded by as many beautiful women as I can get."

"Don't try to charm me." Georgia giggled at the compliment. "As it happens, the kids and I are going your way. We'll eat together, I figure, and then we've got someone to meet. Why don't we all head to the First Night celebration together."

"That someone wouldn't happen to be Robert, would it?"

"Now, that's none of your business, young man." Although the blush gave her away. "Robert and I are renewing our old acquaintance, that's all. We went to high school together. It seems we have a lot in common."

"Good. Everyone needs…friends." He'd wanted to say more, but he didn't want to overstep. Georgia and Shelby were cut from the same cloth—independent, feisty and tenderhearted. Sometimes it was hard to let hopes show when they were new and easily crushed.

As the kids hurried ahead of them—Riley hopping over the cracks in the shoveled sidewalk and Caleb dragging a stick through the snowy fringes of the sidewalk—Ronan's thoughts turned to Shelby. He could only hope that was the way Shelby felt. That his feelings for her, growing bigger with every heartbeat, would—on some level—be returned. Even for just today. One day would have to be enough.

"You didn't have to change the oil in that car." Georgia padded beside him.

"Figured I might as well since I was putting on the new tire." So, Georgia knew he'd fallen for Shelby. That meant she knew, too, that he didn't have a chance.

"You can't fool me, Ronan. You always were a good egg." The older lady kept a close eye on the kids as Riley sauntered across the empty residential street and Caleb left his stick behind.

"You're not so bad yourself, Georgia." His phone buzzed again, and this time he looked at it. A missed call from the mayor and two text messages from his buddy up in Wyoming. When he checked the message, the strength left his knees. The news had been what he'd been hoping for, but it wasn't the news he wanted.

"Bad news?" Georgia asked.

"Only for me." He tucked his phone away, trying not to think about it.

"Ronan, look!" Caleb called out, laughing, holding up a hunk of packed snow. "The perfect weapon."

"But not the only weapon." Ronan gave Georgia the basket, scooped snow into his glove and sent it flying. The snowball sailed through the air, missing the kid by a few inches. "Whoops. Bad aim. I need a do over."

"You're in big trouble now," Caleb warned.

A snowball shot out, whizzing like a little white bomb. It hit him midchest. He grabbed a handful of snow. "Good shot, kid. It's too bad for you that you're playing against the master."

"No, *I'm* the master." The falling snow swirled between them, making it hard to see Caleb's fast pitch, but the icy ball packed some power as it hit.

"Wow, that's one arm you have." Ronan rubbed his shoulder, feigning hurt. "And you're gonna pay for it. Big-time."

"Ooh, I'm so scared. Not." Before Caleb could throw his next icy weapon, one smacked him in the back. "Hey! Riley!"

Riley giggled and took off down the sidewalk, the town's snow maze visible just up ahead, when her brother turned his small arsenal against her. Ronan sprinted to her defense, shielding her as two snowballs thudded against his coat. He slipped and went down in the snow and suddenly both kids were on top of him, pelting him with soft handfuls of snow.

If he could stop laughing, then maybe he wouldn't get any more snow in his mouth. Icy wetness penetrated his clothes as the children stood over him, victors.

"I'm the master!" Caleb punched his fists into the air.

"I'm the master, too," Riley announced, but that was as far as she got as Ronan came to life, rose out of the snow and snatched the girl around the waist with one arm. He caught Caleb in the other and lifted them both from the sidewalk, spinning them around like helicopter blades. Riley squealed, Caleb held out his arms, and suddenly he heard Shelby's laughter. She emerged from the snowy background like magic, bringing color to the gray-and-white world.

"What is going on here?" She tilted her head to one side. "I can hear the pack of you all the way to the bakery booth. Don't think I can't recognize that squeal of yours, honeybee."

"Mom!" The instant her pink boots touched down, Riley took off at a dead run. "Me and Grammy made a surprise."

"You did? What kind of surprise?" She knelt to welcome her daughter's hug. She brushed back her daughter's honey-blond bangs.

Shelby really had changed him. These past few years, he'd never been able to open up, to feel. He'd been numb, and kept everyone at a distance. For some reason, he could let her in. She was like a hint of spring on a cold winter's night.

"Is that so? Did you and Granny make my favorite lunch?" Shelby lightly tweaked her daughter's nose.

"Yep. I put on the crust all by myself." Riley beamed with pride.

"She's gonna make a real good cook one day, just like her mama," Georgia said. "We weren't the only busy ones. Someone changed the oil in your car."

"Ronan," she admonished. "You're meddling."

"Helping. There's a difference." His feet moved him along, following Georgia and the kids, but he was only aware of Shelby at his side. Where he wanted her to be forever.

"I wanted to go over your car since I had the time and the opportunity," he explained. "Just to make sure it was roadworthy should a job offer come along."

"It's a holiday. That's not likely, at least not for a few more days. Not that I've been drowning in offers."

"Did you hear from the Ludwigs? I keep hoping the rumor I heard was true."

"It was. I checked in with them this morning, but they hired someone with more experience."

The downtown had been transformed. Local vendors finished setting up at their booths. The smell of roasting hot dogs, espresso and baked goods mingled on the wind. Fire pits blazed cheerfully to warm the revelers on their way from one event to another. Colorful information stands advertised family-friendly events and directions. A couple bands popular with the teen crowd were setting up inside the mall. Their sound check spilled out the open doors into the street.

Robert waved from the chamber of commerce's booth near the library, where children's author Ellie Summers would be doing a reading after hosting the opening ceremony. Face painting, an ice-carving contest, crafts for the kids, the snow maze, ice-skating, *Winter's Folly* at the playhouse and even a masquerade ball for the grown-ups later tonight at the Wildwood Lodge, culminating in a fireworks display at the stroke of midnight.

He wanted to see everything, Ronan realized, and he wanted to see it with her. To take her kids to get their faces painted and win them stuffed bears at the carnival booths. To wend their way to the ice castle in the center of the snow maze. To take their mother to the masquerade ball, hold her in his arms and never let her go.

The future stretched out ahead of him, cold and lonely and bleak as he took his phone out of his pocket and scrolled down.

"I have a friend up in Jackson. He was in my platoon back in the day." He scrolled through the message menu and showed her the text. "His father is a partner in a law firm. I called him last night asking if they might have a job for you."

"You did *what?*" She skidded to a stop in the street, shaking her head in disbelief. "You went to all that trouble for me? You know you didn't have to. I can't believe you did that."

"It was no trouble at all. My pleasure." She had no clue, not an ounce of what he felt for her. What he would always feel for her. He swallowed hard, trying to keep it all down, and said the words that would take her away from him. "Turns out their receptionist was going to go on maternity leave but just decided to turn that leave into a permanent one, so they have an opening. It's yours if you want it."

"Mine? You really found a job for me?" Tears stood in her eyes. "I have a job?"

"You do, and they're nice folks. They'll treat you

well." He squared his shoulders like a man about to take a hit. "They're offering a decent salary and benefits."

"Benefits, too? Granny, did you hear?" Shelby clasped her hands together. "Did you know what Ronan was up to?"

"Not a clue, but I'm real pleased with him. I'm happy for you, sweet pea." Georgia wrapped her arms around her granddaughter and held on tight. "But now I'm gonna have to let you go. That's gonna be hard, I won't lie."

"I know. But I can't mooch off you, I've got to pay my own way."

"Sure, I was hoping you might stay. You three fill up my house. You've done my heart good."

"You've done more than that for us." She couldn't put into words how she felt. "Now that I have a job with benefits, which means paid vacation, I bet you can figure out the first place I'm heading when I have time off."

"Here to Snow Falls?"

"Here to you." She kissed her granny's soft cheek and caught sight of Robert watching. "Then again, maybe you won't be quite as alone as you think."

"Oh." Granny caught her meaning and blushed. Maybe Georgia was about to start a new phase of her life, full of love and possibilities. Wasn't that what New Year's was all about, celebrating the good things in the year past and believing in the good things to come, and the beloved people in your life?

"And you." She turned to Ronan, wonderful Ronan. He'd backed off a few paces, putting him firmly outside the circle of her family. As if she would let him stay there. She caught his hands in hers, and a connection blazed between them like fireworks in a midnight sky. It lit up everything. The part of her that had been dark for so long filled with flashes of brightness. "You saved my life, Ronan. All the worry and uncertainty weighing me down, it's just gone. How can I ever thank you enough for that?"

"I don't think there's a big enough ice-cream cone you could get me."

"No, it would topple right to the ground it would be so high. That's how much I think of you." Her feet didn't seem to be touching the ground, but she wasn't entirely sure her new job was the reason. Likely it was the man in front of her, good through and through. No matter what difficulty life threw at him, look how he'd turned out. Strong, courageous, the best friend a girl could have. "Thank you. Those two tiny words just don't feel like enough, considering what you've done."

"It's enough, believe me." His gaze burrowed into hers. "I just want you to be happy, Shelby."

"And I could kiss you for that. In fact, I think I will." She bobbed up on tiptoe and brushed her lips to his cheek. His skin was warm, his nearness dizzying and the inner fireworks returned. She lingered, her lips against him, startled at the sensation—startled? Or was it a revelation?

She rocked back onto her heels, gripping his hands so tightly she didn't know how she'd ever let go. What was happening to her?

He broke away. "That's the best kiss I've ever had." Unaware what he was doing to her, he offered her a half grin. "That definitely makes us even. Your break is ticking by, just like your time here. Let's make the most of it—my stomach's rumbling."

"Like a grizzly," Caleb chimed in, taking Ronan by the hand. "C'mon, we're gonna eat."

"In the indoor mall," Granny chimed in, as she handed the picnic basket to Robert and took Riley's hand. "It'll be fun to listen to the band warm up while we eat."

"Sounds perfect." Shelby pasted on what she hoped was the smile she always wore, because she didn't know how everything could change just like that. In one instant, with a single chaste kiss.

## CHAPTER EIGHT

AFTER THE OPENING lowering-of-the-ball ceremony—presided over by the mayor and his special guest, the children's-book author—families celebrated in the streets all afternoon. Ronan's tasks kept him focused, but nothing, not one thing, could make him forget Shelby's kiss. He felt like the man he used to be every time he caught sight of her through the swirling snow. There she was now, handing over a pair of cupcakes, chatting with customers, turning around to pour a cup of hot tea.

Knowing she would have the life she wanted, to support and raise her children, that was what mattered. That was what he wanted, too.

Not true, he corrected himself as he forced his boots to carry him forward, away from her. What he wanted was for her to stay in Snow Falls and to show her over and over again that if she had a problem, he'd be there for her come rain, snow or flood. The end of the world could not stop his devotion to her.

"Ronan!" Caleb appeared out of the snow, speckled with white, his face painted like his favorite superhero. Jolie Godwin had done an amazing job. "Story time was cool. The author lady was real nice."

"Where you headed off to next?"

"We're gonna see Mom." The kid reached out. "C'mon. You gotta come with us."

Once he felt Caleb's smaller fingers curl around his, he was a goner. Riley broke away from Georgia and Robert, who both greeted him, and bolted over to take his other hand.

"Mom's savin' us the best cupcakes." Riley had her mother's smile, wide and dimpled. "The ones with the most frosting."

"Well, guess we can't miss that." He'd been avoiding Shelby for the past handful of hours since they'd shared lunch. It had been torture sitting next to her at the table. It had been everything he wanted. Wyoming was so far away. "I'm partial to lots of frosting."

"It's the best part." Riley skipped along, her face painted in alternating black and yellow stripes. Her nose was berry pink. "Mama!"

"There's my two." Shelby handed over a steaming cup to the sole customer at the counter before she zipped around to hug them.

"Look, I'm a honeybee." Riley dashed into her mother's arms.

"And look at me! Don't get caught in my web." Caleb rushed in to join the hug.

"Goodness, I feel safe knowing you're around." She kissed the tops of their heads.

"They make a nice picture, don't they?" Georgia sidled in.

Likely as not, his longing showed on his face.

"Yessir, they do make a fine picture," Robert answered thoughtfully, rubbing his chin. "I remember when my family was young like that. Time passes so quickly. Before you know it, they're grown and gone."

"That's the truth, Robert." Georgia's voice held a sly note, as if she had everything figured out. "You have to grab hold of those precious years while you can, or love passes you by. *Or* leaves for Wyoming."

"Right." Ronan couldn't deny that. Tomorrow Shelby would pack up her car, make sure the kids were buckled in and hug Georgia goodbye. Would he watch from the shelter of his house, as if not actually saying goodbye to her would hurt less?

"Ronan, my handsome nephew!" Jules leaned on the counter, looking happier than he'd ever seen her. Likely she'd put two and two together, like Georgia. "It figures you'd be still hanging out with this bunch. I spotted you having lunch together when I was hunting down the mayor. Didn't stop to say hey, but you seemed to be having a good time."

"It was just passable," he fibbed, earning Georgia's smile and his aunt's eye roll.

"Look at him, always playing things down. Stoic, that's our Ronan. Georgia and Robert, come up here and order. It's on the house. We're doing a booming business. I hear you found Shelby a job, Ronan."

"Just knew some people, that's all." His throat closed up, making it nearly impossible to talk.

She handed over two brightly decorated cupcakes to her kids, and then she turned to him. "Ronan. I saved the best for you. It's not ice cream, but considering this snow—"

"It's definitely too cold for that," he finished for her.

A band started up somewhere nearby, the melody and harmony, the bass and the drums beat like a heartbeat.

"This tea ought to warm you up." She held out a paper cup along with the cupcake. "I've spotted you walking around, keeping your eye out for trouble and answering questions."

"Just doing my job." He took the offerings. "Cream cheese frosting. That's my favorite."

"I grilled Jules." All she could think about was the kiss, different from the one she'd planted on his cheek on her first night in town.

"Jules survived, so the interrogation couldn't have been too tough." His expressive eyes crinkled at the corners. "Looks like your kids are having fun."

"Are you kidding? They're having the time of their lives with Granny, but then who doesn't, right?" She tore her gaze from the man before her. Somehow she managed to focus on the foursome, of Granny holding Riley's hot chocolate and Robert talking superhero characters with Caleb. "It's funny how things work out."

"What do you mean?" Ronan leaned in, his voice deep and low, only for her.

She shivered. "If my savings account had been able to stretch another month, if I'd decided to stay with Paul's mom instead of my grandmother, if that tire hadn't given out when it did... Then none of this would have happened. I wouldn't be here. You couldn't have stopped to help. We wouldn't be standing here together, you and I."

"True. I'm thankful we are." He reached out, cupping her face as naturally as if he'd been made to do it.

"Otherwise, you wouldn't be owing me, what, a whole gallon of ice cream?"

"That's a fair estimate." And she owed him so much more. She wanted to give him so much more. She could feel his unspoken affection as clear as her own.

At lunch, she'd texted Ronan's friend's father in Wyoming and they needed her to start in five days if she wanted the job. Five days to drive, find a place to stay and someone to watch the kids. That job, that lifeline, was the only certain future she had. "I can see my life changing, and it's because of you, Ronan."

"Just returning the favor." His hand remained, cradling the side of her cheek. There was something in his gaze, something hidden, like a secret he didn't want to share, but she knew what it was. That secret was in her heart, too. Her love for him.

"Shelby?" Jules called as if from a great distance. "I hate to interrupt, but we're getting swamped here."

"Right." She blinked, realizing she wasn't alone with Ronan. Revelers filled the streets. Kids called out, rushing by on their way to the theater. Families sauntered by, stopping to get in line for cupcakes and hot drinks. The thudding bass and percussion from the nearby band punctuated her movements as she pulled away from Ronan. "Guess I'd better get back to work."

"Sure." He nodded, backed away. The veil of snow swallowed him, leaving her bereft when all she wanted, all she needed, was him.

HE HEARD SHELBY'S VOICE above all the others. He stood just out of sight, feeling flecks of snow strike his face. Tomorrow she'd be gone.

"Excuse me, Officer." An out-of-towner approached with his wife and two grade-school-age kids. "Can you point us in the direction of the library?"

"Just up the street. Follow the banners, and you can't miss it." Ronan smiled. The family looked happy together, hurrying along until the snowfall closed around them.

Remembering her kiss on his cheek, his feet carried him forward. The snow broke apart, guiding him to where she stood, huddled near a small space heater in the booth, sipping at hot chocolate between customers. She lit up as she saw him.

"Ronan." She left her cup behind, stepping into the downfall that dappled her with flecks of white. When he took her hands in his, he felt whole. Home.

"I have a confession to make." He'd always had great difficulty speaking what was closest to his heart, but now she made it easy, as natural as breathing. "I regret finding you that job."

"You do?" Surprise widened her unguarded eyes, and in them he saw his future. Their future. She bit her bottom lip, maybe opening up this much was hard for her, too. She took a gulp of air. "I confess. I'm feeling the same way."

"Then don't go." He brought her hands to his chest where his heart beat frantically for her, and for her alone. "Stay with me."

"Believe me, I'd like to, but I need that job. The way I feel about you—" She didn't finish her thought. She ducked her chin, hiding her expression from him.

Didn't she know she could never hide, not from him.

He caught her chin with one hand, nudging it upward until their gazes met.

"I love you, Shelby." No words had ever felt as right or as honest. "I love your kids. I know you need that job, but I've come to realize I need you more."

"You're breaking my heart." She blinked hard against the tears welling in her eyes. "Telling me this when I'm planning to leave tomorrow. I have to go. We could email, talk on the phone, maybe visit now and then."

"No, that's not enough." He drew himself up full height—strong, breathtaking, masculine. "You are too much to lose. I see only two alternatives. I give up my job and come with you. Or you stay here. Either way is fine with me because I want to be with you forever."

"You do?" Her kneecaps wobbled, threatened to turn to jelly. Good thing he was right there so she could lean on him for support. He held her firmly, his hands cupping her elbows, the kind of man who would never let her fall. She had never thought she could have love again. "Forever is a long time. Are you sure you want to put up with me for that long?"

"More sure than I've been about anything." Smoky, tender, dreamy, that voice. "You've brought me back to life, Shelby. You're everything I've ever dreamed of and I've had a crush on you since I was ten years old. That's proof my love for you will last. I want to spend the rest of my life making you, Caleb and Riley happy. Will you marry me?"

"I would be crazy not to, since I love you so much. I do love you." She stood on tiptoe, and their lips met for their first real kiss. His lips brushed hers gently, reverently, the way a happily-ever-after kiss should be.

When he pulled back, his gaze held hers adoringly and she read her future there. A loving marriage, a happy family and each day bright with the joy only true love could bring.

Happy beyond imagining, and this was just the beginning. A new beginning. She let Ronan fold her into his arms, against the steely plane of his chest, and held on to him tightly, to this man who had changed her life with his love, with his heart.

# EPILOGUE

*One year, six hours later*

"DAD!" CALEB'S CALL echoed across the night. Shelby Winters blinked snowflakes off her lashes and watched her son lead the way along the crest of the bunny hill. He looked victorious. "I can't believe you lost again."

"What can I say? I had a bad run. I challenge you to one more showdown." The steady line of Ronan's wide shoulders emerged from the snowfall. His chiseled face brightened when he spotted her. "Hello, beautiful. What are you doing out in this cold in your condition? You should be up in the warm lodge. How did Georgia and Robert let you out of their sight?"

"They were so caught up in each other, I was a third wheel." Shelby thought of her granny, happy with her very serious beau. Robert had begun a sweet old-fashioned courtship that had thoroughly swept Georgia off her feet. After so many years alone, Granny deserved all the happiness and love she could get. The bonus was that in living across the street, Shelby got to personally spy on—er, witness—those flower deliveries, gifts and summer evenings the couple spent together on the porch swing. Robert had confessed to

Shelby just last night that he'd bought an engagement ring, with a proposal to follow shortly.

There was a lot of happiness to go around. Joy filled her as Ronan ambled up, plopped his inner tube on the ground, steadied it with his foot and laid a gloved hand on her rounded stomach. Their baby girl was due in February.

"No way, *I'm* the master." Riley's voice bubbled with laughter as she tromped up to nudge her brother in the side. Caleb laughed back, issuing a challenge. The delight of her children was the best sound in the world.

"Are you sure it isn't too cold out here for you?" Ronan shielded her from the wind, towering over her, her love, her life, her entire world. "I worry about you."

"I'm fine." Blissful. That's how she always felt now as Ronan's wife. They'd married in early January, since she'd turned down that job in Wyoming, and worked part-time with Jules when an employee moved back to Denver to be with family. Just as she'd imagined, her life with Ronan had been flawless. They were a perfect match, kindred spirits, mirrored souls.

"I had to come and see the fireworks with you." She could hear the countdown echoing down the hillside to the town below as the moment of midnight grew near. Folks out on Wildwood's balcony joined in, ticking off the seconds as the best year of her life came to an end, and a new one was about to begin.

"I love you with all my heart." She tipped her face up for his kiss.

"I love you with all of mine." He leaned in, wrapped her in his arms, and the world melted away. As cheers rose up and fireworks exploded, their lips met. Snow fell over them like a promise, a promise of great happiness on this first night and on every night of their lives to come.

* * * * *

To Jillian Hart and Brenda Minton,
two wonderful writers that I had the
honor of working with on this anthology.

# SNOWBOUND AT NEW YEAR

## Margaret Daley

# CHAPTER ONE

*THIS IS NOT WORKING.*

Ellie Summers slammed down the drawing she held on to the bed beside her and bolted to her feet. Pacing to her window at Wildwood Lodge in Snow Falls, Colorado, she stared out at the blanket of snow that covered the ground. Perfect for skiers, but not for this Southern gal. The roads were clear, however, and that was all she needed. Early this morning she'd driven from the hotel airport in Denver. She could drive a little farther and meet with Brody Kincaid, her new illustrator. Who was not working out as she'd thought he would.

Swinging around, she stared at the drawing lying on top of two others, his third attempt to illustrate her newest book in the Barnyard Town series. She needed it settled today. The book had to go to production in six weeks. If he didn't work out...

She snatched up the drawings, her purse and heavy coat, then headed toward the parking lot of the lodge. In her rented car with four-wheel drive, she punched Brody Kincaid's address into the GPS system. They were supposed to meet on January 2, two days after the First Night celebration. Well, she was moving up the meeting, and one way or another their partnership would be settled by the end of the day. She couldn't imagine him not being at his home. From all accounts from John McCoy, her friend and previous illustrator, Brody Kincaid loved living on top of a mountain, practically a hermit, and she knew from the staff at the lodge that he had delivered the manila envelope with the illustrations the evening before.

By the time she reached the halfway mark to Brody's house, a light snow had begun to fall. Life did not come to a standstill in Colorado when it snowed. She would be fine as long as she took it slow. By the time she passed the sign giving the altitude at seven thousand feet above sea level, snow covered the road, but her car was handling it well and hardly anyone else was out.

One glance at the drawings on the seat next to her urged her to get this impromptu meeting over with. Communicating by phone and computer obviously wasn't working. Maybe face-to-face would. She turned on the radio to catch the weather report.

Fifteen minutes later, Ellie gripped the steering wheel so tightly her hands ached from her death hold. Going ten miles an hour, the car crept up the mountain. At least she didn't have to worry about someone crashing into her—she hadn't seen anyone else since the halfway mark. If she went slowly, she could make it. The weatherman had said the snow wouldn't last. By afternoon she'd be safely back at Wildwood Lodge and sitting in front of the large fireplace in the lobby sipping a warm drink. Mission accomplished.

She leaned closer to the steering wheel, squinting as though that would help her see better through the ever-increasing swirling snow—as if someone had shaken a snow globe. Turning around at this point was not an option. As she inched up the mountain, she bemoaned her impulsive nature. What if he wasn't home, after all? She hadn't seen a house in a while. When John had said Brody lived on top of the mountain, he must have really meant *on top.*

She hit a patch of ice, slid to the right and came to a stop in a mound of snow on the side of the highway. She pressed her foot on the accelerator, spinning her wheels but going nowhere.

She scanned the never-ending white landscape, and came to the conclusion she was stuck in a snowstorm—one getting increasingly heavy.

Prying her hands from the steering wheel, Ellie sat in the rented car, trying to calm the trembling that had set in. Her heart pulsated against her rib cage at an alarming rate. What had she been thinking? She should have turned around when the snow started getting heavier at the halfway mark, but her stubbornness had reared its ugly head. It wasn't as if people didn't drive in snow—okay, probably not someone from the Deep South who saw only a few inches at best every few years.

Now that she was here, she wondered how she was going to get back down the mountain, even with four-wheel drive *and* snow tires. Drawing in calming breaths, she laid her head back on the cushioned headrest and tried to compose her taut nerves.

A glimpse of a house off to the right through the tall pines and aspens caught her attention. She blew out her held breath. Maybe it was Brody's place. Even if it wasn't, she couldn't stay in her stalled car waiting for the snow to melt. She glanced around. That might not be until spring.

She stuffed her hands into her thick gloves, zipped up her coat and pulled a wool hat on her head. She tried to open her door but couldn't. The snow blocked it. Crawling over the console, she prayed she could get out the other door. She shoved at it, and it swung open. Ellie climbed out of her car right into freezing-cold snow coming up over her short boots and down into them.

With the snow blinding her vision, Ellie trudged toward the house, keeping herself focused on her destination and, she hoped, a warm refuge and preferably Brody Kincaid's place.

The nearer she got to the stone house the more exhausted she became. The bottoms of her jeans were soaked.

*Splat!*

A snowball struck her in the chest. Another whizzed by her head. She froze.

Off to her right a little girl popped up from behind a wall of snow and started to hurl a third snowball. Ellie ducked, throwing herself off balance. She fell into a snowbank next to her, face forward. Stunned by the turn of events, she lay there for a moment, numb to the bitter cold.

She heard the sound of giggles then a door opening and slamming closed. Ellie rolled over, snow caked to her face. As she swiped her hands across her cheeks, a blurry vision of boots and jean-clad legs came into view. Rubbing her eyes, she trekked her gaze slowly upward, taking in a thick brown coat, relatively dry and probably toasty warm. Her eyes came to rest on a man's face.

A face she'd seen in photos of Brody Kincaid. A

face with intense dark eyes fixed on her. A face with a mouth pinched into a scowl.

"What are you doing here? In a snowstorm. This is December 30. We aren't supposed to meet for three days," Brody said in a deep, baritone voice she'd come to recognize over the phone.

So he knew what she looked like. Did he look her up on the internet or did John give him a photo? "It wasn't snowing like this when I started out." Ellie struggled to sit up. "And even when it started, the weatherman said it would move out of the area quickly." There wasn't one place on her that wasn't wet and cold.

He looked around. "Yeah, I think the weatherman got this snowfall wrong." Brody offered her his hand. "This is not going to pass quickly. I have a feeling it's stalled over us." When his fingers closed around hers, he hauled her to her feet. "But then I might be wrong."

"Are you often?" she couldn't help but ask.

His expression darkening, he lifted one shoulder in a shrug. "I win some. I lose some. C'mon. Let's get you inside."

She followed him toward his house, looking around for the little girl she'd seen—the one who had hit her with a snowball. "I understand you have two daughters." John had told her, but Brody never had said anything about his children. When they talked, it was all business.

"Yes, I knew something was wrong when they ran into the house, leaving the front door wide open, and headed straight upstairs, giggling. Mischief written all over them. That's when I looked outside and saw you in the snow." He stomped up the steps to his wooden deck that ran the length of the front of his cabin and around to the left side. When he opened the door, he said, "After you."

She hurried inside, planting herself on a gorgeous Indian rug in the entrance, which was better than dripping on his beautiful wooden floor. Through a doorway she glimpsed a living area with a large roaring fire in a stone fireplace. The warmth beckoned her, but she stayed where she was.

He came up behind her and said close to her ear, "May I take your coat? I'll get you some towels."

His soft words shivered down her body. She pulled off her gloves and hat then shrugged out of her coat. His nearness robbed her of a decent breath—or it was his disheveled dark brown curls from having removed his hat. She itched to comb her fingers through his hair to bring some kind of order to it. She balled her hands at her sides. The photo hadn't done him justice. He had a powerful presence that commanded a person's attention.

"I'll be right back." He crossed to a hallway that led to the back of the house.

A sound like snickering came from the upper level. She glanced toward the stairs and saw a little girl duck back out of sight. She smiled. Which of his daughters had nailed her?

"Here." He gave her a thick fluffy towel. "You might be more comfortable in front of the fire." He started for his living room.

Ellie looked down at her wet boots knowing her socks were equally drenched. When he paused at the entrance, she bent down, removed both the shoes and socks and carried them with her into the living room.

She slowed as she took in the walls of glass. The view of the mountain and the valley below must be stunning. Not that she could see it right now. White was all that greeted her.

"I imagine when the snow stops you have a fantastic view," she said, setting her shoes and socks to dry in front of the blaze.

"No use being on top of a mountain if you can't see the view."

"I didn't see very many homes the last part of the trip. Doesn't it get lonely at times?"

"With two young daughters?"

"True. But how about them?" When she'd grown up, her childhood home had been in the middle of so many people coming and going. Even now, living near her family, it was never quiet. Except for a few giggles and snickers, his home was downright calm and peaceful.

"They can go to a friend's or their friends can come here." When she didn't say anything, he added, "I used to live in New York City. When my wife died, I came back home."

"I'm sorry about your wife."

There was an awkward silence as he stared into the fire.

"So, uh, you grew up here."

"Yes," he finally said, "part of the year. This land has belonged to my father's family for a long time. When I first moved back, I built this house."

"That's right—I knew you'd lived in New York. My agent and publisher are based there. You must miss it. It's one city I love to visit, and no matter how many times I go, it never loses its magic. How long were you there?"

"Eight years. Getting my career started."

He went from living in a crowded city with his wife to living practically by himself. Why? Because he didn't want to raise his girls in New York? Or was it something else? Life grief, maybe. Painful memories of his marriage? There were so many holes in the research she'd done into Brody Kincaid. Her curiosity aroused, she prodded, "Visiting is one thing—living there must be totally different." She hoped he would elaborate on why he chose to be a recluse. It might help her understand the man and work with him.

*Yeah, right. Who am I kidding? I'm a writer. I love delving into a person's motivations.*

"If I didn't know who you were, I would think you're a reporter." Beneath his soft tone there was a steel wire running through his words.

"And what do you do with reporters?"

"Avoid them at all costs."

"Good thing I'm not or I might still be out in the snowstorm."

He grinned, but it seemed reluctant.

"Daddy, who is she?" One of his daughters appeared in the entrance to the living room. The sound of footsteps pounding down stairs echoed through the house and then another girl almost crashed into her sister—an exact copy of the other. Twins. Why hadn't John mentioned that? Or for that matter, why hadn't Brody? But then everything she knew about the man was from her research—not from the man himself. That only spiked her curiosity more.

"I'm Ellie Summers. What are your names?"

Their wide eyes dominated their faces. They didn't say a word.

Brody motioned them into the room. "I think they're awestruck. They're huge fans of the Barnyard Town series."

They nodded, patches of red on their cheeks.

"And which one of you nailed me with that snowball?"

Brody's jaw dropped and he narrowed his eyes at his kids.

The one with a ponytail squeaked, "She did. Alexa. I'm Abbey and I would never throw a snowball at *you*."

Alexa, her hair in a wild mess, dropped her gaze to an interesting spot at her feet. "I didn't mean to. I meant to hit Abbey."

"Well, Alexa, you have a mean throwing arm. I'm impressed."

The child raised her head. "You aren't mad?"

"No. I could easily see Calvin or Henry doing that. I'll have to do that in my next book that takes place in winter."

Brody nodded his gratitude as Alexa broke into a huge smile. "Because of what I did? I loved *Winter's Folly*. I got it for Christmas."

Abbey stepped slightly in front of her twin. "I did, too. It was my idea to go outside and play war."

Ellie glanced from one to the other, amazed at how similar they were. Only their hair set them apart. "Y'all look so much alike. In school I had two friends who were twins. They used to try to stump me and often did."

Giggling, Abbey put her hand over her mouth. "We've fooled Daddy before."

"You wouldn't be a twin if you didn't attempt that at least once." Ellie slanted a glance at Brody.

Amusement lit his face. "I was just playing along. I know the difference between you two."

"Sure, Daddy," Abbey said, as if she didn't believe him. "We're gonna have a tea party upstairs. Will you come?"

"Of course. I love a good tea party. It reminds me of *Alice in Wonderland,* one of my favorite books," Ellie said before she realized she still hadn't told Brody why she'd driven all the way up the mountain three days early in a snowstorm. He stood looking awfully confused and a little irritated by her intrusion.

"We don't have a Mad Hatter or a Rabbit, but I do let Cindy join us sometimes. My doll is much better behaved than those two," Alexa said in such a serious voice as though she was describing tea with the queen of England.

Abbey took Ellie's hand. "And there really isn't any tea. It's all pretend, but there are real cookies."

"Sugar cookies with icing." Alexa peered at her father. "You can come, too."

"I'll be up in a little while. Don't drink all the pretend tea. Save me some." Brody's gaze was riveted to Ellie's, a quizzical look in those dark depths.

She and Brody were on the brink of ending their partnership before it even began, and she was heading for a play date with his kids? When the snow wasn't letting up and she needed to get back to the resort? Oh, dear. She tried to reassure the man with a smile. "After

I have some tea and cookies, I'd like to talk about the illustrations you left for me."

"I don't think you'll be going anywhere for a while." He didn't sound pleased. "I'll let my housekeeper know you'll be staying for lunch. We can talk after that."

Mounting the stairs, Ellie decided to use this time to pump the girls about their daddy. Other than his professional credits and the fact that his mother had been a famous actress, she knew next to nothing about Brody Kincaid. And she wanted to know a lot more. Even John had been evasive, telling her to make up her own mind. She'd known what her friend had been doing. If he'd turned Brody into enough of a mystery, she'd be intrigued and work with him just to solve the conundrum of Brody Kincaid, an exceptional illustrator, who was coming into his own as a painter. Well, she had teamed up with Brody, but the real mystery had become why he couldn't deliver the kind of exceptional illustrations he was known for. Something was clearly wrong. And she wanted to find out what that was.

## CHAPTER TWO

BRODY WATCHED ELLIE LEAVE, their eyes meeting for a few seconds before she disappeared with his daughters. For that brief moment, he felt bound to her, unable to look away. The sensation left him unsettled and even more leery of illustrating this children's author's books.

*John McCoy, what were you up to suggesting we collaborate?*

His old friend used to be her illustrator but had retired a few months ago after surviving a heart attack, right before he was going to illustrate Ellie's latest book. Brody's name had been on a shortlist of potential illustrators for her wildly popular children's series. He illustrated to make money, but his passion was his acrylics, which were finally selling. He'd agreed to fill in for John because they needed someone right away and he needed the money, but he just couldn't seem to give the woman what she wanted.

No doubt his third attempt hadn't been what she was looking for, either. He was trying very hard to emulate John's style. He was quickly discovering it had been a mistake to agree to work with her, especially when she started talking about having him accompany her on her next book tour. Too bad John didn't live in Snow Falls. If he did, he would insist his longtime friend be here to mediate between them. He had a feeling he and Ellie Summers would need a mediator.

He much preferred being left alone on his mountain with his daughters and drawing. Being the center of attention wasn't for him and even made him reconsider this kickoff to a gallery tour in the spring for his paintings. Certainly he had no intentions of touring with Ellie.

As a child of a famous film star, he'd had more than his share of the media. If he illustrated the Barnyard Town series, he would be in the public eye again. John had usually traveled with Ellie to draw the characters for the children. Brody wasn't ready to jump into that frenzy. And yet he needed the money. His painting had only just begun to sell.

But if he couldn't produce what she wanted, then the touring would be a moot point. He headed toward the kitchen in frustration to talk to Marta.

"Who was that I heard in the living room?" his fifty-year-old housekeeper asked. "Didn't they realize we're in the middle of a snowstorm?" Marta waved her cooking spoon at the bay window.

"It's Ellie Summers."

"The children's author? Why is she here?"

Marta was a little gruff around the edges, but his daughters adored her. "She came to see me."

"Her timing is lousy."

"She'll be staying for lunch."

Marta frowned and stared outside at the swirling snow. "I suspect she'll be staying for dinner and maybe even breakfast."

"You might be right." And that bothered him. She

seemed decent enough. Alexa had knocked her over with a snowball and yet she hadn't been upset about it. Why did her being kind make him want to get rid of her all the more?

"Lunch won't be for another hour."

As he mounted the stairs, he stopped in his room to get her a pair of his sweatpants. They'd swamp her, but at least they had a drawstring. She had to be uncomfortable in wet jeans.

He paused outside the girls' door and listened to Alexa declare in a tone full of authority, "But Petunia needs to be Henry's girlfriend."

"Farmer Brown and his wife rescue Petunia and bring her home to help with the mice problem in the barn," Ellie replied patiently. Ah, Petunia. He just couldn't seem to draw that character the way Ellie needed. He had no idea what he was doing anymore if she didn't like his third attempt. "I'm not sure what I'm going to do with Petunia in the series."

"But Henry needs someone." Alexa's voice rose. "He's all alone."

"Like Daddy. He shouldn't be alone."

*Henry or him?* Abbey's plea struck him in the chest. He wasn't alone. Unless Abbey meant… Brody charged into the room before his daughters said something he didn't want them to say.

He forced a smile to his face. "You two don't need to monopolize our guest."

"What does monopolize mean?" Alexa ate the last bite of her cookie.

"Want a person's attention all for yourself. Miss Summers and I have some business to talk about." After

Irene's death, he didn't want to become involved with a woman seriously. It took all he had to raise his two daughters who both shared the same middle name—Trouble.

"What business? Uncle John's business?" Abbey asked, looking from him to Ellie to him again, her ponytail swishing.

"None of your business."

"Aw, Daddy, that's not fair. We don't like secrets." Alexa pouted. "Ellie said she came to see you about some drawings."

"Ellie?" He frowned.

"Yeah, I told them to call me by my first name. I hope that's all right with you."

Before he could say anything, Alexa asked, "Why didn't you tell us you were drawing for the Barnyard Town series?"

*Because I would never have a moment's peace with you two hounding me about the pictures.* "We're still in the talking stage. Nothing is finalized."

"What's there to—finalize?" Abbey cocked her head to the side. "You draw pictures and she needs someone to draw since Uncle John can't anymore. It's wonderful." She exchanged a look with Alexa. "We can help you."

Alexa nodded.

*That's what I'm afraid of.*

Abbey patted the small chair next to her and pretended to pour some nonexistent tea. "The cookies are great."

Ellie's lips pressed together in a thin line as he settled his large frame on the tiny seat. "I can attest to that," she said. "I didn't have breakfast and I had two. I'll take some more tea, Abbey." Was she laughing at him?

While his daughter filled Ellie's cup, the woman's attention focused on Abbey, he studied her. Twenty-nine and a huge success, yet it seemed as though she went to pretend tea parties every day. Her smile encompassed her whole face and made it appear as though it was only for the child she was talking to. But what arrested him were her gray eyes. Expressive.

As if she realized he was staring at her, she glanced at him. He read amusement in those startlingly compelling eyes. He would love to draw her in charcoal. No oils or acrylics. A portrait that captured that face—not beautiful, but intriguing. From an artistic point of view only, he thought, and broke eye contact.

He swallowed hard, shifting in the chair and almost tipping it over. He steadied it and snatched up a cookie while his other hand clutched the sweatpants in his lap. "I brought you something to wear until your jeans dry. I know they'll be too big for you—" his gaze skimmed her petite frame, hardly out of place at the children's table "—but they're dry." He thrust the sweatpants at her. "There are socks in the pocket."

"That's sweet." She scanned the room. "Where can I change?"

His daughters hopped to their feet saying in unison, "We'll show you."

Ellie left the playroom with Alexa tugging her hand. Half a minute later he heard footsteps pounding down the staircase. Brody relished the ensuing silence because it wouldn't last long. He sensed Ellie had returned to the playroom before he turned and saw her by the doorway, a pensive expression on her face. She needed to talk to him. She'd come all the way up the mountain in a snow-storm and it wasn't because she'd loved his new illus-trations. He could use the money, but was it worth it?

"The girls took my jeans to put them in the dryer."

She was wearing his sweatpants, the pant legs pool-ing on the floor. She must have them clinched as tight as the drawstring allowed, but his long-sleeve T-shirt hung down covering her waist. Not bad. At all. Again he thought she would be great to sketch. High cheek-bones. Pert nose. Beautiful eyes. A long, slender neck. Short auburn hair that framed her face perfectly. He shook his head. They were business partners—at least for the time being. He'd loved one woman and her death had taken his desire to appreciate high cheekbones and a pert nose. Ellie was unsettling him.

She moved across the room and retook her seat, her hand resting on her thigh. "This is much better than those wet jeans. Thanks for thinking of it."

He glanced toward the door. "I wonder what's tak-ing the girls so long."

She chuckled. "Probably something else caught their fancy. They were telling me about the ice-carving con-test at the First Night celebration tomorrow."

"That's one of their favorite events. Last year some-one made a castle like one in a fairy tale. They loved it and were sad to see it melt. I can't imagine spend-ing hours on something like that and it only lasting a few hours."

Her elbow on the table, Ellie settled her chin in her palm. "I know what you mean. I want something I cre-ate to last."

"Yes, I guess you would." A connection sprang up across the short distance that separated them. He wanted to deny it, but he couldn't. She understood the creative mind.

"Once I was working on a story, and before I had a chance to save it, my screen went black. I lost it. From that day forward an automatic online service backs up my computer constantly."

"You didn't save as you were going along?"

"I usually do, but that day I got caught up in the story and lost track of time."

"I know what you mean. Sometimes I'll be working, and before I know it, the girls are home from school and the whole day has flown by." He paused. This connections was more than unsettling.

"I love it when it's like that. It beats eking out a few words at a time. That's murder."

"Or staring at a sheet of paper or canvas and nothing inspires you." Which was what was happening with her book.

"Right. You get what it's like to be blocked." Ellie relaxed her shoulders and sat back. "You have two cute daughters. I bet they keep you on your toes."

"I hardly have to work out, that's for sure. We're outside a lot—active. And they have vivid imaginations. We discovered a cave once and, of course, a treasure chest had to be inside. But before we'd taken a couple of steps into the dark cave, they decided it was the home of a bear and ran down the mountain screaming. I could hardly keep up with them."

"Ooh, that's good!" she said, smiling. "I may have to use something like that in one of my Barnyard Town books. Have Henry and Calvin go on a hike and discover a cave filled with adventure."

"I love Henry," Alexa said from behind Brody. He hadn't heard them come back in. He really should put bells on their shoes.

Abbey sat in the chair next to him. "Calvin is better than Henry."

Brody released a long sigh as his daughters launched into an argument about it. He tuned out what they were saying and assessed Ellie's reaction as Alexa and Abbey went back and forth. She seemed intent on keeping up with them—something he usually gave up on after a minute. But not Ellie.

"So which one is your favorite?" Abbey finally asked Ellie.

She tapped the side of her chin. "Hmm. That's a tough one. I like each one for a different reason, but I guess if I had to pick just one it would be…" Pausing, she pursed her lips.

"Who?" both girls asked, each bending closer to hear.

"My newest one. Petunia."

"Henry's girlfriend." Alexa drilled her gaze into Abbey.

Abbey's mouth turned down. "Why can't she be Calvin's?"

Alexa perched her fist at her waist. "Duh. Because he's a dog."

"Girls, no arguing," Brody said, secretly relieved his daughters had interrupted. When Ellie had talked about the creative process, he'd felt a kinship with her that he refused to feel with a woman again. When Irene died giving birth to his daughters, he vowed he wouldn't get that close to anyone again. Her death had ripped a hole in his heart. He'd been the one who had wanted children.

"Tell you what, Abbey. I'll think about introducing a girl dog after Petunia settles in at the farm."

"You will?" Abbey sat up straight and tossed a smug look at her twin. "Ha. Calvin doesn't need Petunia. He'll get his own girlfriend. A better one."

Before his daughters launched into another argument, Brody turned to Ellie. "I thought I could show you my studio. We have time before lunch."

Abbey jumped to her feet. "We've been in his studio tons of times, Ellie. He's been giving me and Alexa drawing lessons in there." She leaned toward Ellie and whispered, "We can't go in the studio without Daddy."

"Right now I need to talk with your daddy. Later I'll tell you a story I'm thinking of doing next and you can give me your opinions. Okay?"

Eyes like saucers, both girls nodded, quiet for a few seconds.

Ellie rose. "I had fun. Y'all throw a great tea party."

Abbey blinked. "We can help you with your story. Is that what you said?"

"I love getting kids' input. After all, these books are for y'all."

"Will you sign our Barnyard Town books?" Alexa darted toward a bookshelf at the other end of the playroom.

"Girls, we'll see you later. If she wants to sign them, she can then," Brody said before his daughters had Ellie's attention again.

Abbey opened her mouth to say something. He held up his hand, palm out. "Later. Right now go downstairs and help Marta set the table."

Alexa and Abbey looked at each other. Seconds later they rushed out of the room with Abbey saying, "Maybe she'll let us help her mash the potatoes."

"That probably wasn't my wisest suggestion. We may not be eating until one or two."

Ellie glanced toward the window, a frown lining her face. "It's snowing harder. Even if it stops soon, how am I going to get my rented car out of the snowdrift?"

He turned to stare at her. "A snowdrift? You didn't tell me you went off the road."

"I was so startled by the snowball, I must've forgotten to mention it. That's why I walked past the girls' fort. I had to abandon the car. Didn't you see it? It's not far, through the trees."

He'd been so wrapped up with Ellie's unexpected visit he hadn't noticed. Striding to the window, he peered outside. He couldn't see the end of his driveway because of the driving snow.

"Let's check the weather station and see what's happening in Snow Falls. It may be too late for you to leave, even if we could get your car unstuck, especially if they've closed the road."

"Closed the road? You mean I might be trapped here?"

## CHATPER THREE

"IT LOOKS LIKE YOU'RE STUCK," Brody said, turning off the weather station. He sounded nonchalant about it. Of course. He wasn't a woman stuck at a relative stranger's house without her makeup and clothes, which were sitting in her room at the Wildwood Lodge.

"Overnight?" Ellie stared out the window at the thick, falling snow and knew the answer to that question—had when she crawled out of her rented car and trudged toward his house.

He nodded. "Unless it lets up all of a sudden and the snowplows can get out. Even then it will take a while because my house is at the top of the mountain. I do have a friend who lives farther down who can pull your car out of the snowbank, but not in this weather."

"Why couldn't you live right in Snow Falls? Then this wouldn't be a problem." Ellie dug into his sweatpants' pocket and pulled out her cell. No bars. She gritted her teeth. "No reception."

"There never is up here."

"How do you get internet? I know you have it. We've emailed back and forth."

"I have a landline and my internet is dial-up."

She breathed a long sigh. "Then I can call the hotel and find out what's going on down below."

"Sure. One is downstairs in the hallway." Ellie marched out the door into the upstairs corridor, which was a feat in itself with the oversize sweatpants.

Making her way down the staircase carefully, hoping she didn't trip, she couldn't shake the notion she was wearing what he usually did. The thought accelerated her heartbeat.

There was something about Brody Kincaid that appealed to her and yet at the same time warned her off. John had said he was reclusive, especially after his wife died in childbirth. She'd known he was a father, but nothing about how old or adorable the two girls were. Maybe that was it. She wanted to have a family—be a mother—but she'd never found the man who would fit into her life. She'd dated an accountant once, but he'd never understood her creative needs. The way Brody did.

She was nearing thirty. Time was running out if she wanted more than one child, and she did. She lifted the receiver to her ear and called the lodge. Five minutes later she hung up from talking to a staff member at the front desk with the verdict. She was trapped. With a single man who shared her creativity. A single dad who clearly liked children. *Interesting.*

"What did they say?" Brody asked behind her.

She spun around, embarrassed by her train of thought. "It's snowing in town, too, but not as much as up here. The weatherman has changed his forecast to snow for the next twenty-four hours on this side of the mountain. The town should be fine."

"I know that one of the events for the First Night celebration is a play from your book *Winter's Folly* because the girls insisted we go there no matter what. What time do you have to be at the playhouse?"

"Five. The play starts at six. I'm narrating it and then having a book signing afterward."

"My drawing lesson for the kids at the lodge is at three. If it stops by ten or eleven, that'll give the snowplows several hours to get the main road cleared. We may be last, but it shouldn't take more time than that."

"I have to be at the town square in the early afternoon to open the festivities by starting the ball countdown to midnight at one."

"That may be a problem. It's eleven-thirty right now. Even if the snow stops in twenty-four hours, I don't see how we'll make it. But it could stop earlier. There's no telling with the weather around here."

"Great. What should I do?"

"Call your contact and let him know what has happened."

"That's the mayor. I left that info in my hotel room."

"I can get you in touch with him. One of my cousins is a friend of his." After Brody placed a call to his relative, he punched in some numbers then passed the receiver to her.

"Mr. Richards, this is Ellie Summers. There may be a problem with me making the opening ceremony tomorrow."

"What?" the man said in a booming voice.

"I'm at my illustrator Brody Kincaid's house on the mountain, and it's snowing up here so much the roads are impassable."

"Why in the world are you there in the middle of a snowstorm? Didn't I put you up at the Wildwood? The children have been looking forward to seeing you. Does that mean you won't make the play, either?" His tone held a frantic ring mixed with a touch of anger.

"I didn't plan this. I'll be there if it's at all possible."

"You're the mistress of ceremonies. That's an honor we only bestow on one celebrity."

She pulled the phone away from her ear. "I know. I don't want to let the children down."

"Then don't. Call me tomorrow. The snow isn't too bad here. You'll be able to make it. All you have to do is drive slowly and allow yourself plenty of time. I'm certainly not telling my two grandchildren you aren't coming."

When she hung up from talking with the upset mayor, she faced Brody. "I think he thinks I planned this."

Brody frowned. "I should have known. He doesn't handle change well. He's the one who started the First Night celebration a while back."

"Well, I'd *hate* to disappoint the kids tomorrow. They're why I agreed to participate in the celebration." She wouldn't tell him he was actually the main reason she'd agreed. She'd known with his family it would be easier if she came to him, and she wanted to meet him in person to figure out why he couldn't deliver what she wanted.

"My girls and I have been going since they were babies except for one year when Abbey was sick. They'll be disappointed if we can't get down the mountain."

A sudden thought caused her to suck in a deep breath. "I just remembered I have a speech I'm to give and it's back at the hotel." Panic set in. "I was going to rehearse it this evening."

"Where are you staying?"

"Wildwood Lodge."

"Oh, then there shouldn't be a problem. We drive right by there on the way to the town square."

She clenched her jaw so tight pain shot down her neck. "You don't understand. I hate giving speeches."

"Then why did you agree?"

"My agent insisted I do it. 'Great publicity,' he said. I need to practice saying no more often. I'm afraid the publicity won't be favorable when the press catches me babbling nonsensically. Of course, that might not be a problem when I don't show up."

Brody glanced in the direction of the kitchen where they could hear giggling. "Let's go to the studio. We can talk where two little girls won't hear everything we say." He strolled into the great room off the foyer. "The weatherman has been wrong before. This storm might fizzle out."

"Do you believe that?" Ellie followed him toward a door at the other end of the large room.

He shrugged and let her go through first. A short enclosed breezeway separated the house from his studio. Chilled from the storm outside, she hugged her arms to her chest and was glad she had on a pair of warm sweatpants and socks—even if they were his.

He hurried past her and unlocked the door. "I tried working in the house. It didn't happen. If I didn't have a separate place even though it's only five yards from the house, I would never get anything accomplished. I usually lock both doors, and if necessary, Marta pages me on the intercom."

The studio was toasty warm. Slowly rotating, she saw several finished paintings as well as some in various stages of completion. One caught her attention—a large painting with slashing lines and vibrant colors of a view looking down on a lake surrounded by mountains. She couldn't pull her gaze away. The scene stole her breath. He had captured nature's beauty—raw and powerful. Should she look at doing something different for her books? How would this style translate into a children's book?

She finally walked to a bank of floor-to-ceiling windows along the back of the studio and stared out at the driving snow. "What's out there?"

"The best view of the valley. My studio is perched at the edge of the mountain. It drops off there. When it isn't snowing the natural lighting is great."

"I imagine it would be." She turned from the window to face Brody.

He stood in his element—his canvases, drawing board and paints all around him. From across the room, his gaze held her transfixed. He cleared his throat. "You didn't come all the way up the mountain to exchange pleasantries. What's wrong with those illustrations I left for you at the lodge?"

She nibbled on her lower lip and tried to think of how to compose her response. "There wasn't anything wrong with them."

"But? There's definitely one at the end of that statement."

"But there is none of your passion and emotions in

the illustrations." She waved her hand at a painting hanging up behind him. "Not like that one. That's what attracted me to your work when John mentioned you."

"And yet you wanted the same thing you got from John—pastels, soft. Safe."

"Safe?"

He frowned. "I'm not John. That became obvious when I've tried to emulate his style." He indicated his work around the room. "I can't be something I'm not. Soft pastels don't excite me. I do my best when the colors are bold, the lines dramatic. My drawings pop off the page. Have you considered modernizing your illustrations? Kids are into manga. Maybe something more like that."

"Manga? That might fit for my new series for older kids, but I don't know about Barnyard Town."

"I don't see how I can do what you want. I've tried. It isn't working."

Her heartbeat began to hammer against her rib cage. "What do you mean? You knew John's style before you accepted."

"You told me what you wanted in the two scenes. A skunk spraying Henry and Calvin. Mary Ann trying to bathe Henry in tomato juice. That's a funny scene. I couldn't express it without using some of what I'm used to. Time is running out. You know it. I know it. Maybe we need to cut our ties now so you have time to find someone who can deliver what you want."

"Just change your choice of colors, soften the lines."

"You should know it isn't that simple when you're creating something. Your heart has to be in it. Mine isn't. I didn't think it would be a problem, but…" He shook his head, staring at the falling snow outside. "This partnership is not working. You need to find another illustrator. You still have time. I don't want to leave you in a bind at the last minute."

A gasp at the door, which Ellie now realized was ajar, intruded on the moment. Brody marched toward it and yanked it open.

Fists on his waist, he glared down at the pair of girls crouched by the entrance, huddling together because of the cold in the breezeway. "I thought I made it clear this was a private meeting between me and Miss Summers. Go to your rooms."

"We came to let you know dinner was ready. Marta asked us to get you," Abbey said, straightening as she rubbed her hands up and down her arms.

"We didn't want to inter—" Rising, Alexa looked toward her sister.

"Interrupt you," Abbey finished.

"So you decided to listen to what we were talking about instead?"

Both girls dropped their heads and mumbled, "Yes."

"Tell Marta we'll be there in a minute, and we will have a talk later."

Brody's two daughters plodded down the breezeway, their posture expressing their disappointment. He waited until they disappeared before closing the door all the way, its click splicing through the now-unnerving silence.

"I think it's best if we sever our ties," he repeated as he turned toward her.

Ellie squared her shoulders and moved into his personal space. "I came all this way and now I'm stuck here overnight. The least you could do is give this another chance. I'm willing to. We can talk after lunch. Frankly, the book is due the first of March, so no, I don't have that much time to hunt for someone else. Where am I going to find another illustrator as talented as you who can do it right now? I know the holidays are hectic and take a lot of family time, but things ought to settle down now that the new year is almost here." She fortified herself with a calming breath and continued. "Creatively I've had to make changes at my editor's request. That's similar to this situation."

He sighed, a frown creasing his brow. "Let's eat. We'll discuss this later."

As Ellie walked down the breezeway, she felt the way Abbey and Alexa must have as they had trudged away a few minutes ago. She'd been so busy herself promoting *Winter's Folly* during the holidays that she didn't spend the time to cultivate her new partnership with Brody as she had with John in the beginning. Now she had to woo him to stay on the job. He was good, and a good illustrator/artist could adapt. The last set of illustrations was an improvement. Maybe another attempt would finally work.

"No dessert for you two," Brody announced to his daughters at the end of lunch, which was a full-course meal. "I need to finish my meeting with Miss Summers, and under no circumstances do I want you to think you can eavesdrop on it."

"I'll make sure they don't." Marta shot Ellie a look as though this extra work was all her fault.

Brody wasn't clueless—Marta wasn't pleased Ellie

was here. It had become evident when Ellie sat in Marta's chair at the start of the meal. When his housekeeper came into the dining room with the last bowl of carrots, onions and potatoes, she came to a halt and glared at Ellie. Routine was important to Marta, and she had helped bring some of that to his household. His girls had desperately needed the structure. Abbey piped in before he could that the seat Ellie sat in was where Marta sat. But when Ellie moved to the other vacant chair, the tension hadn't dissipated.

"Do we have to go to our rooms?" Alexa asked, breaking into Brody's thoughts.

"No, I want you two to help Marta clean up the dishes. That way, Marta, it will be easier for you to keep tabs on them. You can start by taking the plates into the kitchen." When he had pronounced that he and Ellie end their business relationship, he'd thought he would feel relieved. But he wasn't, and it really didn't have anything to do with the money. That in itself scared him. Now he probably would give it a fourth attempt instead of focusing on his upcoming tour for his paintings.

*Run* kept sounding in his mind, especially when she fixed her full attention on him with those gray eyes that conveyed so much of what she was feeling. But this was his house and there was no place really to run.

Alexa stood first, collected her plate and Ellie's and hurried out.

Abbey got to her feet but didn't move. Instead, she tilted her head and studied him. "Why don't you want to draw the pictures for Barnyard Town? That has got to be the best job in the world."

He'd known his daughters wouldn't remain quiet

about what they'd overheard earlier. What had surprised him was that Abbey had waited until the meal was over. That had to be a record. Probably because she and her sister had been whispering to each other through lunch, in between pumping Ellie for more information about Petunia and a possible girlfriend for Calvin. Scheming no doubt about a way to get him to change his mind.

"Daddy, aren't you going to answer me?"

"No. This is between Miss Summers and me. It doesn't include you."

Abbey planted one hand on her waist in disbelief. "But it concerns me."

"How so?" he asked and clamped his lips together to keep his laughter inside.

"I won't get to tell the kids at school that you're doing the pictures in the books. It would help your status if you did."

Brody's mouth dropped open. "My status? Where in the world did you come up with that?"

"TV. I heard it on a show."

"Young lady, I believe you have a job to do." He turned to Ellie. "Let's continue our conversation in my office." His studio was too personal—not as business-like as his office. That ought to help him not give in to what she wanted—illustrations he now realized he couldn't do.

He wanted to make it clear to her he didn't want the job, especially now that he'd met Ellie in person. She reminded him of his deceased wife with some of her mannerisms and those eyes that told him what she was feeling. But even worse, Ellie enthralled his two daugh-ters. They'd tried to fix him up with their best friend's divorced mother last fall. They were six and a half. Where did they come up with these ideas?

Shaking his head, he made his way to his office on the other side of the house, checking the snowfall at a window as he passed by. Short of a miracle, Ellie would be staying tonight. Which would only give his daughters more time to concoct a plan to get him to work for her. But knowing them, they wouldn't stop at that. The disaster with their best friend's mother still haunted him. He needed to get Ellie to town and away from Abbey and Alexa.

Alexa appeared in the hallway from the kitchen. "Daddy, before you go into the office, Marta wanted to know if you wanted coffee," she said in her sweet voice.

Boy, he was in trouble. Something was up with Alexa. And if her, then Abbey, too. He started to say no, but Ellie interrupted him.

"I'd love some. Maybe it will chase away the cold."

"Daddy can build a fire. There's a fireplace in his office. He's good at stuff like that."

Ellie slid a glance toward him. "That would be nice. I don't think I've completely thawed out after my intimate encounter with the snow today."

He gritted his teeth. Next, his daughters would turn on soft music. At least the snow would keep the great room bright so there'd be no dimming of the lights. They'd done that when Kelly's mother came to pick her up and the three of them begged her to wait in the living room while they finished cleaning up the mess they'd made upstairs.

Alexa swiveled around and raced toward the kitchen, yelling, "I'll be right back with the coffee!"

"Your girls are so adorable. You're lucky to have them."

"Yes, I am." *Most of the time.*

"So sweet and friendly."

"Yes, they are." *When they want something.*

"And smart. The stories they were telling me at our tea party were hilarious. I could see them becoming writers."

"They do know how to fabricate stories." Brody gestured toward one of the overstuffed chairs while he took the one across from it, as far away from her as he could be and still carry on a conversation without raising his voice. That would only entice his kids into the hallway to listen.

Alexa came in with one mug while Abbey brought the other one. Marta carried the sugar and cream.

Abbey carefully placed his cup on a coaster on the desk near Brody. "Just like you like it, black." She smiled sweetly, which set off alarm bells. He knew that look. He glanced at his other daughter. The same expression. A double whammy.

Abbey stepped back while Alexa gave Ellie her mug. "Have Daddy show you the drawings he did of us playing in the yard. He's very good." She pointed toward a binder on a shelf behind him. "He keeps them in there," Alexa added then joined her sister while Marta put the cream and sugar on the table next to Ellie.

"Girls, I know what you're doing, and as I said earlier, this is between Miss Summers and me." He sent them a "don't say a word" look.

They both lowered their gazes to their shoes, not a meek bone in their body.

"We're leaving," Marta said while herding the twins toward the exit. "Don't forget about dessert. A French silk pie. Your favorite, Mr. K."

"We won't. And Abbey and Alexa—" Brody waited until his daughters peered back at him with that meek expression on their faces that spelled trouble, before continuing "—no listening at the door. Help Marta clean up then go to your rooms. I haven't forgotten we need to talk."

"But, Daddy—" Alexa started to say, but Abbey yanked her out into the hallway.

He heard Abbey say, "Don't make him any madder, or we'll have to stay in our rooms the whole time Ellie is here."

"I'll make sure they behave," Marta said before shutting the door with a little more force than normal.

A laugh escaped Ellie the second they were alone. A light, musical sound that made him think of Irene. She'd been so full of life. In fact, Ellie's smile reminded him of Irene. His wife's eyes sparkled the same way as Ellie's. They both had a dimple in their left cheek. He frowned. He didn't like the direction of his thoughts. This was why he needed to end this partnership before it really got going.

"May I see the drawings?" Ellie's question pulled him away from his thoughts about his deceased wife and how he was the reason she wasn't here enjoying her two daughters, anchoring him in the present—one where he had a problem.

"They're really nothing, just some I did for the girls. We made a book out of them."

"I'd love to see them."

The look she gave him—just short of her batting her eyes at him—coupled with her soft tone of voice was lethal. Irene could do that to him. There he went, comparing Ellie and Irene. He gritted his teeth again and pushed to his feet. If for no other reason, this was why he shouldn't collaborate with Ellie Summers. Too hazardous to his well-ordered life.

After sliding the binder off the shelf, he handed it to her then took his chair, wishing he were anywhere but in his office at the moment. The pictures were something special between him and his daughters. Moments of their life he'd captured, not with a camera but with his acrylics. A work of love.

She opened to the first illustration and her gaze lifted to his. "I thought you were talking about a pencil or pen drawing. These are small acrylics." She flipped through a few more pages. "Beautiful. I feel like I'm right there with the girls, playing on the swing. In the pile of leaves. Oh, this one with the snowman is adorable. And the one trying to catch a squirrel." Radiant. That was how she looked when she smiled. "Did they?"

"What? Catch a squirrel?"

"Yes. When I was a little girl, I tried to do the same thing but with a skunk. It wasn't a pretty picture when I got too close and it defended itself."

"Is that where you came up with that scene with Mary Ann and Henry after the skunk incident?"

Nodding, she waved her hand at the binder. "I've imagined building snowmen and chasing squirrels with my own children. Or the children I dream of having. Like what you've captured here. I envy you your kids. They're full of imagination and life."

And in that second the wall he'd built around himself cracked. He swallowed several times. Ellie Summers was dangerous. He didn't want to care about a woman ever again. He was just fine living on this mountain with his two daughters and painting in his studio. He didn't need anything or anyone else. Especially not a woman who wanted her own children. Two were plenty. As his painting career grew, he wouldn't even need the money from his illustrations.

He surged to his feet and snatched the binder from Ellie's grasp. "I don't think we have anything to discuss."

## CHAPTER FOUR

"I THINK YOU'RE RIGHT." She couldn't believe she was admitting this, but she couldn't deny what she'd derived from looking at his personal drawings. She hadn't even realized that was what she wanted—at least not consciously. But maybe she had subconsciously when she went with Brody in the first place. "It's time for a change."

He snapped his fingers. "Just like that. Are you really sure?"

"Those drawings are exactly what I want to see in *Petunia Comes to Town*. I want to spark children's imaginations and emotions with the pictures that go with my words. Please reconsider working on the book. Petunia's arrival will shake things up." She rose and tapped the binder he held. "I want the story's illustrations to do the same thing. But the only way we'll know is for you to sketch a few samples."

Only a foot separated them, the air charged with tension. She half expected him to put some space between them. He took a deep breath but remained silent and where he was.

"May I finish looking at the binder?" She held out her hand.

His gaze drilled into her, but beneath the hard lines on his face she saw a softening in his expression.

"Please?" Ellie added with a look she hoped persuaded him.

The stiff set to his shoulders relaxed. "I don't normally show this to others." He gave her the binder. "Not even Marta."

"But your daughters made it difficult for you not to?"

"Exactly. That's Abbey and Alexa. No doubt they're somewhere plotting some other scheme to get me to illustrate your book. I want you to be one hundred percent sure you want to go in a different direction."

"I want something along these lines." She tapped the binder. "I *know* you can do this."

He backed away. "I don't know. This was so personal."

"You get it. These drawings make that evident. If you can give me two illustrations, I'll fax them to my publisher to get his okay. But I know there won't be a problem. He'd been talking about the direction for my new series for older children. This will sync well with our ideas and then perhaps you'd consider doing both. It could be a bridging of styles."

"You're good at steamrolling people," he mumbled, finally putting space between them.

Ellie sat again and opened the binder. "Please just reconsider. Think about it. Don't give me an answer until after the First Night celebration. We can meet at the original time, and you can let me know. Maybe if we got to know each other that would help."

Surprise flitted across his features, and he took another step back. It was as if he didn't want to get to know her.

"I know working on the book together is a professional partnership, but when John and I became friends, it made our partnership work so much better. We knew what the other wanted before they did."

*Like a marriage* popped into Ellie's mind. She could never say something like that to him. This man was a recluse. The idea would send him running toward a higher mountain to perch himself on.

"Maybe we could discuss the first illustration again in person, then you could try redoing it. If it works, great. If it doesn't, I won't say another word. I'll ride off into the sunset as Buster, the horse in my new series, would say. Deal?"

Brody sighed. "We're stuck here together for at least the next twenty hours. I guess we can put the time to good use. I warn you, I don't work well under pressure."

She held up her hands. "No pressure here. You don't have to finish it in the next twenty hours. Just start it maybe or at the least we can talk about the scene and what I was thinking when I wrote that part of the story."

"Did you do this with John?"

"Sometimes. But like I said, we became friends and that helped. I know not all illustrators and writers do, but it worked for us."

His lips thinned, he stared out the window behind Ellie for a long moment. "Okay. One more illustration."

"Yippee!"

Brody pivoted toward the intercom system, mounted by the door with a full-fledged scowl.

"Shh, Alexa," a little girl's voice whispered.

Ellie chuckled. He glared at her, strode to the door and yanked it open.

The sound of footsteps pounding up the staircase

resonated through the house. In a few short hours Ellie had gotten more material for her next book than when she visited her nephews. What if Petunia and Henry had twin kittens? And an intercom. She could think of tons of mischief for them to get into.

Brody reappeared in the entrance to his office. "They're hiding. They don't know I know where their latest hiding place is. I think I'll let them stew for a while."

"Where is it?"

"They've taken their toys out of a cabinet and they hide in there."

Laughter bubbled out of her. "You must never have a dull moment with them."

"There's nothing wrong with dull."

"Do we still have a deal?"

"Yes. If we did work together, I'd be my daughters' hero."

"I have a feeling you already are." Ellie turned to the next drawing and burst into louder laughter. "Oh, my. You do have your hands full," she said, pointing at an illustration of one high in a tree while the other hung from a branch about ten feet off the ground.

He glanced at it. "That drawing I did from memory because I had to get the ladder and climb up to rescue Abbey. She was stuck. Of course, that was after I saved Alexa from falling and breaking something. They were supposed to be in their rooms reading, their homework for school. Marta about had a heart attack when she looked out the window over the sink and saw them. And to think at one time I wanted four or five children."

"You've changed your mind? I think three or four

kids would be great." With her biological clock ticking down, she'd be lucky to have one or two. Although she was still young. Twenty-nine was still young.

"Yes. Two children are enough for me."

"You might change your mind when you meet the right woman." The second she said it Ellie snapped her mouth closed. Why didn't she censor herself better? Who was she to give him advice about his love life? Hers was all but nonexistent.

"Not likely. Don't get me wrong. I love Abbey and Alexa so much, but it was hard raising two babies. Until Marta, I couldn't find a housekeeper who worked well with them. The stories I could tell you about some of the women I tried out, especially since I wanted a live-in housekeeper-nanny. Don't tell the girls that's the way I think of Marta. They think they are way too old for a nanny. When I hired her, I made it clear to the kids she would just be a housekeeper. Somehow they bought that."

"Or they genuinely liked Marta enough to tolerate having her as a nanny. She's a terrific cook and seems to care about your daughters." Although she didn't think the woman cared for her unexpectedly dropping in to see Brody and disrupting her routine.

"She's a jewel, but I had to go through a whole treasure chest before finding the gem."

"I used to say I would never do a certain thing, but low and behold I was proven wrong."

"What?" He took the chair across from her.

"I told my publisher and agent I would never do author tours or give speeches. I'm now doing both even though I hate to get up in front of an audience."

"I have a feeling you can wrap an audience around your finger."

His compliment warmed her, and she began to relax. "Maybe children. I don't know so much about adults."

"But children are your audience. My daughters were enthralled with you." He cocked a grin. "I'm thinking they would be even if you read a telephone book."

She laughed. "And I thought you were giving me a compliment."

"Oh, but I am. This has been a treat for them to meet you in person. When their uncle John came to visit, they pestered him into telling them all about you. They couldn't believe he was working with you."

"Is that why you agreed to our partnership even though it isn't something you usually do?"

"Yes. Why did you ask me?"

"John recommended you, and I trust his opinion. He's never steered me wrong before."

Brody frowned. "Until now."

"I'm not so sure he was wrong. Like I said—" she held up the binder "—sometimes John could tell what I wanted before I even knew it."

"We'll see."

"Tonight would you let me read Abbey and Alexa a bedtime story?"

"If I said no, I'd never hear the end of it."

"Good. That's something I don't get to do unless I'm visiting my sister. She has two boys. But they're nine and eleven, getting too old for my books. So I started making up stories instead. That's why I'm thinking of expanding into books for that age, too. One of my favorite books growing up was *Charlotte's Web*."

"The pig, right?"

She nodded. "And the spider."

"So you have a sister. Any other siblings?"

"Just Kathy, and she's five years older than me, so we weren't close growing up. But now we are. How about you?" She didn't want him to know she'd read all about him. Some of his childhood, mostly publicity shots with his mother and quite a bit while he lived in New York before dropping out of sight and living in Colorado on top of a mountain. But nothing recent.

"I have a few cousins. Two of them live in the area. But other than that, no immediate family."

"Isn't your father alive?"

Brody stiffened, clutching the arms of the chair. "Yes, somewhere in Europe. When he and Mom divorced, he left the United States. I hear from him sometimes at Christmas. Not this year, other than some presents arriving for the girls."

His hint of vulnerability touched her. "So neither of us has a large family."

"Yeah."

"Did you ever regret that? Quite a few of my friends had a ton of cousins. At the holidays they usually went from one family member's house to another. Our place was always so quiet compared to theirs."

A chuckle eased his tense features. "Living with my mother was like living in a circus with crowds looking on. People coming and going—constantly. It was rarely quiet. My mother was a whirlwind that swept everyone along as she moved through life. She needed those people around her. Up until her death I didn't know what calm and peaceful were." He swept his arm to indicate his office. "That's why I'm living where I am."

"Didn't you tell me you had a tour this spring for your paintings?"

"Nothing like your schedule. But yes. I cut it down to the bare bones, though, which my agent wasn't excited about. I know my limits and have learned to respect them. Besides, I can't be away from Abbey and Alexa long. The spring tour will be the first time I've left them for longer than an overnight with Marta. I would never have been able to do the tour if she hadn't come to work for me."

"I do love meeting children and seeing their smiles. I love getting them excited about reading. I've even worked with young elementary-school students writing their own stories. It's all the other stuff I don't like."

"Then don't do it. Focus on what you like to do, but let the other events go. I'm just starting out but you've established yourself as a writer. The one thing I vowed when Abbey and Alexa were born was that I would be there for them. I wouldn't let my work take me away like my mother's did when I was growing up. Or like my long-distance dad. It hasn't always been easy but I've made it work."

"Is that a second reason why you wanted to back out of working with me—because John toured with me?"

Brody pushed to his feet and paced to the floor-to-ceiling window. His back to her, his hands clasped behind him, he stared out at the snow-blanketed landscape.

Ellie nibbled on her lower lip, wondering why Brody wasn't answering her question. Twisting in her chair, she looked at him. "I'll understand if it is, especially after meeting your daughters."

He unclasped his hands and pivoted toward her. "If my style ends up working for you and your publisher, I don't see how I can be part of your tour. I know how much the children enjoyed John drawing the characters for them, but I can't leave Abbey and Alexa."

A strong knock reverberated through the office.

"I wonder which one of my daughters that is." He strode toward the door.

A few seconds later Alexa stood in the entrance, her shoulders slumped forward, her hair even wilder about her face. "Daddy, why didn't you try to find us? I fell asleep in the cabinet."

"Because I thought you and your sister needed time to reflect on how you listened in on a private conversation. Twice. Who flipped on the intercom in here?"

Abbey stepped into the doorway slightly behind Alexa. "I did while Marta was giving you the sugar and cream."

"It was bad enough when you listened in at the studio, but then you did it again. This time purposefully. No accident."

"Please don't turn down working with Ellie because of what we did," Abbey said, keeping her gaze glued on her father as though her look could convince him not to.

And if any expression could change her dad's mind, it was Abbey's sorrowful one. Ellie covered her mouth to hide her grin.

Alexa squared her shoulders and lifted her chin. "Yeah, Daddy, Ellie needs you."

The fervent way the child spoke caused a blush to

creep up Ellie's face. The heat singed her cheeks. She dropped her head to hide her reaction. Maybe in a strictly professional way she needed him, but for some reason he was making it clear that even friendship might not be possible between them.

There was something about their conversation earlier that made her feel a connection to him. He was an intriguing man, and under different circumstances, she would be attracted to him. But she didn't date to just date. She wanted to get married, have a family, so any man she dated was prospective husband material to her. She didn't waste what time she had on men who weren't. And Brody Kincaid didn't want more children. That was number one on her list.

Vaguely she was aware Brody was talking to his daughters. When he said her name, it pulled her back into their conversation.

"Miss Summers and I are working on it, but if there's any more eavesdropping, the answer will be no."

"We've been so excited she's visiting," Abbey said in a dead-serious voice.

"Yeah, Daddy. Our excitement got the better of us."

"That seems to be a problem for you two."

Abbey shrugged. "What can I say? We get excited." Leaning to the side, she peeked around her father and said to Ellie, "We're sorry, Miss Summers."

A few seconds passed while she tried to come up with something solemn to say. "Remember in future not to listen in on others' conversations. You might hear something you don't want to hear."

"Oh, like Calvin did when Buster and Zoey were gossiping?"

Ellie snapped her fingers. "Exactly."

"I need to work for a few hours. Can I count on you to behave and keep Miss Summers entertained?"

A pout turned Alexa's mouth down. "Work? But this is the day before New Year's Eve."

"I promised Miss Summers I would try something with one of the illustrations—" he paused, then added "—to see if we can work together going in a new direction."

"Great. Daddy, you need to hurry up. We'll take care of Miss Summers. Don't you worry at all." Abbey hurried toward Ellie and grasped her hand, tugging her out of the chair. "Tell us all about Petunia. We can help you with her. We love cats. Too bad Daddy is allergic or we would have several."

Ellie glanced back at Brody as his daughters, each one taking a hand, pulled her into the hallway. "If you have any questions about that first scene, you know where to find me, especially if you want to show me what you've done so far."

"I will when I'm finished."

As she followed Abbey and Alexa up the stairs, she already missed the lively exchange she'd had with Brody. She liked him, but he was used to being alone—raising his children, working. She wanted more of a partnership.

A partnership like the one she'd had with John.

# CHAPTER FIVE

"I'VE GOT A FRESH POT of coffee for you," Ellie said when she came into Brody's studio hours later, "and a sandwich for dinner."

Seeing Ellie brought a smile to Brody's lips. It had been several hours since he'd holed up in his studio to work on the illustration. The first hour all he'd done was stare at the paper. And then an idea had sparked him. "Thanks. I'm starved. What are Abbey and Alexa doing?"

"Playing."

"Behaving?" She'd changed back into her own clothes and handed him back his sweatpants. He lay them in a chair by the door. Suddenly his eyes were drawn to them. Very distracting.

"They're being little angels."

With her short auburn hair framing her face, her gray eyes big and expressive, her mouth full with a hint of dark maroon lipstick, she appealed to him. For a few seconds he couldn't look away from those luscious lips. Finally he returned his gaze to hers, scrambling to come up with something coherent to say. She was definitely becoming a distraction all round. "I'm surprised they haven't come out here to see what's going on."

Ellie averted her gaze.

He put his brush down. "What happened?"

"Oh, nothing. Really."

"Your tone of voice doesn't imply nothing."

"It wasn't anything. I caught them whispering about getting us alone. They have quite creative minds."

"I'm afraid to ask what they came up with."

"Abbey was going to have me come to your office while Alexa told you I needed to talk to you in your office. Then when we were in the room, they were going to lock the door. They know where the key is to that room."

"You're kidding." Alexa and Abbey wanted a mom, but they were going to have to be satisfied with their single dad and Marta. He wouldn't go through what he went through with Irene's death ever again. Losing her put him in a dark place that he was only now beginning to come out of. But even now the guilt still plagued him. If only he hadn't wanted children, she would be alive today.

"No. I pointed out to them that would only make a situation worse. That forcing us together wouldn't cause us to work together. Most likely the opposite would happen. They immediately scratched that off their list."

"They had more schemes? A list of them?" Brody took a gulp of the warm coffee, needing the caffeine to keep alert—obviously to stay one step ahead of his daughters and their matchmaking.

"A couple. They talked about running away so both of us would come looking for them, but Abbey thought they better not do that. It was too cold outside and dark."

Brody shook his head. "I should be used to this by

now, but they continually amaze me. They're each other's best friends."

"Abbey suggested hiding inside and only making it appear as if they went outside, but Alexa said that wouldn't work. You'd figure it out and when you came back you'd find them because you know all their hiding places."

"And they're alone right now. Probably hatching some other kind of plot as we speak. Maybe I need something stronger than coffee."

"They're quietly sitting at the kitchen table drawing me illustrations of *Winter's Folly*. They thought if you didn't work out, they might."

He was in the process of sipping his coffee and nearly spewed it all over the illustration he'd been working on for hours.

Taking one of the napkins she'd brought him, she dabbed it across the drawing table. "I did ask them why they needed to get us alone." Ellie pulled a stool toward the drawing board, then sat. "They thought if we became friends we would do things for each other because that's what friends do. That you'll draw the pictures for my books as a friend. They think you need a friend."

*They want someone to be much more than friends.* He still shuddered when he thought of the incident with Kelly's mother, not to mention their couple other attempts to get him to date. Six years old and they were thinking about dating. What was next?

"Yep. Then they started telling me about all their friends. They sure have a lot."

"They've never met a stranger. When they had their

birthday party at the Ice Castle in town, they invited all their classmates. That was forty children from two different classes. Try keeping an eye on that many kids at one time. Thankfully some of the parents took pity on me and stayed to help. And I had Marta. That was their first and maybe their last birthday party. I think my hearing was permanently impaired from all the noise."

"That sounds like a lot of fun. I can only remember a few birthday parties."

"I never had one that wasn't a media event for my mom." The touch of sadness in his voice made him realize he was letting his guard down around Ellie. He quickly tried to shore it back up. If they worked together, it had to be a professional relationship only. She might have been good friends with John, but he couldn't afford to be this attractive woman's friend. Too risky.

"How about friends?"

"Contrary to what my daughters think, I do have friends. A lot of them live in different parts of the country but not all. But I have to admit, lately I've been more focused on my family and career. There's just so much time in a day."

Leaning against the drawing board, Ellie settled her elbow on it with her chin in her palm. "What do you do for fun?"

"Go on adventures with the girls. Read when I can, usually when they're finally in bed. Cross-country ski. I'm teaching Abbey and Alexa how."

"If the snow doesn't let up, we could always ski to Snow Falls."

Brody laughed. "Have you ever skied downhill?"

"Well, no, but how hard can it be? I've water-skied. I'm quite good at keeping my balance."

His laughter grew. "It's nothing like waterskiing. Snow Falls is miles away. I doubt you'd have the stamina to make it."

She looked him in the eye. "I beg your pardon. I'm a quick learner. I'm in very good shape. I exercise."

"Oh, what?"

"Yoga mainly. But I also lift weights a couple times a week and power walk three or four miles three times a week."

"Snow Falls is eighteen miles down a mountain."

"It's that far? I didn't realize. I thought it was taking me so long to get here because of the blizzard." She glanced toward the large window that revealed the snow—a lot—was still falling. "I have a feeling the mayor isn't going to be too happy with me."

"He'll have to get over it. If it's not possible, then it's not."

"I like your attitude, and if it was just the mayor, that would be okay, but the children... You really don't think we could ski down? I mean, if the roads haven't been cleared yet? We could probably hitch a ride once we got to the bottom since it's not snowing as much in Snow Falls. By the way, who in the world named the town?"

"Did anyone ever tell you that you talk a lot, from one subject to another?" he asked, laughing, a twinkle in his eyes.

"As a matter of fact, yes, they have. Once I get comfortable around a person, I'm pretty much like that. I love talking to people. I guess I never met a stranger, either. Maybe that's why I like your daughters so much. Kindred souls."

Her last statement panicked him. His daughters already loved Ellie's books. It wouldn't be too much of a stretch for them to want much more. He'd never hear the end of it from them after she left. "You might keep that to yourself. They'll want to visit you." Brody moved his arm away so she could see the illustration.

"Oops. They may have already said something about that, and I may have told them they could." Ellie peeked at the unfinished drawing. "I'd love to have them visit me in South Carolina, maybe in the summer when they can swim in the ocean."

For a moment he had visions of him and his daughters on the beach with Ellie. His heartbeat sped up, and he could swear the heater in the room was working overtime. He grasped onto the reality of her staring at his illustration. "Don't tell them that. We still haven't decided where we stand on this partnership. I don't want to get their hopes up." Especially about a relationship beyond friendship, because that wasn't going to happen. Encouraging them and even Ellie wasn't fair to them. "I know you're dying to tell me what you think about the illustration. Go ahead. I can take it."

"This is starting to look like what I envisioned when I saw your drawings of your girls and we talked about a different direction."

"But?"

"More vibrant. If I'm going to make a change, then I really want it to be big. I want the colors to dazzle the children. Don't hold back. I want to make a splash."

She met his gaze. "I want Petunia's arrival to shake up Barnyard Town. When I went with you, I might not have consciously thought I wanted to go in a new direction with the series, but your drawings have convinced me I should."

"Okay. I think I can do that."

She covered his hand on the drawing board. "I know you can. I've seen it. Think of your daughters when you sketch."

For a long moment his gaze held her immobile as though she'd been too long outside in a snowstorm. Slowly the warmth from his skin seeped into her dazed mind, and she realized what she had done. She yanked away, anchoring both hands in her lap.

"I'm glad you have faith in me. This isn't really like anything I've done before."

"But it is. Think about Abbey and Alexa and what they love about your paintings. They told me you're the best artist they know."

His laughter filled the air, dissolving the "moment" they had shared. "I'm the only artist they know besides John."

"Ah. I won't tell John where he stands with your daughters. It'll be our little secret they preferred their daddy over him."

He intrigued her. When you peeled away his protective layers, there was so much depth to him. Those barriers most likely were there because of his unusual childhood, living in the limelight with the media wanting to know everything about him—the only child of a star.

His mouth quirked into a grin. "I'd say you're safe.

I think he knows how the girls feel about my talents. He was staying here once when my daughters decided to charge their friends to tour my studio. I was running late and when I walked into the house there was a parade of kids coming out of the breezeway. That's the last time I left John in charge of watching my daughters."

The amusement in his voice spoke of a deep friendship between him and John, a man whose age was closer to Brody's father's. "How did you two meet? He never told me."

"He dated my mother for all of two months when I was a teenager. Their relationship didn't last, but ours did. I know this is cliché, but John was the father I never had."

"It's not cliché. I had adults in my life other than my parents who were important to me. I had an English teacher who saw potential in my writing and encouraged me."

Brody nodded and took another drink of his coffee. "Thanks again. Should keep me alert so I can finish this before you leave tomorrow."

When he mentioned tomorrow, her heart instantly began to pound. She would have to make her speech without her usual preparation. That is *if* she even made it into town. At the thought of disappointing her young fans, she had to take some deep breaths. "My cue to leave and let you work."

"Would you mind taking those sweatpants on the chair by the door to Marta?"

She glanced down at her watch and hopped off the

stool. "I'm late for a tea party. See you later." She scurried to leave.

"A tea party? It's eight at night."

"I know. But the girls insisted we have another one. They had a proposition for me." Besides, it would take her mind off her predicament.

"A what?"

"Proposition. My word, not theirs. They said they had a deal I couldn't refuse."

His laughter followed her out of the studio along with a warning to beware. Yes, good advice, because she was quickly getting sucked into this family.

There was no reason to dive into a personal relationship that was doomed to fail from the beginning because the man didn't want to make any kind of commitment. She'd been through one like that. Never again. Only a professional one with Brody, if she could get him to agree. That was the way they both wanted it.

LOOKING AT THE RAPT expressions on his daughters' faces, Brody stood in the doorway, listening to Ellie read to Abbey and Alexa, who should have been in bed an hour ago. He'd lost track of time trying to finish the illustration. Almost there but not quite.

Ellie closed the book. "Okay, time for bed. You said you'd go to sleep if I read one more story."

"But we have to hear the last one." Abbey produced the fourth in the series from behind her back. "Daddy always reads it."

Brody cleared his throat and said, "It's way past your bedtime. You'll have to hear it tomorrow."

Both girls swiveled their attention to him. Alexa's

eyes grew round while Abbey tilted her head and said, "How long have you been eavesdropping?"

"Five minutes. You were engrossed in the story."

Abbey shifted. "I knew the whole time."

Alexa giggled. "Then why did you ask him how long he'd been there?" She continued in a solemn voice, "Daddy, you know you shouldn't eavesdrop on other people's conversations. But I'll forgive you if you let Ellie read the last story." She opened the book she wanted Ellie to read and passed it to her.

"While that is big of you to forgive me, Alexa, it doesn't change my mind. Bedtime. You've monopolized Ellie enough for one day."

"She doesn't mind, do you?" Abbey asked.

Ellie looked from the twins to him. "I don't." Then she added, "But you always need to do what your dad says. Remember when Susie didn't do what her father told her? A fox almost got her."

Alexa nodded. "It was a good thing she was small and could hide in the hole in the henhouse. What made you think of a mousehole?"

Brody moved into Abbey's room before his daughter managed to steer the conversation in a wild-goose chase to delay going to bed. "Girls, tell Ellie good-night. Then under the covers."

They did as they were told but grumbled under their breath. While Ellie shelved the books she'd read, Brody leaned over and kissed each daughter, then started to leave. Alexa popped back up.

"Daddy, I need to show Ellie where everything is in my room."

"I'll take care of it. Go to sleep."

"Are you sure? Don't forget to show her the night-light in the bathroom."

Abbey punched her sister in the arm. "Ellie is a grown-up. She doesn't need a night-light like you do. Daddy, I don't need one, either. I don't want it on. It is *my* room."

"But Alexa likes it—" Brody switched on the soft light on the table "—so it stays on."

"You're such a baby," Abbey mumbled and turned her back on her sister while pulling the covers up over her head.

"I am not. We're the same age. In fact, I'm older than you are."

"By five minutes. You're still a baby."

"Girls, no more or you two will stay here with Marta tomorrow instead of going to the First Night celebration."

Alexa pushed at Abbey. "See what you caused."

Abbey shot up in bed and shifted toward her sister. "Nothing. I'm being quiet." Then she made a motion by her mouth as though she were turning a key in a lock, then buried herself under the covers again.

"Let's get out of here," Brody whispered close to Ellie's ear.

Her scent like apples and cinnamon teased his senses. He pulled back. This woman attracted him—more than he should let her. They lived with a country between them. She lived in South Carolina—hot, humid—sultry, like the woman. He shook that thought from his fried brain and strode toward Alexa's bedroom. She wanted a family while he had no interest in having more children. He barely kept his head above water. More children would drown him for sure. Whoa. Why was he even thinking about children and Ellie?

"With Marta living here, I don't have a spare bedroom. When we have guests, Alexa bunks with Abbey. I hope that's okay with you," he said as though he were conducting a business transaction.

"It's fine. I would even sleep on a couch if I had to. It beats sleeping in a car buried under snow."

He chuckled. "I guess it does." That was another thing about Ellie that he liked. In one day with her, he'd laughed more than he usually would in a week.

But what if they could work together? Keep it strictly professional? The only way was if he could illustrate to meet her needs. He didn't do a job unless he could do his best. Was that why he told her they shouldn't work together after all? He wasn't pleased with what he'd produced originally. Now, though, after meeting Ellie in person, it just might work out, especially because she now wanted what he did naturally. At least he hoped that was what she meant.

Ellie made a full circle in the middle of Alexa's bedroom with its canopy bed and white furniture. "I love pink. Definitely a little girl's room. Lots of frills."

"Yeah, Alexa embraces being a girl while Abbey struggled with it. She told me the other day she wanted to play football. I heard that and nearly scalded my throat when I gulped my coffee."

"What are you going to do? Do they have football for girls?"

"Not in Snow Falls, thankfully. I suggested soccer or softball. She's thinking about it."

"What does Alexa want to do?"

"Dance."

"That makes sense." Ellie flicked her hand at the Degas ballet dancer reproduction.

"That's her favorite picture."

"Even over your paintings?"

He nodded. "I can't complain. She's got good taste. I love that period of art." Heading toward the door, he said over his shoulder, "I've got something for you to wear. Be right back."

In his bedroom he dug around in his dresser drawer until he found what he was looking for. When he returned, Ellie was sitting on the bed, surrounded by stuffed animals, staring out the window. Watching her with his girls earlier had attracted him to her even more. Dangerous thinking, but he couldn't seem to stop it.

"It amazes me how bright it is outside even though it's night. It looks like the snow isn't coming down as hard as before." She swung her gaze to him. "Or is that wishful thinking on my part? I do not want to call the mayor and tell him I'm not going to make the opening ceremony. Does he have the power to ban my books in Snow Falls?"

"No," he said with a chuckle, then crossed to the window and looked out. "Besides, his grandkids would kill him." The snow fell in a steady stream, but the wind had died down and he could see the pine trees that surrounded his house. "I think you're right."

"Oh, I'm going to have to remember you telling me I was right."

"Because it might not happen again," he said in deadly seriousness right before a smile spread across his face.

Her laugh warmed him. He couldn't take his eyes off her. Her beauty came from within. A kindness shone in her expression that he hadn't often experienced growing up among vultures who always wanted something from him—to them he'd been a way to get close to his mother. Ellie would be a good mom. She should have all those kids she wanted. The thought sobered him.

He tore his gaze away from her and moved the few feet to her, thrusting his pajama top toward her. "If you want, use this to sleep in."

She took the soft blue shirt and examined it, holding it out to check its size. "Yours?"

"Yes. Since you don't have any extra clothes, I thought you might want something comfortable to sleep in."

Pink dusted her cheeks. "I am getting kind of tired of these jeans and sweater, especially since we don't know how long I'll have to wear them tomorrow."

"Hopefully not too long, especially if the snow continues to slack off."

"I'm not even worried about my speech as much as just showing up at one."

"We'll get there somehow. I guess I'd better go. Let you get some sleep." But he didn't want to leave. He was just getting to know her, and tomorrow, the First Night celebration would be hectic.

She rose. "Yeah, I'll need to rehearse my speech in the morning. Maybe the girls wouldn't mind being my audience. I think I remember some of it."

"We all will if it'll help. I certainly understand how you feel about not wanting to speak in front of strangers." The more he thought about her the more he decided they had a lot in common. She understood the creative process and had given him space tonight, entertaining his daughters for him. If he weren't so attracted to her, she would be a good friend.

"Thanks." She rubbed the oversize flannel shirt between her fingers.

The action riveted his attention. He imagined those hands touching him. He imagined those lips... He wrenched his thoughts away from where they were going.

When he started for the door, he mumbled, "Good night," and increased his pace. He didn't breathe decently until he was in the corridor, striding toward his bedroom. What was wrong with him? Snowbound one day with a woman and he began to envision her in his life?

DRESSED BACK IN HER JEANS and sweater early the next morning, Ellie paused at the large window in Alexa's bedroom to see if it was still snowing. When she opened the blinds, white greeted her everywhere, but the snowfall had tapered off quite a bit and the gray clouds weren't dark like the day before. Hope blossomed in her. She might be able to get back to the lodge and even possibly change before the opening ceremony.

Then she craned her neck to see the road that ran out in front of Brody's house. The snow still covered it. Where was the snowplow? When she checked her watch, she realized it wasn't even dawn.

With a sigh she decided to go downstairs and get some coffee. If they cleared the road soon, she wouldn't have to try to rewrite her speech. She could get the one she had in her room at the lodge.

The door to Abbey's room was closed. The quiet in the house wouldn't last long. Those two precious girls were a handful. Being with them the past day made her realize she wanted a husband and children even more. But the prospects weren't promising. Writing was a lonely job. Then when she was on a book tour, she spent maybe a day in one town then moved to the next one. Certainly not conducive to meeting Mr. Right.

When she thought about Mr. Right, Brody flashed into her mind. Laughing at something his daughters did. His smile reaching deep into his eyes. His head bent over his drawing board as he tried to come up with an illustration.

But what was she thinking? Granted, she would be in Snow Falls several days—not one—but she would still be returning to South Carolina to finish her latest project.

When she reached the first floor, she noticed a light on in the great room and made a detour to check it out. Brody sat on the couch with his drawing pad in his lap, working. Not wanting to disturb him, she started to back out. He glanced up.

A smile lit his face. "You're up early."

"So are you. I don't want to interrupt your work. I certainly know how that can be."

"I think I'm through. Something was bothering me last night about the illustration. During the night I figured it out and came down here to finish it."

She bridged the distance between them and eased down beside him, his leg pressing against hers. He peered at her, his dark eyes luring her toward him. The atmosphere shifted. She wanted to see the illustration, but for the life of her she couldn't look away from him. His attraction grew stronger, his lips so close she felt the whisper of his breath over hers.

Kissing him wouldn't change their circumstances. She managed to close her eyes, severing the link between them. When she reopened them, she saw the illustration in his lap and latched onto it to distract her from what she really wanted to do.

"This is perfect!" She grabbed the pad and held it up. "Just what I wanted. The scene comes right off the page." Swinging toward him, she didn't realize how close he really was.

Her lips inches from his, he took the drawing from her, then his hand delved into her hair, tugging her even nearer. His mouth captured hers, and any resistance to the idea of kissing him vanished, replaced with a deep need to connect. She'd been alone for so long. She wanted so much more than her career. She wanted it all—love, family and a career.

Vaguely she heard the pad plopping onto the table in front of them, then Brody entwined his arms around her and plastered her against him. Her heart pounded so hard she was sure he felt its beat. As he deepened the kiss, she surrendered to the sensations bombarding her—the all-consuming touch of his lips on hers, his faint scent of lime, the rough texture of his thumbs framing her face.

When he finally parted, his breathing labored like hers, she still swirled in an overload of senses. Everything seemed sharper, more vibrant, rich—like his illustration.

Ellie looked into those dark eyes and couldn't deny her feelings. "I've wanted you to do that since I saw you with Abbey and Alexa. Nothing is more appealing than a single father who cares so much for his children."

His art spoke of a man with a lot of passion, reined in but there beneath the surface. Leaning in, she wanted to feel that fiery connection again. Her lips tasted his while she brought her hands up to cradle his face.

When his palms covered hers, he pulled back. "This isn't a good idea. I should never have kissed you."

"Why?" she managed to say.

"I'm not what you want—not really. My life is settled into a good routine. I have my girls and work I enjoy. I'm…"

"Content? Resigned? Scared to commit?" She waved her hand toward the pad on the coffee table. "I think you're afraid to feel. When you do finally let go, look what you're capable of. Such beauty and passion. Full of emotions. Why are you scared to feel?"

"Because it can be ripped from you in a second." All the feelings he'd bottled up inside exploded out of him. He jerked to his feet, his arms rigid at his sides, his hands opening and closing.

His wife died in childbirth. At a time when a couple should be elated and celebrating, he had to bury her. After six years, Ellie had thought he'd be ready to move on. "We can't stop living because something bad might happen. Life is full of trials and tribulations. We don't hide from them. We embrace them and learn from them."

He sucked in a deep breath. "You don't couch your words in niceties."

"Part of the reason I write for children is to teach them ways to handle their problems. Each book has a lesson couched, as you say, in an entertaining story." She pushed to her feet to be more at eye level with him. "You've essentially holed yourself up here on your mountain. You've all but admitted that to me. You should come down every once in a while and partake of real life. Yes, you may be hurt, but you could also enjoy yourself and get a new sense of rejuvenation. You owe that to your girls." Her feelings flowed from her because she cared about Abbey and Alexa. But she also cared about Brody. Too much, if the stabbing pain in her heart was any indication.

Anger marked deep lines into his face, his eyebrows slashing down. "My girls are fine."

"Then why do they need to find you a friend? You've been buried in your sorrow and haven't realized they want more. Last night they kept telling me all about you. One story after another. They love you and they sense your sadness." She realized she'd probably blown her chances of having Brody illustrate her books. She could still work with him, but she didn't know if he could.

"I was the one who wanted children. Irene wanted to wait. She died because of me."

"Is that what you've been telling yourself? Are you so sure about that? Did you force it on her? Or, did you two talk about it and decide the time was probably right? It was a tragedy. No one was at fault. Blame doesn't have to be given here."

His scowl evened out into an unreadable expression.

He stared at his illustration, probably trying to form the words to tell her he quit. She pulled herself up tall and prepared herself for his rejection.

A high-pitched scream ripped through the house, coming from upstairs.

# CHAPTER SIX

A CHILL FLASH-FROZE BRODY. The sound of one of his daughters crying out resonated through him, sending panic to every part of him. After a few seconds he leaped to his feet and raced for the stairs, taking the steps two at a time.

Abbey ran down the hallway, tears flowing from her eyes. Pointing back to her bedroom, she said, "Alexa hurt herself."

Alexa's sobs coming from the room spurred his pace. Behind him he heard Abbey mumbling, "I'm sorry. I'm sorry," and Ellie consoling her.

When he saw Alexa, she was sitting on the floor, wet tracks streaking down her face. The overhead light was on. "Baby, what happened?"

"It hurts, Daddy. Make it stop."

"What hurts?" He knelt down next to her.

She touched her left ankle. "I can't walk."

The area she indicated was already swelling. "How did you do this?"

"Couldn't see in the dark. I tripped over that." Alexa gestured toward a box that held a game the girls loved to play.

"The night-light went out?" He looked toward it and it wasn't on.

"I guess."

Ellie immediately came to Alexa on her other side while Abbey hung back. "I can get some ice for the ankle."

"Thanks. That might help the swelling until we can get her to the hospital."

"Hospital!" Alexa screamed as Ellie left to get an ice pack. "I don't want to go there."

"Daddy, you fix her. She'll be okay," Abbey said behind him, crying more than Alexa.

"I can't fix this. Alexa, I'm going to call Harold to see when he can get the road plowed. The snow has slowed down somewhat so he might be able to start now as a favor to me." If he had to beg the man, he would. He couldn't stand to see his child in pain. "You need to have X-rays taken of your foot and leg. You might have broken a bone."

"I'll get a cast?"

"Maybe, depending on what's wrong. It could be a sprain. Either way, a doctor needs to look at it."

"I don't like hospitals. I don't want to go. I'm better now." Alexa tried to stand.

Brody held her down. "No. I don't want you making it worse."

When Ellie returned with the ice, she placed it gently on the child's ankle. "This will help, honey."

Brody stood. "Will you stay with her while I call about the snowplow?"

Ellie nodded.

As he strode into the hallway, Abbey ran after him. "Daddy, I didn't mean for Alexa to get hurt."

He stopped and turned toward her. "I know. She'll

be all right. We'll get her to the hospital and they'll patch up her leg."

Abbey dropped her head and mumbled, "I turned the night-light off. It was bothering me last night, and I couldn't sleep." The words rushed out as her shoulders hunched more and more.

"We'll talk about this later. First, I need to see to your sister."

She lifted her head. "I'm sorry."

The pain in Abbey's expression mirrored Alexa's, but for a different reason. He knelt in front of her and clasped her arms. "I know you are. I also know you wouldn't want anything bad to happen to Alexa. Later you can tell your sister you're sorry."

"I'll make it up to her. I promise." She wiped her tears away. "I can do her chores while her foot is hurt."

"I think that's a good suggestion. Now I need to call Harold and wake up Marta." He rose and started for the staircase.

That's when the penny dropped. How different was he from Abbey? He hadn't meant for Irene to get hurt. All he had wanted to do since Irene died was try to make it up to her.

As Brody drove his SUV on the snowplowed road down the mountain, Ellie sat in the backseat with Alexa and Marta while Abbey was in front. Snow still fell, covering the highway with another layer, making it slick.

Harold was going to wait until it stopped, but he couldn't refuse Brody's plea. Luckily in Snow Falls the roads had been cleared and weren't nearly as risky as the steep one coming off the mountain. The one they were on. Ellie kept her gaze on Alexa, who cuddled up next to her. When Ellie dared to look out the windshield, her heartbeat accelerated and sweat coated her forehead. It was one thing going up a mountain in the snow, but a totally different experience coming down one in the snow, especially with the treacherous curves Brody had to navigate.

Brody hit a slick spot, and the car fishtailed. Her breath bottled in her lungs, Ellie pressed closer to the child as though that would make this trip go faster.

Ellie smiled at the child between her and the housekeeper. "We're nearing the highway into town. It won't be long before you get to the hospital."

"I wanna go home." Alexa buried her face against Ellie, who would love to bury hers in someone but was trying to present a brave front for the children.

"How long?" Was that her voice that quavered?

"Fifteen minutes," Marta said, her expression not as harsh as it had been the past day.

They'd already been in the car over an hour and a half—a trip that was normally only thirty minutes. "I think there's a reason I live in South Carolina. I don't think I'm a snow bunny."

Alexa and Abbey giggled, breaking some of the tension in the car.

Abbey turned in the front seat and peered back at her. "Daddy is an expert at driving in bad weather."

At that moment the SUV slid toward the bank of snow the plow had created on the side of the road. Ellie tensed. Was this one of those trials and tribulations she'd told Brody was part of life? She hoped wrecking the car wasn't one. Although Brody was going slow because it was downhill, he had to brake a lot—sending the car sometimes into a slide. She remembered her rented car still buried in a pile of snow at his house—not near a drop-off. A shiver ran down her spine as she stared at the next sheer drop only yards from the car.

Alexa glanced up at her. "We'll be all right."

A hurt child was comforting her. The gesture swelled Ellie's throat. She swallowed several times and murmured, "I know."

"We've come through the worst part. It didn't snow down here nearly as much as up the mountain."

The sound of Brody's voice, full of assurance, eased the tight hold fear had on her. A little. The hard angles of his face, his white-knuckle grip on the steering wheel made her angst return full force. The road still looked steep, the incline at times a sixty-degree angle.

"I don't want to miss the celebration," Alexa said, the ice pack sliding off as they went around another curve. "I want to see your play."

Ellie picked up the ice pack and placed it on Alexa's propped-up foot again. "I'll make sure you have a front-row seat. The doctor will fix you up. You might end up with crutches, but you'll have all of us to help you get around." She said that in confidence that Brody would want to have something to do with her once they reached Snow Falls. Why had she spoken her mind?

*Because I care. Because I want more.*

"Yeah, sweetheart. I know how much you're looking forward to this afternoon and evening," Brody said as he took an S-curve, a tight thread woven through the last part of the sentence.

"Why wasn't the night-light on?" Alexa asked.

Quiet descended.

Brody threw Abbey a look. Alexa saw and sat up. "You turned it off?" Alexa shrieked and punched the back of the seat Abbey was in. If it hadn't been for her injured foot, Alexa would have probably gone over the seat to get to her sister.

"I couldn't sleep with it on and you were asleep. I'm sorry."

Alexa folded her arms over her chest and glared at Abbey. "I'm not speaking to you."

For the next ten minutes silence reigned while Ellie chewed on her lower lip. As Brody went around probably the twentieth curve in the road, a cliff on her side of the car caused her to clutch the door handle as though she was trying to make sure it stayed closed. Her heartbeat thundered in her head. What if he went into another slide—right off the mountain?

"How do y'all do it? Unless it thaws a lot, I don't know how I'm going to be able to drive my car back to town. Snow is fine for about an hour, then I'd like it to melt completely away."

"You get used to it." Brody threw her a glance, which made her even more tense.

"Keep your eyes on the road." Ellie fisted her hands, her nails digging into her palms.

"It's like your humidity in South Carolina. When I've been in a place with a lot of humidity, I wonder how the people living there can stand it. I was in Florida last summer, and I sweat continuously. There were times it was oppressive. Same thing as snow in the winter in Colorado."

"You can have your snow. I'll take my humidity over

it any day." Although, if Brody gave her a reason, she'd learn to get used to snow. The thought didn't surprise her nearly as much as it would have a day before.

"I don't mind—humid-ity," Abbey piped in. "I still want to come visit you in South Carolina and go to the beach. I've never seen the ocean."

"Honey, you don't invite yourself to someone's house." Brody clipped each word as he spoke.

Abbey looked at her dad then back at Alexa. The girls were smart. They could feel their father's anger—directed at her.

"What about Florida?" Ellie asked to cut through the sudden strain. Seeing the main highway up ahead, she forced her hands to relax. They were going to make it in one piece.

"We went to Walt Disney World. There were a lot of lakes but no ocean." Alexa uncrossed her arms and cuddled against Ellie again.

"I love that place. I haven't been in several years."

"We had so much fun."

The four of them began to talk about what they saw and did at Walt Disney World. As Ellie listened to them, obviously the fifth wheel, a heaviness settled in her chest. She wanted to do that with a family. When she'd visited the place, she'd been by herself and wouldn't have even gone then, but her publisher had set up an event with her, promoting her new Barnyard Town book on the Disney property.

The camaraderie among the others in the car con-firmed what she wanted. A family—husband and chil-dren. For years she'd been writing for kids and yearning for them. When she returned home, she needed to connect with others—enter the dating game. At least this twenty-four hours with Brody made her realize that.

She looked at Brody's profile—strong, all male. If only things were different...

"We're here." Brody drove into the parking lot of the small hospital. "The good thing about Snow Falls is that the doctors are used to broken bones and know what to do."

"Daddy, I think I'm much better now. I'll be running around in no time. Let's go to the Ice Castle for breakfast."

"We can do that *after* we see the doctor I drove the past two hours for you to see."

A couple of minutes later Brody strode into the E.R., carrying Alexa while the rest of them trailed behind. After telling the nurse at the counter why they were there, they took a corner of the waiting room. Only a few people were in front of Alexa. The twins huddled together on a small two-seat couch across from the adults, while Brody sat with Marta between Ellie and him, his arms folded over his chest.

Keeping the world at arm's length. His body language shouted out he didn't need anyone but his daughters. And Ellie realized she had a lot to give to someone who needed her.

Soon a nurse came to get Alexa. As the child was ushered into an exam cubicle, she said, "I don't want a shot. I'm okay. Really."

Brody followed, glancing back once before vanishing into the hallway. The look he gave her—full of that vulnerability always there under the surface—tore at her heart.

Wishing she could be there for Alexa, Ellie inhaled a calming breath. The past twenty-four hours seemed an eternity and yet...

Her eyes glistening, Abbey plopped down next to Ellie. "I didn't mean for this to happen."

"I know." Ellie slung her arm around Abbey. "What if I ask your dad about me and you going to the Ice Castle for breakfast then you can come with me to my hotel? I have to change my clothes and get my speech. I still have to give it and I should go over it." She couldn't leave them until she knew Alexa would be all right.

"I'll help you. I'm a good listener."

"Let me talk to your dad and see if it's okay if you come with me for a couple of hours."

After telling Marta where she was going, Ellie left the waiting room to see if she could talk with Brody. A nurse directed her to the cubicle Alexa was in. Ellie paused outside in the hallway to wait to get Brody's attention. When he saw her, he said something to Alexa and stepped out into the corridor.

Frowning, Brody asked, "Is something wrong?"

"I thought while Alexa is being checked out by the doctor that I would go to my hotel. It's within walking distance. I need to change, grab my speech and let the mayor know I'm in town. Abbey wants to come with me, so I was going to grab some breakfast at the Ice Castle. Is that okay with you?"

"You figured this all out with Abbey?"

"We talked about it. I had a broken arm as a teenager, so unless E.R.s are a lot faster than they were then, it'll be several hours before Alexa will be released. Abbey is hungry and needs to do something other than sitting."

"Do you have children?"

She narrowed her eyes. "You know I don't."

"Then how do you know what's best for Abbey?" He was scowling.

The sound of Alexa calling him drew his attention to the cubicle. "Fine. Take her. You're right." He strode toward the room.

"I'll leave my cell number with Marta. Let me know when y'all are through here. I can have Abbey back then."

He didn't say anything else but disappeared inside, drawing the curtains for privacy. She'd felt as if he'd shut her out of his life—had since they'd shared a kiss that screamed something the opposite of indifference toward her. What had transpired between them had been anything but that. He just didn't want to acknowledge it. He would then have to admit to himself that he cared for someone—was attracted to her. That just possibly there was life beyond Irene. That it was time to let his guilt go and move on.

Ellie took a moment to compose herself, counting to ten slowly. She didn't want Abbey to know what was going on between her dad and her. Of course, the child would have had to be driving down the mountain in a totally different car than the one she and Brody had been in not to know it wasn't going well.

And on top of having her ego damaged, Ellie had probably lost her illustrator—one perfectly suited for what she wanted. It had taken him to show her that, and now she didn't want another one.

WHEN ALEXA RETURNED to the cubicle after tests were run an hour and a half later, Brody smoothed his daughter's hair behind her ear and sat next to her to wait for the doctor. "Honey, they said you fractured your ankle in one place. They can't put a cast on for a few days until the swelling goes down, so they're going to wrap it and you'll use crutches. You aren't to walk on it. You'll need to sit and prop your foot up to help the swelling go down. When it does, we'll come back to get a cast on it. We shouldn't be too much longer here."

"I want to see Ellie at the lodge. It's not fair that Abbey gets to and I don't."

"If Ellie has time before the opening ceremony, she's coming back as soon as you're through with the doctor."

"She is?"

"Do you think she'd leave without saying goodbye to you?"

"No. She's so nice and pretty. Don't you think, Daddy?"

"Yeah," he said slowly, seeing a gleam in his daughter's eyes.

"Are you going to draw pictures for her books?"

He didn't have the heart to say no in the face of her eager expression—not after being brave about her ankle. She was actually smiling in spite of the pain the medication hadn't quite disguised. But he wouldn't lie to her, either. "I don't know." How could he work with Ellie when all he wanted to do was kiss her again and again? He shouldn't have earlier. But her mouth was so tempting.

The kiss changed their relationship, shifted it to a level he didn't know he wanted to reach. She wanted a husband and children. What did he want? That's what he needed to figure out. What Abbey had said this morning

about not meaning to hurt her sister made him reconsider how he was beating himself up over Irene's death.
He'd never imagined he'd lose Irene because of having
children. When she died that was what he'd focused on.

"You should, Daddy."

"It would elevate your status with your friends?"

"Yes."

"You know what I would say to that."

She grimaced. "Yeah, they aren't my friends if they
don't like me for who I am."

"Right."

"The real reason is I like her. So does Abbey. We
talked about it. That way, Ellie could visit and we could
go to her house and the beach. You need a friend. I have
Abbey. She'll listen to me. Even though she turned off
the night-light, I know she didn't mean for me to break
my ankle. But don't let her know just yet that I forgive
her. She needs to squirm some." Alexa grinned from
ear to ear.

He'd certainly done his share of squirming since his
wife passed away. When was it enough?

"Ellie likes you a lot. It's like in the movies when
two people kiss. So it would be fun to go to her place
and for her to come here. But maybe not in the winter.
I don't think she likes snow."

Heat scorched his face. Suddenly all he could think
about was the hot kiss they had shared. "I'm not promising anything. It's not just my decision."

"I DECLARE THE FESTIVITIES open. Go have fun." Ellie
pushed the big red button to start the ball ascending

toward midnight when the new year would arrive and fireworks would color the sky.

A cheer went up from the crowd gathered in the square. Afterward the mayor shook Ellie's hand as if he'd never freaked out on the phone, and posed with her for a photo opportunity. Ellie made her way to Abbey sitting on the stage next to where Ellie sat through the other dignitaries' remarks.

"You were wonderful." Abbey smiled up at her.

She wasn't so sure. She'd stumbled over a couple of words but otherwise gave her short message about greeting a new year with family and friends. "You were my inspiration. Thanks for listening to me rehearse earlier. You're a good listener."

Abbey thrust back her shoulders. "I saw Daddy, Marta and Alexa arrive in the middle of your speech."

"You did?" She had fixed her attention on a couple of children near the front and hadn't seen anyone else because that was the only way she got through giving a speech. Ellie glanced at the crowd slowly dissipating, moving away from the podium. In the midst of the throng, she spied the trio threading their way toward them with Alexa on crutches.

"Will you come with us when Daddy gives a lesson about drawing different animals that live around here? We get to try our own drawing. After that we can go with you to the play. I can't wait until I get to go backstage."

"I'm not sure." Glancing toward Brody, she tried to read his expression, but his dark sunglasses hid his face. "This is family time. I probably should get to the playhouse." Although she didn't know what she would do. Most everything had been taken care of by the production team. She was only there to be the narrator at the beginning and end.

"Daddy is a good artist. You can pick your favorite animal. Daddy helps a lot of my friends. He comes to my school once a month. He's so good with children. He's a good daddy."

Ellie mashed her lips together to keep from chuckling at Abbey's blatant attempt to tell her all about what was good about her father. She didn't have the heart to tell Abbey it wouldn't make any difference. That her dad didn't want to get involved. That she was already sold on what a nice guy he was. And that was why it hurt so much. She wanted to work with him. She wanted to see if a relationship could go beyond friendship. She wanted to be in his life as well as the girls'.

Alexa planted herself just below the platform and shouted, "Ellie, we made it. Well, almost. I heard a little of your speech. You did great."

Ellie descended the steps with Abbey. "Good. Y'all missed my mess-up."

Brody took off his sunglasses. "I bet you'll have standing room only at the play later. I, uh, I've got to go to the Wildwood Lodge so I can get ready to teach. I also need to make sure my paintings were set up in Aspen Hall there for the art exhibit." His gaze roped her to him. "I hope you'll join us, Ellie."

The male look he gave her warmed her in spite of the cold weather and gave her hope that at least he would agree to be her illustrator.

"You've got to, Ellie," Alexa prodded. "I may need help."

She glanced at Alexa. "Help? It looks like you're doing fine on your own."

"You never know," the little girl said with a laugh.

"Are you going to be up for all this excitement?"

Alexa's eyes widened. "No way would I miss any of this. I've been waiting weeks."

Abbey tugged on Ellie's arm. "I'm going to make a grizzly bear."

Alexa moved in front of Ellie. "I'm drawing a mountain lion."

"I'll go with y'all if you'll come with me to the playhouse."

Abbey swung around to her father. "Can we, Daddy?"

"You two don't want to go through the snow maze?"

"Only if there's time after the play," Alexa said, "because we've done that before."

Abbey exchanged a look with Alexa as if they were reading each other's minds. "And the ice carvings. We can't do everything, but that's okay. We want to be with you two."

"Sounds like a plan to me. I'll let you kids and Marta lead the way to the lodge. The ice carving is on the way. We could stop for a little while."

Brody hung back with Ellie. "Are you sure you weren't kidding me about not liking to get up in front of an audience? No one knew you were nervous about speaking. You were a pro."

She blushed at the praise. "That's your daughter's influence. She gladly listened in my hotel room while I went over and over my speech for at least forty-five minutes."

He smiled. "Now I know you're kidding me. Abbey never sits still that long."

"I didn't say she was sitting still. She was on the move, exploring or bouncing on the bed the whole time."

He chuckled. "That's my Abbey." Stepping closer, he closed his hand around hers. "Later, when the munchkins have exhausted themselves, I'd like to talk."

"About what?"

"Our partnership and other things." He winked and started toward the Wildwood Lodge, still holding her hand.

LATER THAT NIGHT IN the living area of Ellie's suite at Wildwood, she hovered over Abbey and Alexa, curled up on the long couch. "I thought they would make it to the fireworks."

"Actually I'm surprised they kept going, especially Alexa. I think at the end they were functioning on pure adrenaline. They were determined to see and do everything they could."

"I loved the snow maze. It reminds me of a maze I went through in England. I was threatening to cut my way through the hedges to get out, but I didn't want to end my vacation in jail, so instead I screamed for help. Some lovely older British gentleman came to rescue me."

He laughed. "I'm surprised you liked that maze then after that experience." He hesitated. "Let's go outside on the balcony. It's nearly the new year and time for the fireworks display."

"Should we wake them?"

"Not just yet. We haven't been alone all day."

"Alone?" Ellie's heart rate kicked up a notch. "Marta should be back soon from visiting her friend."

"Yes, and soon the girls and I will have to leave."

On the balcony, music from the masquerade ball drifted on the night air, adding a magic to the evening. Ellie's throat constricted. The First Night celebration had been perfect. She had spent it with Brody and his daughters as though they were a family. For a few hours he had shared something special with her and for once she had no words to describe the emotions swirling inside her.

He pulled her toward the love seat. After they sat, he covered them with a blanket lying on the couch. "Warm?"

She nodded. "This lodge has a perfect view for the fireworks. Did I tell you how much I love fireworks?" She shifted toward him.

His dark eyes held her immobile. The tightness in her throat threatened to cut off her next breath.

"Two years ago we couldn't make it to Snow Falls on New Year's Eve because Abbey was sick, so we watched them from our deck."

"That almost happened this year with the snow. One of my favorite holidays is the Fourth of July because of the fireworks. I'm like a—"

Brody laid a finger over her mouth. "Shh. You're chattering. Why are you nervous?"

"You're about to tell me whether you're going to illustrate my books or not. I'm not sure I want to hear the answer."

He cradled her face. "I want to illustrate your books

now that I have a good idea of what you want and I know we can work together."

"You do?"

"Yes, but more than that. I hope that we can get to know each other a lot better. Would you consider staying for a week or so…or coming back very soon so I can make sure I'm on track with what you want?"

She couldn't help it—she was disappointed. To him, this was just business. "We can video chat. That would probably work."

"Let me put it another way. I like you a lot. And while I want us to be friends, I'd like more than that because I care about you. My daughters care about you. You've made me realize how much I've shut myself off from others. How I was blaming myself for my wife's death. All that was doing was hurting my girls and me. Life goes on and I'd stopped living part of mine. You opened my—"

She put her hand over his mouth. "Shh. You're chattering. Yes, I would love to stay."

Winding an arm around her, he dragged her to him and kissed her, releasing all his bottled-up emotions. As the fireworks exploded in the sky announcing that it was midnight, he laid claim to her, stealing her heart. This kiss, packed with feelings long denied, overwhelmed her with the sense that she was where she belonged—finally.

The sliding glass door opened, and Abbey and Alexa came out onto the balcony.

Abbey rubbed her eyes. "The fireworks have started. Why didn't you get us up?" The child's eyes grew round as she took in her father holding Ellie. She tugged on

Alexa, nearing causing her to lose her balance on the crutches. Then she leaned toward her sister and whispered loud enough for everyone to hear, "Daddy is hugging Ellie. You know what that means."

Alexa angled around her sister to stare at them. Brody kept his arms around Ellie while he lounged back and snuggled her closer.

"It means it's cold out here, and we are sharing the blanket," he announced to his two daughters whose mouths had dropped open.

Alexa ignored her father and replied to Abbey, "Yeah, they like each other. They're friends."

Brody inched close to Ellie's ear and murmured, "Much more than that, but I'm not telling them. Yet."

His words cemented her decision to stay in Snow Falls to see where their...partnership...led them.

Three days ago she would never have imagined being snowbound at the new year would be an answer to her dream.

\* \* \* \* \*

To Doug, for always being my hero,
for encouraging me in this dream,
for keeping me sane.

# A KISS AT MIDNIGHT

## Brenda Minton

# CHAPTER ONE

A YEAR HAD PASSED and Jolie Godwin still remembered a stolen kiss and a moment of lost sanity. Of all the men, why did it have to be Jake Wild's arms she'd found herself in at midnight last year? Why did it have to be his kiss she couldn't forget?

It didn't help, being back at the Wildwood one year later. What kind of fool decided to walk into the lion's den and set up shop? Oh, that's right, Jolie Godwin did.

"What are you wearing tonight?" Cassie Douglas elbowed her as the two walked through the doors of the outside entrance to the boutique attached to the Wildwood Lodge.

Jolie stomped her feet on the welcome mat. Snow had fallen during the night, putting two more inches on top of the six inches already on the ground. That's what happened in Snow Falls, Colorado. Snow. Jolie happened to be the one person in town who didn't ski, so she didn't get all giddy over the white stuff.

She also didn't get too excited over shopping before nine in the morning. Which she was, for some crazy reason.

Only in a tourist town like this would a store be open before 9:00 a.m.

The quiet store smelled like a pine forest and new

clothes. Christmas music played, even though the holiday was over. Trees were still decorated with twinkling lights and garland still hung across the windows. Warm colors, soft lighting. The aroma of really good coffee blended with scented candles that brought to mind cinnamon rolls or sugar cookies. Coffee sounded far better than shopping.

"Jolie, I asked you a question," Cassie said a little too loudly, pursing her berry-red lips and arching her well-waxed brows.

Jolie smiled and searched the room for the coffeepot.

Cassie cleared her throat, not letting her off the hook.

"I'm not going." Jolie looked away. "You talked me into it last year. Not this year, my friend."

She couldn't handle a repeat of last year. Besides, she didn't fit into this world. Cassie's world.

Mannequins in the window were dressed better than Jolie ever hoped to be dressed. They wore beautiful sweaters, skinny jeans and furry boots. She glanced around for an excuse to leave before she accidentally bought something that cost more than she made in a month.

She wondered if Jake Wild actually liked the things he sold in the Wildwood Boutique. Not that it mattered. But really, the owner of Wildwood Ski Lodge was more of a jeans-and-flannel guy than designer suits and silk ties.

She walked away from Cassie, but her friend followed, grabbing Jolie's sleeve to prevent her escape.

"What do you mean you're not going? I already bought your ticket. Remember, Merry Christmas from me?" Cassie stopped long enough to touch a dress of shimmery red with starry-looking sequins. "With your dark hair, you'd look gorgeous in this."

Jolie flipped the tag so Cassie could get a good look at the four-digit price. "Not in this lifetime."

"Fine, but if you sell one of those magnificent wall hangings—"

"I'll make the next payment on my house."

"He kissed you," Cassie reminded her with a smirk.

"It wasn't real. It was 'Cinderella at the ball' kind of stuff. Not reality. The clock struck twelve and there I was, the person standing in front of him." She touched the dress. "I'm going to enjoy my day, so let's stop talking about this."

"But he did invite you to display your art."

"Not exactly an invitation. I applied and got accepted to display here." And of course she'd questioned herself, wondering if he'd allowed her a booth because of old feelings of guilt.

"I think he might like you because you aren't chasing him. I think it probably gets old, being Jake Wild, Colorado's best catch."

"People catch trout, not men, Cassie."

"That's very cute."

"I don't know why you insist on believing he likes me."

Cassie examined another gown and didn't look up. "Because he just walked by and peeked in the window and it was you he looked at. Now, let's talk about what you're going to wear to the ball."

Jolie shot a quick look at the window and saw nothing but snow. "I'm not going to this ball. I'm going to town with you. We'll go through the snow maze, watch the ice sculpting and I'll paint superheroes on sticky faces."

"Lighten up and live a little. You're not getting any younger."

No, she wasn't getting any younger. And she felt far older than twenty-nine. Sometimes Jolie felt as if she'd been an adult her entire life. A hand touched her arm. Cassie smiled a softer smile.

"You okay?"

Jolie smiled through her tears. "I'm good. Now, let's forget this imaginary world of romance. You need a very real dress for your very real date with your extremely handsome fiancé."

Cassie smiled and her eyes glittered a little. "Lance is perfect, isn't he?"

"I suppose. If you're into handsome, rich and kind. Yeah, sure, call him perfect."

"Jake Wild is…"

Jolie shook her head. "No more about Jake Wild. We're worlds apart, he and I. Besides that, I'm too busy for fantasy romance."

Jolie would always be the mousy girl studying hard to make it out of her real life and into something better. She'd been the girl taking the long way home so people didn't know the truth. She'd been the girl living in a travel trailer with her dad, after her mom had died and they'd lost everything.

Perspective needed. Jake Wild couldn't be the memory of a perfect kiss, not when he was the man who had helped to destroy her father. No, she had to give him a break. He hadn't destroyed her dad. Alcoholism had destroyed Mac Godwin. Alcohol and a broken heart.

She turned away from Cassie and headed for the door that led out of the boutique into the main lobby of the lodge.

"Where are you going?" Cass called out, not caring that she was the only loud person in a place of soft whispers, soft lighting, soft music.

Jolie glanced back over her shoulder. "I'm going to look at my booth to make sure everything is ready for this afternoon."

The First Night celebration in Snow Falls was a big event. Not only were they celebrating New Year's Eve, they were displaying local art and talent. The entire town would be involved. There would be music, vendors and the Wildwood Ball. Last year she'd worn one of Cassie's dresses and a mask from New Orleans. She'd pretended she belonged in that shimmery, starlit world.

As she escaped the boutique, she hit the solid wall of a male body, knocking the breath out of her lungs. Strong hands gripped her arms. She looked up and the world went a little off-kilter. But then his face came into focus. Strong features, eyes the color of a stormy sky, thick dark lashes.

Wow, he smelled good. Wrap your arms around him and breathe deep kind of good. Proof that she needed to get out more often. She needed to do something else, something more social than sitting alone in her studio 24/7 bending copper into art.

"Oh, sorry," she whispered and tried to remove herself from his strong grasp.

"How are you, Jolie?" He stepped back, gave her a long look and smiled. "Is your exhibit ready to go?"

"Yes." She tried to move past him. What was it about

this man that always turned her into a self-conscious teenager?

"I wanted to talk to you about the copper art and the light fixtures you make."

"Is there a problem? The exhibit coordinator told me I could have a ten-by-ten booth and showed me where to place the hangers." She looked up, holding her breath as she waited for him to tell her she couldn't have her exhibit at the Wildwood because he didn't want Mac Godwin's daughter on the place.

"Relax, you're good. I just hadn't realized you did this type of work. In school you were…"

"Dark?" she supplied when he seemed unsure of how to say it.

"Not really." He smiled when she raised her brows. "Okay, yes, that might be the word. You painted abstracts, people with long faces and no eyes."

"Teen angst. I've worked through that." She pinched the hem of her sweater and held it out. "See, no more black. All grown up."

"I've noticed." He cleared his throat and Mr. Unflappable seemed to disappear for a moment. "We're building a new addition to the lodge. I'd like to talk to you about light fixtures and wall hangings for the rooms."

"Oh, okay. Here's my card." She dug into her purse. "Give me a call."

He laughed but took her card. "I meant in person."

She heard footsteps behind her and turned, breathing a sigh of relief when she saw Cassie. Her relief was short lived because the look on Cassie's face warned her that her friend had picked the two of them for a fantasy romance. Great.

"I'm her manager." Cassie smiled big and winked at Jolie.

"Right, Cass, and the price just doubled." Jake stepped back to let a customer into the boutique. He relaxed, leaning one shoulder against the doorway. Cassie knew how to handle him. She'd been in his league since forever. Cassie's family owned a restaurant in town and a gondola lift for people who really didn't ski but wanted to see the world from above.

"She is the best." Cassie switched her new dress from her right arm to her left and put a hand on Jolie's back. "So if you're interested, it's going to cost you. Maybe the two of you can talk at Wildwood's New Year's Eve ball."

"I'm not going." Jolie frowned at her friend. "Remember, I have other commitments."

"Volunteering to paint superheroes on the dirty faces of little children is not a commitment, it's torture. And you're doing that this afternoon."

"It's torture that I love."

Jake pulled a card out of his pocket and wrote something on the back before handing it to her. Most people wouldn't have pegged him for the owner of the resort, not in his hiking boots, faded jeans and button-up shirt.

"I'll be around most of the day," he said. "If you're going to be here working on your exhibit, call my cell and we'll discuss what I need for the new addition."

She took the card and slid it into the pocket of her jeans.

"Thank you. I will call."

"Good. And, Jolie…" He pulled his phone out of his pocket.

"Yes?"

"I have to take this. We'll talk later?"

She nodded, scanning the area for Cassie. Time to escape. Not that she wanted to call it escaping. More like…
Yes, escaping.

JAKE GLANCED AT HIS watch as he walked through the lodge an hour after bumping into Jolie and Cassie. He doubted Jolie would call him. He'd read it in the panic-stricken look on her face. She had no intention of spending time with him, not even for business.

He understood her hesitation but had hoped they could put the past behind them for business. All around him people were gearing up for New Year's Eve. Years ago he'd heard a saying that how you spent New Year's Eve was how you would spend the rest of your year. It must be true because he spent most years working through the holiday followed by working through the next year.

As he passed the ballroom that was receiving last-minute touches, he stopped to watch the progress. Candles were being set out on the tables. A buffet dinner would be set in the adjoining room. The band had already done a sound check. He entered the room, checking off everything that still needed to be done. In the center of the dance floor he stopped, remembering last year's ball and a kiss.

A year ago on this very night he'd stood alone as the clock struck twelve and then he hadn't been alone. Jolie Godwin had been in front of him. She had turned to face him and he'd given in to the moment and pulled her close.

One year later he still couldn't get past that kiss. Nothing unsettled Jake. Nothing got under this skin. But for a year the least likely person had been a reminder that maybe he wasn't always in control.

Jolie Godwin had somehow gotten to him.

He couldn't afford to let her get under his skin. The lodge needed him focused. All around him people were going about their lives, doing their jobs, and they depended on him to not be his mother.

For the past ten years he'd been busy rebuilding a business his mom had ignored and his first stepfather had tried to bleed dry. The two of them had nearly destroyed a family legacy. Jake's hard work had brought it back to life.

One last look at the ballroom and he left the room and turned down the corridor to the Aspen Hall, a room in the convention center that would be used for the local art exhibits.

As he walked through the double doors he did a double take and nearly turned to leave. But he didn't. If he was going to be in control, he would also control this situation and whatever it was she did to him. He watched as Jolie climbed a ladder, a hammer in hand and a cup of coffee on the utility shelf where most people kept paint. Her sweater, soft and deep red, clung to her body. Talk about blooming late. He remembered her as an awkward teen, a loner a few years younger than himself.

And he remembered her at nineteen, not really a flirt, just a girl sitting on the edge of the pool, sweet in her modest one-piece swimsuit.

She reached to string what appeared to be silk aspen

leaves to a backdrop. The ladder wobbled and she tee-
tered on the top step, arms swaying and the silk vine
dangling.

Jake hurried forward and put one hand on the ladder, the other on her waist. She gasped, her eyes wid-
ening in surprise.

"I didn't see you," she exclaimed, breathless and
pale.

"You were too busy falling off the ladder."

"I wasn't falling."

*Let it go.* "You were falling."

"I wouldn't have," she assured him as she climbed
down from the ladder. "At least not far."

*She wouldn't have fallen.* He gave her space as she
picked up a few bits and pieces of silk greenery and
pulled pins out of a package.

"Have you had breakfast?"

She gave him a quick look and then went back up.
"No. I usually go with coffee."

He held the ladder as she stretched to stick a pin in
the backdrop.

"If you're almost finished we could grab a bite to eat
and discuss business."

She pulled the straight pins out of her mouth and set
them on the utility shelf of the ladder. "I'll be done in
fifteen minutes."

"That sounds good. We can meet in my office."

"I don't know." She looked around, at everything but
him, as if trying to come up with a reason to back out.

"Jolie, we can eat in the restaurant, but I have a dining area in my office. It's private and we can talk without being interrupted."

Without answering, she climbed down again and went back to work on her booth. She pinned colored cloth to the backdrop, draping it carefully, ignoring him. He reached to help, holding the cloth for her to tack it in place. He let her settle the thoughts in her mind, because he knew this wouldn't be easy. It wasn't any easier for him. Maybe it was time to clear the air.

"I'm sorry about your dad." He watched her as he said it. She looked straight ahead, biting her bottom lip. Finally she turned to face him. Her dark eyes held his for a brief moment.

"You apologized at his funeral."

"I know, but I think it had to be said again."

Jolie picked up the hammer, the extra cloth and a few other items. She stored them all in a rubber tub.

"You had no choice." She released a shaky sigh. "You had to fire him. I didn't realize it at the time, so of course I was angry."

"Jolie, I could have pressed charges, but I didn't. I got why he did it."

She picked up a box of tacks. "He did it for me, but that wasn't who he was. A long time ago, he was someone different."

"I know he was a good man."

"It's over. Please, just let it be over. You don't have to feel guilty. I miss him, but I'm doing what he would have wanted me to do."

"I know."

He'd lost his dad, too. Building this lodge into something special was the way he paid tribute to a man who had left them too soon.

She wiped a finger under her eye and returned to

pinning cloth. He didn't know how to undo what appeared to be a truckload of guilt on both their parts. He had fired a man who had already lost too much. She'd probably spent a lot of sleepless nights blaming herself because her dad had stolen money to help her pay for college.

Jake should do more than give her space, he should walk away. He had a business that needed him focused, not distracted. He had a child upstairs, wanting his attention. Not his child. He shook his head. He always managed to be the one picking up the pieces for everyone else.

Jolie didn't need him to pick up the pieces. She'd done a great job putting her life back together.

He studied her again, at the fall of dark hair she brushed back with an artist's hand, long-fingered and graceful. For the first time in years, Wildwood Ski Lodge was the last thing he wanted to think about.

The thought brought him to his senses. Business.

"I'll meet you back here in thirty minutes and we'll go to my office to discuss the artwork. I'll order breakfast from the restaurant."

She nodded, a pin stuck in her mouth.

He left it at that and walked away.

# CHAPTER TWO

LATER SHE'D PROBABLY kick herself for agreeing to this meeting, but with Jake leading her through a maze of halls, she didn't have time to rethink, or escape. Even if she wanted to go, she couldn't find her way out on her own. Not without a map or a GPS.

Jake opened a door of the office with a key card. Jolie walked through the double doors ahead of him and into the world of Jake Wild. She'd been here once before. She'd confronted him after he'd fired her dad. She'd yelled. She'd called him names. She'd pushed him and hit him. He'd stood next to his desk and let her take her anger out on him.

She didn't learn until later that he had fired her dad because Mac had stolen a deposit bag full of cash. When her dad finally confessed, Jolie had made payments to Jake, eventually getting it all back to him. Her dad. She glanced around the large suite that was Jake's office. Her dad had lost himself in a bottle of whiskey.

She had loved her dad. He'd had his faults, but she loved the man he had wanted to be.

Nine years brought a lot of clarity to a situation. She breathed deeply to clear her mind, to push past the surge of pain that hit her as she stood in that room again and remembered. Her father had been an alcoholic long before Jake Wild fired him. The drinking had started during her mother's illness and continued until he drove his car off the road six years ago.

"I'll order breakfast." Jake picked up his phone, still watching her. "Omelet?"

"Fine." She walked to the double doors that led to a patio. In the distance she could see the small outdoor ice rink, empty at this time of the morning. At night, twinkling lights surrounded the ice and old-fashioned post lamps added more light.

"Do you skate?" Jake walked up behind her.

She didn't turn to face him because he stood too close, and turning would put her in his arms. She remembered being held by him. She remembered how it had felt to have his lips on hers, his scent clinging to her.

After midnight last year, the magic had ended. As everyone else took off masks, laughing and hugging, the two of them had released hands and stepped away from each other.

"No. I don't skate."

"You should learn."

She turned and stepped around him, back to the center of the room. "Jake, can we just take care of business and I'll go."

"Of course." Someone knocked on the door. "Come in."

A waiter pushed a cart into the room. The wonderful aromas made Jolie's stomach forget that she didn't usually eat breakfast.

"Thank you, Ted." Jake tipped the young waiter. "We'll serve ourselves."

Ted nodded curtly after glancing in her direction,

and then left them alone, closing the door behind him with a finality that sent a shiver down Jolie's spine. She rubbed her arms. She'd forgotten her jacket in the convention hall.

Jake noticed. He reached for a remote and seconds later a gas fire blazed in the fireplace. She smiled because it was cheesy and yet…

"I promise, I know how to build a real fire." Jake moved the food cart close to a small table and chairs in front of the fire.

"Of course you do." She laughed in spite of herself. "You don't have a dimmer switch and music on that remote, do you?"

He grinned. "No, I'm not that much of a player. I don't have the time or inclination. And I think if I did, I'd be more old-fashioned."

"How?" She winced, wishing she hadn't asked.

Jake moved to her side. He pulled out her chair and motioned for her to sit. "Like this. I'd pull out your chair, open doors for you. I'd probably send you a dozen roses."

"I believe that. Only a true romantic could come up with a masked ball."

Jake lifted the domed top off the tray of food. "I hate to disappoint you, but I didn't think it up. I have a marketing team headed up by my very unromantic cousin Tansy."

"I'm crushed."

"But if you wanted it to be my idea…"

She shook her head. "No, I'm good. And really, we should get back to business."

He sat down across from her. She watched as he

poured coffee. He really did have strong hands, she thought again, suntanned. No rings. His shirtsleeves were rolled up, exposing arms that matched the hands. Last year he'd held her in those hands.

She accepted the cup of coffee, clutching it in both hands.

"Jake, I don't want your charity."

He drew back and looked at her. "It's breakfast and business, Jolie."

"We're talking about my art. I don't know if you think I need this and you're trying to make up for the past, but I don't need it. Wildwood is a beautiful place and your buyer travels all over the world looking for suitable pieces for the rooms. I've talked to her and she isn't interested in local art. 'It doesn't meet Wildwood standards,' I believe were her words."

"She was wrong." Jake pointed to the plate he'd set in front of her. "Eat your eggs and stop being so defensive. I'm a businessman, Jolie, not a charitable organization. I buy what works for this resort, and what you're doing works. End of story."

She would like to believe that, but guilt could cause a man to do crazy things.

So what was her excuse? Why was she sitting with him, about to enjoy a meal that smelled heavenly? She could get up, walk away. Instead, she remained seated and waited to see what would happen. Maybe because it was almost a new year and she wanted something in her life to change. She wanted the broken pieces to heal. She wanted the walls she'd built to crumble a little. She wanted light back in her life, not just in her art.

BREAKFAST AND BUSINESS, nothing more. Jake called that a success. As he walked Jolie to the car he'd had brought around for her, he started to ask if she would be at the ball. He stopped himself. Asking her would have been a mistake. She would see it as an invitation. Especially after she'd already told Cassie she wouldn't be going.

She thought his buying her artwork was a form of charity. He'd tried to let that slide off his back, but it bugged him. Or maybe it forced him to question his motives, to question himself.

"Next week, after New Year's is over, we'll meet and I'll look at your sketches." He opened her door for her and she slid into the compact car.

He wasn't sure the car was the most suitable. True, the town of Snow Falls was at the base of the mountains, so she didn't have to worry about climbing hills, but the roads could still get snow-covered fairly quickly.

Wisely, he kept the comment to himself. She was a grown woman and he didn't have a say in the decisions she made. Nothing had ever made her his responsibility.

"Yes, next week. I have a few things to take care of, but I should be able to find an hour."

"Of course, an hour." He nodded once, his hand on the car door. "Be careful, the snow is coming down pretty hard."

Yeah, he couldn't help himself.

She smiled and laughed. "Thank you, I'll try to remember that."

He laughed. "Yeah, I know, you've been driving these roads for years."

"Exactly, but it was very romantic of you to mention it." She winked and reached to pull the door closed.

Jake stepped back onto the sidewalk and watched as she drove away. That felt pretty crazy, standing there without a coat, watching as her car pulled out of the parking lot.

He turned and walked back into the resort, brushing snow out of his hair and stomping it off his boots. His cousin Tansy stood in the doorway, watching him. She shook her head. His cousin, the only female he really trusted—other than his niece. She slid an arm around his waist and they went to his office together.

"She's a sweet woman." Tansy sat at the table he'd recently left. She reached for the cinnamon roll he hadn't touched. "You left a perfectly good pastry. She must be nice."

"I'm only interested in Jolie's artwork." When Tansy raised one well-defined eyebrow, he smiled. "For the new addition to the lodge."

"Oh, of course." She picked up a fork and took a bite of the cinnamon roll. "Do you like her, or feel guilty?"

"Take that and go. I don't need internet-counseling sessions."

"I am so hurt by that. Yes, I learn a lot from the internet, but I happened to take an introduction to psychology class when I majored in business."

They both laughed and he sat down across from her, in the seat Jolie had sat in a short time before. "Maybe guilt. Maybe something else."

"Maybe you have a hard time believing there are people who aren't out to use you. Not without reason. Exhibit A—your mother. Your stepfather. Your stepsister. That woman you dated a few years ago whose name we don't mention." She smiled and flipped her auburn hair back off her shoulder. "Have I missed anyone?"

"No, you haven't. And it could be that I'm too busy building a business to date. When I do date, I don't want it to be a woman who thinks I'm buying her breakfast or her art out of guilt."

"Give yourself a break. Stop working and enjoy your life. Take out a pretty woman. Remember, you're the most eligible bachelor in Colorado."

"My romance gene is unfortunately stifled. And that article just complicated my life. The crazies came out of the woodwork."

Tansy laughed, flipping her dark hair to the side. "There have been a few that could almost be described as stalkers."

"Exactly my point. I don't have time for this."

"Send her flowers." Tansy licked the fork clean and set it on the table. "She likes fall flowers, not roses."

"How do you know?"

Tansy shrugged one shoulder. "I have my ways."

"Tansy?"

"Do you think she became an overnight success on her own? I know your lack of a romance gene, and your unfortunate guilt gene, so I took care of things."

"What the…"

She narrowed her eyes. "I do have a few connections in the hotel and resort business, so I spread the word."

"And people think you're heartless." He shook his head but he smiled. "Tansy, you restore my faith in humanity."

"Not everyone is out to use you, Jake."

"Only ninety percent of them?"

"You need to learn to trust a few people. Make that your New Year's resolution. Must trust people. Start easy, with someone like Jolie Godwin." She got up and walked to the door. "Remember, you offered to give her the money. She paid it back."

"I'll think about it."

"Good boy. Now, go get Anna. She's ready to go to town. It's New Year's Eve and you can't always be in control. And Jake, remember that Anna's a victim, too." She paused, a hand on the doorknob. "Introduce her to Jolie. Anna's only artistic outlet is a coloring book and markers, but the two of them might hit it off."

"Go."

At his command she saluted and walked out. Jake leaned back in his chair and watched the fire licking at the gas logs in the fireplace. Thoughts rolled through his mind. The new addition to the lodge, New Year's Eve, his stepsister's child and a kiss. It all came back to the kiss.

If he let Tansy deal with Jolie and the art purchases, he could move on. He could keep his focus on business. The plan made perfect sense.

And it was the last thing he wanted.

## CHAPTER THREE

JOLIE WENT HOME AFTER the meeting with Jake. She didn't have a lot of time. So much for a nice leisurely pace on New Year's Eve. She had promised to meet Cassie at the Ice Castle Café and then she had offered to do face painting at the library, where they were having several events.

She would much rather stay home, even if it meant missing a workshop by illustrator Brody Kincaid. She wanted to support a local artist, but staying home was tempting beyond belief. A hermit, that's what Cassie called her. She had her little house, her studio and a great coffeemaker. What more could she want out of life?

If she'd asked her best friend that question, Cassie would have had an answer. Cassie lived in a world where men were there to pick up the pieces, to hold things together. Jolie had held things together for her dad. After her mother's death she'd made sure he ate, that he had clean clothes and that he sometimes got up and went to work. She couldn't remember ever having a man to lean on, to count on.

So when asked what more she wanted out of life, a man was not at the top of the list. She'd love to make more money with her art. She didn't need to be rich, she just wanted to pay her bills and have something left over at the end of the month. She would like to be able to go on vacation. She'd love to have a fashion sense, but mostly she threw on whatever she pulled out of her closet.

As she drove to the Ice Castle restaurant, she thought about all the times her dad hadn't gone to work. She remembered how happy he'd been when he landed the job at the Wildwood and how he'd presented her with money for college. She'd been naive enough to believe he'd saved up enough to pay for her tuition for a semester.

She'd worked two years and two jobs to pay back what her dad had stolen and to keep the electricity on. Mac Godwin had stayed drunk. Most of the time he'd been passed out on the small sofa in their travel trailer.

Through it all, she had loved her dad. Sometimes she'd resented him, resented taking care of him, but she'd loved him.

Cassie waved from inside the Ice Castle. She had her niece and nephew with her today, which explained why they were eating here. The restaurant had an amazing play area for children. Later in the day they would have an ice sculptor.

Jolie slipped a little on the packed snow right outside the entrance. She shivered as she stomped her snow-covered boots and walked through the door that Cassie pushed open for her.

"It's about time." Cassie hugged her tight. "Where have you been?"

"I had to run home. And then I had trouble getting out of my driveway."

"You need a truck, not that little car of yours."

"It's what I have, Cass." Jolie smiled at the two children behind Cassie. "Are you guys having fun?"

"Are you going to paint our faces?" Lana asked, her blond hair parted on the side and curling around her face. "Aunt Cassie said you would."

"Later."

"I want a fairy princess." Lana touched her cheek.

Jolie groaned, then muttered, "A fairy princess…"

Cassie laughed and took her niece and nephew by the hand. "We have a table at the back. I ordered already. Did you want something?"

"I had a late breakfast."

Cassie shot her a look, but Jolie ignored her and followed the children through the restaurant. She smiled because Cassie's niece and nephew, like Cassie, were blond and pretty, even Jason. At seven, he didn't want to be called pretty. They were getting situated at their table when the front door opened again.

"Hmm, imagine that." Cassie glanced from the door to Jolie. "Jake Wild and the adorable Anna."

"Who is Anna?"

"You need to get out more often." Cassie looked up from the menu to Jolie. "She's the niece he got custody of a few months ago."

"What? I…I hadn't heard."

"That's because you stay in that studio of yours and I always forget to tell you what's going on in the real world. And I usually avoid the topic of Jake."

"Thank you. I appreciate your sensitivity." Jolie forced the dry tone, but she wanted to smile. She wouldn't let herself look at Jake Wild or the precious little girl, maybe four or five years old, standing next to him in a picture-perfect red wool coat, black stockings, mittens and a cap.

Okay, maybe she did look.

But she didn't look at Jake. She wouldn't think about how cozy it had felt to sit in his office. She wouldn't think about hands that were strong…or a smile that…

Cassie waved. "Jake, join us."

"Cassie—you're impossible."

Jolie started to leave, but Cassie grabbed her by the arm. "He's a nice guy and a family friend. Relax."

"Right, relax. He's going to think this is a setup."

Jake held the child's hand as he threaded his way through the tables. A few people called out to him. He waved, but he looked tense. She wondered why. She'd always thought of him as the guy who took life for granted and never had a bad day. Why would he have bad days? He was Jake Wild.

"Are you sure you have room?" he asked when he reached them.

"Of course. We have the entire back wall." Cassie still held Jolie's arm.

Jake shrugged out of a heavy canvas coat and then leaned to help the little girl standing next to him. He pulled off her stocking cap and shoved it in the pocket of his coat. He said something quiet and she shook her head and then raised her hands, flashing words at him in sign language. Jolie caught her breath. She saw Cassie glance her way, head cocked knowingly. Because, of course, Cassie knew.

"Ice cream it is." Jake lifted Anna off the ground and held her close as he took a seat. The girl was tiny but her expression seemed more mature than her size. She had big, dark eyes, an elfin face and long, dark hair.

"Hi, Anna." Cassie touched the child's hands. "Remember me?"

Anna nodded. She looked at Jolie. Cassie squeezed Jolie's arm. "This is my friend Jolie."

Anna signed to Jake and leaned close to him. He laughed and hugged the child as he translated. "She says you're pretty."

"Thank you." Jolie smiled at her.

"She thinks you look like Cinderella."

Jolie nearly choked on her cola.

"Thank you."

Jake Wild, a nice guy who understood sign language and had custody of his stepsister's child. Jolie had been judged a lot in her life, and as she watched Jake she realized she'd been doing some judging of her own.

AFTER EATING BURGERS, probably too quickly, the kids ran off to play. Cassie cleared the table and made the excuse that she had to go supervise. As she walked away she smiled, very sly. Jake gave her credit, she could occasionally do almost subtle. The kids probably did need to be supervised. Not that Anna would go far.

"She's a beautiful child." Jolie nodded toward Anna, who wandered through the play area watching the other children. She occasionally looked back, searching for him as if he might disappear.

"Yes, she is."

He needed to find a way to spend more time with Anna. She needed security. She had a terrific nanny. She had Tansy and she had him during every free moment of his day. But she needed more. The way he had needed more at her age. His mother hadn't been a drug addict, just nonexistent. She'd never liked Colorado so she stayed gone as much as possible and left his up-bringing to his father and a succession of nannies.

His dad had died young. Jake had pretty much been on his own since his teen years. He wondered if Jolie ever thought about how similar their lives really were.

Jake watched as his niece stood at the base of a slide, not really wanting to go, but maybe thinking about it.

"Cassie said you have custody. I didn't know."

"It isn't common knowledge."

"I see." But she didn't. He could see the questions forming, and knew she wouldn't ask.

"My stepsister is a drug addict," he finally said. "Right now she's living in a halfway house in Denver. She didn't have any other family to take Anna, so I pe-titioned the court for custody. I didn't want her lost in the system."

"She can't speak?"

"No, she can't. She's hearing impaired, but with hear-ing aids she's gained some hearing. Being born deaf, she never learned to speak." He watched Anna take a step up the ladder of the slide. "I should go help her."

"I'll come with you."

They walked to the play area together. Children ran, playing and laughing. Moms tried to keep track of their offspring and keep some semblance of order. Anna moved back when another child pushed through to take a turn on the slide. Jake wanted to yank the boy up by the collar, but he also didn't want to be attacked by moms.

He wasn't a dad. He hadn't really planned on being one. But it was easy to love Anna and want to protect her. He'd learned quickly that he would hurt someone for her.

"Go ahead, kiddo." Jake stepped close to his niece, shielding her, giving her a minute to think about the ladder. She signed with lightning speed and he laughed. "No, I'm too big. You go and I'll be right here."

Jolie stepped close. She smelled like herbal shampoo and flowery lotion. She squatted to Anna's level. "I'll wait at the bottom for you and your uncle Jake can help you climb."

Anna smiled big. Man, he loved that smile. For a long time he'd thought she might never smile. She'd been through a lot with his stepsister. From what he'd been told, Anna had been homeless at times. She'd been left with people she didn't know. Her father was a man who sometimes drifted into her life. And she was afraid of him. That was the thing Jake knew most about Anna's dad.

But she was adjusting. Jake made sure she felt safe. She even sometimes laughed now. A few months ago she'd known very few signs, so she basically had no communication skills other than what she'd made up.

She signed to him now.

"She said I should buy you an ice-cream cone." Jake cleared his throat, well aware a child was pushing his buttons.

"I love ice cream." Jolie looked up. "I'm sorry, it slipped out. I'm not trying to get ice cream out of you."

"It might break the bank." He lifted Anna onto the

ladder. "Better get down there. She's expecting you to catch her."

Jolie walked to the end of the slide and waited. As Anna came down she held out her arms. His niece slid right into her embrace and Jolie hugged her tight. Yeah, for that he'd buy her ice cream and more.

"Time for that ice-cream cone, Ms. Godwin?"

"No, I really can't. I have a lot to do today."

"Like what?" He smiled at Anna, who now stood next to Jolie. "You'll break her heart if you don't have ice cream with us. And you'll break Cassie's heart, because she's behind you eavesdropping."

She turned quickly and of course Cassie wasn't there. "That wasn't nice."

"You're right. But we would like for you to stay."

He should have let it go. He didn't have to beg a woman to spend time with him. He really didn't have to use a kid to get the job done. At the moment, he would have done just about anything to get Jolie to have an ice-cream cone with him. Or with Anna.

Jolie reached for Anna's hand and the child let her take it. "For Anna, I'll stay for ice cream and then I have to go."

"What do you have to do on New Year's Eve?" he asked as they walked back to the table. He motioned their waitress over.

"I'm signed up to paint faces for an hour, remember? And then there are a few exhibits I want to see." Jolie slid into the booth opposite the two of them.

Anna tugged on Jake's sleeve. She signed fast, her eyes big. He could have ignored her, not asked the question, but she tugged at his sleeve again, insisting.

He should tell her no. There were things a child didn't get, wouldn't understand. Shoot, half of what he felt at the moment, he didn't understand.

The waitress took their order and left. He cleared his throat and glanced down. Anna's eyes were on Jolie and her little fingers flew again.

"Anna would like to know." He watched her sign and then switched his attention to Jolie. "We would like to know if you'd join us for an early dinner and then ice skating. I promised her skating before she goes to bed and I go to the party."

He knew he'd put Jolie on the spot. Who could say no to Anna? Obviously he couldn't. And he should have. He should have told her that Ms. Godwin had other things to do and that he needed to get back to work. Instead, he was letting a five-year-old child arrange his social life.

## CHAPTER FOUR

JAKE WILD LOOKED ABOUT as cornered as a man could look. But Jolie's gaze didn't linger on Jake. Not really.

But only because looking at Jake turned her inside out. Anna made things easier. Anna was a little girl wanting to do fun things. And Jolie remembered how it felt to be a little girl who wanted so much.

She was the last person Jake Wild wanted to spend time with. Anna didn't know that. Anna, with her big eyes and flashing fingers.

"She says she won't let you fall." Jake grinned and that grin undid all Jolie's reservations.

"Of course she'll go!" Cassie picked that moment to jump into their conversation. "I don't even know what the two of you are planning, but the answer has to be yes. It's New Year's Eve."

"Cass," Jolie began, but Cassie scooted her over. Her niece and nephew sat at the table next to theirs. "I didn't see you."

"Of course you didn't and stop making excuses. You find things to fill your time and you need to learn to relax. Jake has a staff to oversee the art displays at the lodge. You're going to face paint for an hour."

Jolie remembered the final payment she'd sent to Jake Wild. The relief at having returned every dime of his money. She remembered that day thinking he was finally out of her life for good. And then last year she'd kissed him.

He had kissed her back and then he'd backed away and it was as if it never happened. She didn't want a repeat of the kiss for either of them.

Really.

A sharp elbow jabbed her ribs. She moved away from Cassie, in case there happened to be a repeat.

"Okay." Her voice? Her answer? She opened her mouth to retract it, but Anna's hands were flying again.

Jake looked from his niece back to Jolie. "She said we'll have corn dogs."

"Corn dogs sound wonderful."

Jake's dark eyebrows arched. "Yes, every woman enjoys corn dogs for dinner."

"If they don't, they should," she countered.

"Let's stop the chitchat and get down to planning," Cassie said as the waitress returned with their ice cream.

"Planning?" Jake looked and sounded perplexed.

Jolie thought it had to be about time for her to escape. She couldn't, not with Cassie sitting on the outside of the booth, blocking her in.

"The date." Cassie handed Jolie a sundae smothered with hot fudge and peanut butter. "That looks fattening."

"It looks wonderful." Jolie watched Anna, who had ordered the same, dig in. "This isn't a date."

"Ice-skating lessons," Jake agreed. "That's all." His eyes twinkled, and she wondered how she would escape this evening with her heart intact.

She concentrated on the sundae. Her traitorous mind kept replaying being held in his arms.

"What are you wearing to the ball?" Cassie prodded, taking the conversation in a new direction.

"I told you I'm not going."

Jake handed Anna a napkin and pointed to the chocolate on her chin. Did he really care if she went?

"You have to. I bought you a ticket," Cassie continued, and Jolie questioned why the two were friends. They were complete opposites, and yet here they were, nearly twenty-five years after that first day of preschool, still friends.

Cassie had grown up with a silver spoon. Jolie joked that she had grown up with a plastic spoon. But she loved Cassie because Cassie had always been there for her. From preschool on, the two had been inseparable. Cassie had kept Jolie from feeling alone in the world. She'd made sure that Jolie had moments to remember. Jolie had been the friend Cassie knew she could always count on.

"I'll think about it, Cass." She looked at her watch. "And now, I have to go."

"I'll send a car for you. Would four o'clock work?" Jake stood, the way a gentleman would. Jolie slid out of the booth and stood in front of him.

She glanced at her watch again. Four o'clock. That would give her a few hours to enjoy First Night in Snow Falls. She could see the art exhibit, paint faces and maybe try the snow maze.

"That sounds good."

"We'll be around town for a while. Maybe we'll

bump into each other again. I think Anna wants her face painted."

"She should definitely get her face painted." Jolie waved at Anna. "See you later. Remember, I've never skated."

Anna signed something that made Jake smile. He signed back to his niece rather than answer with words. Anna giggled and signed. The two of them had a quick conversation that left everyone out of their little world, and convinced Jolie that she needed to learn this language.

"What did she say?" Jolie asked when he turned his attention back to her.

"I think I won't tell."

"Oh. Maybe I'll find out later."

"Maybe." Jake's stormy eyes met hers and she couldn't think past those eyes, or how good it felt to stand in front of him.

She glanced at her watch. "I should go."

Cassie stood to hug her goodbye. When she leaned in close, Jolie's friend whispered, "Chicken."

"You betcha."

With that, Jolie hurried out of the restaurant, and away from temptation in the form of Jake Wild.

JAKE LEFT THE RESTAURANT a short time later. Anna had hold of his hand, so for the time being there was no conversation. Now that she knew sign language, she seemed to be making up for lost time. For years her mother had assumed she was developmentally delayed, or just didn't want to talk.

Selah had never bothered having Anna checked by a physician.

It still made him angry. If he had his way, he'd keep permanent custody of his niece.

Anna pulled her hand from his and signed. He answered by both signing and speaking, because both were important to her development at this point.

"Yes, we can go through the maze. Let's go to the library first and see if they're having story time yet. Remember, the lady who writes books is here to read her stories."

Anna signed, "And face painting."

He wasn't getting out of this. One way or another, Anna would include Jolie Godwin in their New Year's festivities. He wondered if a five-year-old child could be in cahoots with his cousin and Cassie.

He reached for Anna's hand again.

The sidewalks of Snow Falls were increasingly more crowded as they walked. The town had been planned years ago to be in the style of a European village. The streets were cobblestone. The sidewalks were brick and stone. The street lamps resembled gas lanterns of the Victorian era.

Freshly fallen snow covered everything, making it more perfect than the event planners could have dreamed. He led Anna through the crowd, surprised when she pulled back. He turned and saw that her eyes were wide.

"What's wrong?"

She shook her head but remained frozen to the spot.

"Anna?"

She signed, "My daddy." He shook his head because

he'd seen her father once, in court, and never again. And he couldn't see the man here now.

"I'm not going to let anyone hurt you."

Anna moved in close to his side.

"You know that, right? You're safe."

She nodded, but still those dark eyes darted back and forth.

"Do you see him?"

She shook her head.

"Okay, we'll go to the library, but if you see him, you let me know. Anna, please remember that I won't let him hurt you."

She held tight to his hand. Jake scanned the crowd as they walked. Anna's father wasn't there, just as he hadn't been there the other times she thought she'd seen him.

She finally relaxed and was fairly skipping as they approached the library.

"Would you like hot apple cider?" He led her inside.

Anna shook her head and signed that her belly hurt. He gave her hand a light squeeze.

"Because you ate too much ice cream."

They passed a long line of children waiting to buy a book that they could get signed by the author and then a line for face painting. He peered over the children and moms, looking for Jolie's dark head.

She stood behind a table, a child seated on a stool in front of her. He watched until Anna pulled his hand in another direction.

"Don't you want your face painted?"

She smiled a little bigger and signed, asking him if he would get a superhero on his face. He gave in.

"Yes, I'll get my face painted. You can pick."

And then they were in line, waiting. He ignored a few looks from the women around them. Finally they were at the front of the line. Jolie looked up and smiled.

"Is Anna ready to get her face painted?" She reached across the table to touch Anna's hand.

Anna signed and pointed at him. He met Jolie's gaze, saw the twinkle in her dark eyes.

"Is Uncle Jake getting his face painted?" Jolie asked Anna.

Anna nodded rapidly and reached to flip through the book of designs. She found one of a superhero mask and pointed at the picture. Jolie chuckled.

"I think that's perfect. What picture do you want, Anna?"

She picked a cat for herself.

Jake took a seat on the stool because Anna insisted he go first. She stayed close to his side, her eyes trained on his face. Jolie rinsed her brushes and leaned in close. He could smell her floral perfume and mint gum as she worked.

The brush stroked his cheek. She held his chin with her left hand, tilting his head. He closed his eyes because it was easier than watching her, the fall of dark hair, the way she bit her bottom lip when she concentrated and the tiniest flutter of a pulse at the base of her neck.

Her hand moved up his jawline. He inhaled but kept his eyes closed. Face painting shouldn't be foreplay, he thought. But her breath was soft, her hands gentle. She was so close he could feel her as she moved to get a better angle.

It would be good if the torture ended sooner than later. He opened his eyes and she looked away. Her lips were moist from wetting them with her tongue. He wanted to hold her close and kiss her breathless.

She moved, bumping her hip against his knee. If it had been any other woman, he would have thought she'd done it on purpose, to drive him over the edge. But it was Jolie's innocence that pushed his buttons.

If ever a woman wasn't after him, it was Jolie.

"I'm almost done." She dabbed more paint on his cheek. "There we go."

Anna made a sound, her voice rusty from lack of use, but he knew that sound as laughter.

"What's so funny?" he signed.

She signed that he looked silly. He looked into the mirror that Jolie held up. Yeah, he guessed on a thirty-three-year-old man, a superhero mask might be a little over the top.

"I feel like I should go rescue people," he signed and spoke, for Anna's benefit.

"I think you do enough rescuing." Jolie dabbed the brush in paint. "One more spot to fix."

He knew she was remembering the Christmas when he'd left a basket on their porch. It had been just a year after her mother's death, a year before his father's, and he'd heard people in town talking about what Jolie and her dad needed. He'd watched Jolie, just a kid, trying to hold on at school.

"Who rescues you, superhero Jake Wild?" She put her brush in water and pink climbed her neck to her cheeks.

Jake stepped off the stool and lifted Anna so that

she could become a cat for the day. "If I'm a superhero, Jolie, I don't need to be rescued."

Anna looked from Jolie to him and back to Jolie. Her smile had faded as she watched, listening to their conversation and probably sensing that the joking had ended.

Or maybe the joke was on him, because he wanted to kiss Jolie Godwin right then and there, with the entire town of Snow Falls as witness.

## CHAPTER FIVE

LONG AFTER JAKE LEFT with Anna, Jolie felt shaken. With hands that trembled she'd painted lady bugs, ponies, cats and cartoon characters on little faces. As her shift ended, she said a few hurried goodbyes and walked out of the library unsure of what she would do next.

She glanced at her watch as she buttoned her coat. The snow had stopped falling, but the sky remained gray and the air felt cold and damp. It could snow again and probably would.

In the past she'd thought about leaving her hometown for somewhere warmer, a place where people didn't know her as Mac Godwin's daughter. She'd thought about starting over in a town where she would just be the artist in some little house. But she'd stayed in Snow Falls and she'd weathered the storms, the real and the emotional.

She had friends here. She had roots. In the end, those two things meant more to her than a warmer climate and anonymity. For some crazy reason those thoughts made her mind return to Jake. Did he ever want to leave, to go live in a place where he wasn't known as one of Colorado's most eligible bachelors?

"Hey, where are you going?"

She turned and saw Cassie, who looked beautiful,

as usual. Blonde, elegant and always together, even in jeans and a heavy sweater. Jolie envied Cassie's ability to throw on anything and look as if she'd spent hours getting ready.

Jolie shoved her hands in her pockets to warm them. She'd forgotten her gloves in her car still parked at the Ice Castle. "I painted faces, now I think I'll take a break before I catch the illustration workshop Brody Kincaid is giving."

"You promised a child you'd have dinner and go ice skating."

Jolie pushed her hands farther into her pockets.

"I haven't forgotten. But my toes and hands are freezing. Where are the kids?"

"Their mom took them. Will you go through the snow maze with me before you leave?" Cassie rummaged in her purse and pulled out a pair of gloves. "I always have a spare."

"Who does that?" Jolie took the gloves. "Seriously, Cass, who has extra gloves in their purse? I don't even have a spare car key."

"You should learn to be more prepared." Cassie held out two tubes of lip balm and two rolls of mints. "You never know what will happen."

"I should learn to be more obsessive, you mean?" She took one of the tubes of lip balm. "Thank you, don't mind if I do."

Cassie laughed and hooked her arm through Jolie's. Together they headed across the square in the direction of the ice maze. Snow started to fall again. People walked in groups, going in and out of shops. First Night was a big event in Snow Falls. It brought more than the normal skiing crowd; it brought people who wanted to be a part of a New Year's celebration that was meant to be family friendly.

"You have to go to the ball tonight, Jo." Cassie still held her arm. They were close to the maze. People were laughing as they came out the exit.

"Why do I have to go? I have a great book that I'd love to finish. I have a wonderful new coffee blend."

"You should get a cat." Cassie glanced at her. "I mean, if you plan on being the old artist spinster, shouldn't you have cats?"

"I'm allergic."

"Why don't you want to go? Are you afraid?"

"No, I'm not afraid. I don't want to be a third wheel. I don't want to be the person without a date so all my friends' boyfriends and husbands feel as if they have to take a turn dancing with poor lonely Jolie."

Cassie's smile had long since disappeared and they'd stopped walking. Jolie knew she'd messed up. She'd put that serious look in her friend's eyes.

"Are you lonely, Jolie?"

Jolie frowned and closed her eyes. She shouldn't have said that. "No, Cass, I'm not lonely." Maybe sometimes. At night when she was sitting alone with a glass of wine and a book about fictional people falling in love, yes, maybe then.

"There's no reason for it. You're beautiful, sweet, talented and going places with your art."

"I promise I'm just fine with my life."

"There are men who would love to share their lives with you."

Jolie smiled at that. "Yes, and I do go on dates. It's

just, you know—" what could she say "—I want something special. I don't want to settle."

"I'll let it go. I don't want you to sit in your house alone tonight. Not on New Year's Eve. Take a chance that love will find you, Jo. Take a chance on a second kiss."

She should have known that was where this conversation would end up. Jake Wild. It always ended there.

"Jo, I saw the look in his eyes when he kissed you."

"Right, the look of shock because he realized he'd just kissed Mac Godwin's daughter?"

"No, the look of shock because the kiss rocked his world."

"We saw two different things, Cass."

"I saw reality. You saw what you always believe about yourself. And what you believe isn't the truth. Being Mac Godwin's daughter doesn't mean you aren't good enough."

"Being Mac Godwin's daughter means that the stolen money will always be between Jake and me. It's always in my mind, on my conscience."

"You paid it back. You didn't steal that money, but you paid back every dime. You need to let go of the guilt."

Jolie looked away from her friend and swiped at tears sneaking down her cheeks. "Let's not talk about it anymore. Let's not do the whole New Year's thing where we examine our lives and pick apart every little thing we think we need to change before the next new year rolls around."

"Okay." Cassie reached for her arm again. "But come

to the ball with us. It won't be the same for me if you're not there. And you know how selfish I am."

"Right." Jolie laughed and sniffed back tears that caused everything to blur for a second. "You're the least selfish person I know."

"Which is why you won't be upset when you get home and find a dress hanging in your closet."

"A dress?" Jolie glanced toward the maze in time to see Jake walk through the arched entrance with Anna.

"I used my key and hung it in your closet. Don't kill me."

"I won't kill you, but really, Cass?"

"I had to buy it. That red is going to look beautiful with your coloring."

The dress from the Wildwood Boutique. "Cass, not that dress. Not the 'costs more than I make in a month' dress."

Cassie nodded. "Yes, that dress. I got a great deal on it, so don't argue."

"A great deal?"

"Yes, a discount."

"How?"

Cassie didn't answer. Instead, she tightened her grip on Jolie's arm and dragged her toward the maze. The very same maze Jake Wild had entered moments earlier.

Not that it mattered.

JAKE TRIED TO CALL TANSY just before they went in the maze. The idea of not being at the lodge, not having his hand on the reins, didn't sit well with him. Not that Tansy couldn't be trusted to take care of everything. He just liked knowing what was going on.

She didn't answer anyway.

Anna held tight to his hand, a tiny reminder of why he had to take time off, why he had to let go a little. It didn't mean he wasn't still in control. He knew every aspect of his business.

He just needed to relax and focus on the other important things in his life.

As they walked through the maze, the tall, snow-block walls towering over them, Anna rubbed at her ears. Jake stopped walking and leaned to sign. People rushed past them, talking and laughing. He moved his niece closer to the side.

"What's wrong?"

She clenched her hands at her sides and shook her head.

"Anna, something is wrong. Tell me."

She moved her fingers in hesitant gestures, unsure. "It's too loud."

Of course it was. For years she'd lived in silence. Now there were echoing sounds, probably overwhelming at times. The hearing aids weren't an easy adjustment and with her severe hearing loss, the doctors had explained that they didn't produce the clearest sounds.

"Do you want to go back to the lodge?" he signed, still squatted in front of her.

She shook her head. "Turn them down?"

He nodded. "Yes, turn them down."

They continued, Anna holding tightly to his hand. He could tell when she relaxed. She walked a little quicker and turned to look up at him, smiling. Eventually her hand loosened and then she let go.

The maze went on forever, splitting, turning back

around, dead-ending. Jake stopped once to get his bearings. He pulled out his phone and checked the compass. Anna looked up at him and he signed that he thought they should be close to the middle and the castle.

Other groups passed them and then came back around, shaking their heads, lost. Anna looked up again and he smiled to let her know that everything would be okay.

"We'll find it," he signed.

She nodded and he wondered if she looked pale or if it was the dim light inside the maze. He stopped her and knelt to face her.

"You okay?" he signed.

She shrugged. Okay, not a good sign, and he had limited experience when it came to kids who weren't okay. They were learning together, he and Anna.

"After this we'll go listen to the lady read the story she wrote."

She nodded, but there didn't appear to be an ounce of excitement in the look.

"Or we can go home."

She nodded. He touched her forehead and it felt cool.

"We'll get through the maze and go home."

Again she nodded.

His phone rang, buzzing in his pocket. It was Tansy returning his call. He straightened and stepped aside, pulling his niece with him.

"You rang?" Tansy sounded as if everything in the world was great.

"Anna and I are going through the maze. I wanted to check and see how things are at the lodge."

"We don't need you, Jake. Everything is running

smoothly. People are starting to arrive for the art exhibits. We have hostesses serving drinks. A few of the artists are wandering around talking to people. It's all going as planned. Are the two of you having fun?"

"I think we're having fun, but maybe too much fun. Or too much ice cream. Anna doesn't want to hear the author read her book. She wants to come home."

"Maybe she's feeling insecure?"

Jake rubbed a hand over his eyes. "Of course. I should have thought of that. Anyway, as soon as we figure out how to get out of here, we'll be heading that way."

"If you don't get back soon, I'll send out a search party."

"I might need it." He hung up and looked down, hoping Anna would return his smile.

Anna wasn't there. She couldn't have gotten far. She'd been standing right next to him. He came across several groups of people but not one little girl in a red coat. He'd dressed her in red because the nanny said red would be easy to spot.

So where was she? He remembered her fear when she thought she'd seen her daddy. What if it had been him? What if Jake had blown off her fears and now it was too late?

"Anna!" He cupped his hands around his mouth and shouted. She had just been there. She'd been holding his hand. He shouted again and then remembered he'd given her permission to turn down her hearing aids.

Someone ran up behind him. He turned, hoping to see his niece. Instead, it was Jolie and Cassie. His gaze immediately went to Jolie.

"What happened?" she asked with those searching dark eyes.

"She walked away while I was on the phone." He started walking and the two of them hurried alongside him. "She turned down her hearing aids, so she can't hear me calling for her. Crazy. I can't believe I let her do that."

"Jake, we'll find her." Cassie reached for his arm.

"I know, but I also know how afraid she is. Hell, I'm an adult and I'm scared right now." He pulled the cell phone out of his pocket and called the city police to ask them to watch the exits and to hold on to Anna if they found her.

"I'm going this way. You two go that way," Cassie indicated with a nod of her head.

"Cass…" Jolie started to step toward her friend, but Cassie was already hurrying away. "Hey."

Cassie turned to walk backward a few steps. "Jo, it'll be better if we split up. We'll find her sooner."

Jake took off in the direction opposite the one Cassie had taken. He slowed when he heard Jolie's footsteps behind him, but he kept moving. He started to yell his niece's name, but remembered she wouldn't hear him. But then maybe she would turn her hearing aids back up when she realized she was lost.

He gave it a shot. "Anna!"

"We'll find her, Jake."

"It was a stupid mistake, taking that phone call."

"You didn't know she'd walk away."

Jolie's hand somehow managed to be in his as they continued through the maze. He stopped people as they passed, asking if they'd seen a small girl alone. No one had. Either they hadn't seen her or they hadn't really been watching for a lone child.

"Where in the world could she be? She was right there with me and then she was gone." He shook his head. "I don't remember looking away for more than a second."

"Kids are quick, Jake. She might have seen something interesting and maybe got too far away without realizing."

"She's already afraid that her birth father is here. She thought she saw him earlier."

"Was it him?" Her hand tightened on his.

He'd thought about that a lot. "No. I think she's afraid of him and she's always worried he'll show up."

"It's so much for a child to deal with. She's lucky to have you. Eventually she'll realize that you're the one keeping her safe." Her voice was soft and she moved closer to his side.

If things hadn't been so crazy he would have let himself think a little longer about the woman next to him, the fact that she thought he was the man who kept people safe.

He'd been taking on the world alone for the past ten years and he'd been doing it without any regrets. Until now, this moment when alone was the last thing he wanted. For the first time someone made him feel stronger just by having her next to him.

Crazy thoughts, he decided. He had never experienced this kind of fear. He didn't know how to process this amount of worry. His mind had to be grasping, reaching for something that wasn't.

"I didn't realize when I got custody of Anna how I would feel."

Jolie looked up at him. "What do you mean?"

"This instant need to make her happy, keep her safe."

"Like being a dad?" She smiled as she said it.

"Yeah, exactly. Crazy."

"I'm sure she's easy to love."

They kept walking. The farther they went into the maze the more he worried about his niece. He thought about that fearful look on her face earlier. The psychologist he'd taken her to said it was natural for her to be afraid. Her life had been nothing but chaos for the first five years. It would take her time to trust in the stability and constant love he provided.

He wondered if she would think he'd let her down.

His phone buzzed again. He answered but kept walking. The city officer identified himself.

"We have her at the exit, Jake. She found her way out."

"Thank God. I'll be there as soon as I find my way out." He looked around for a quick way out, even if it meant going through a wall of snow.

"We'll be waiting for you." The officer hung up.

Jake stopped walking and drew in a deep breath.

"She's okay?" Jolie asked quietly as she stood there next to him, shivering in her down-filled coat, a stocking cap pulled tight over her dark hair.

"Yes, they found her. Now we have to find our way out. Once we're out of here, I'm buying you hot chocolate."

"Coffee, please." She sniffled and her nose was pink.

"Coffee it is."

"At my place. It's close and Anna probably needs to warm up somewhere that isn't crowded and chaotic."

Her place. He had hold of her hand and they were walking, following others who seemed to know where they were going.

"That sounds good."

He'd completely lost his mind.

## CHAPTER SIX

JOLIE WATCHED AS JAKE wrapped his arms around Anna and held her close. Cassie had got out first and she'd stayed with the child, knowing she'd feel safer with someone she knew. Now she moved to Jolie's side and the two watched as Anna and Jake had a long conversation, probably about safety and never doing that to him again.

Now, how did she get out of the invitation she'd offered? Of course she couldn't. Anna's cheeks were red, her eyes still swimming with tears, and her teeth chattered from fear and from cold.

Jake picked her up. He turned to Jolie and half smiled but clearly worried about his niece. "Is that offer still open?"

"Of course it is." Jolie ignored the look Cassie shot her.

"What offer?" Of course, Cassie had to ask.

"We're going to my place for coffee and to get Anna warmed up."

"I see." Cassie's eyes widened. "Well, okay, I should go home then."

"Come with us, Cass." Jolie reached for her friend.

Cassie shook her head. "No, thanks, I have so much I need to be doing to get ready for tonight."

"You're ready."

"I have to curl my hair."

Jake had walked away with his niece. Jolie watched them go, the man in his heavy jacket, the little girl held tight, her arms around his neck. A crazy warmth flowed from Jolie's head to her toes. She wanted to laugh, and to sing off-key show tunes and dance.

It really didn't make sense.

"Interesting." Cassie leaned in close. "I think this might be a promising new year."

"Go away, Cassie." Jolie smiled at the man who had stopped a short distance away and turned to look for her.

Cassie gave her a little push and Jolie stumbled forward. She caught herself and turned to give her friend a meaningful look.

"I'll get you for this."

"You did it to yourself. Now, go catch yourself a man."

People around them stared and Jolie's face warmed. She had no intentions of catching herself a man.

"Sorry…" She didn't know why she apologized when she got close to Jake. Of course she knew why. Because of Cassie's obvious attempts to push them together.

"No need. Cassie always has the best of intentions."

"She's clueless. She thinks…"

Jake pulled a remote car starter from his pocket. "She thinks I plan on kissing you tonight at midnight."

Heat climbed from her neck to her cheeks and she couldn't answer.

"I'll drive." He pointed to the Escalade parked a few parking spaces from her compact car. "Mine will be warm when we get inside."

"Warm sounds good. I've often thought about moving somewhere warm."

Jake opened the passenger door for her and then the back door for Anna. As Jolie got in, he buckled his niece into her booster seat. Before closing the door he kissed her brow.

He would never let that child down. Jolie's heart caught at the thought and others that followed. She looked out the window as Jake got in and shifted into Reverse. She watched the town square and the buildings drift from view.

Because Jake protected the people he cared about. Her heart ached and she couldn't explain it. She wasn't this person, wanting something out of reach. She knew how to survive and to be happy. She was happy.

Why did New Year's Eve do that to people—make them think about their lives, their future, what they still wanted? And what she wanted was someone to love her. A strong person who would be there for her, hold her tight when she got scared, cheer her on when she accomplished something.

She wasn't twelve. She was past needing those things. Wasn't she? After all, she'd been alone a long time.

"Jolie, are you okay?"

She turned, smiling at him. "Yes, I'm fine. Just thinking."

"About?" He stared at the road in front of them and she looked away.

"Life and why it is that we use New Year's Eve to examine our lives, as if this one day a year should be the day we all think about changes we need to make. And then forget them the next day."

"I'm of the opinion we should always be changing and looking for ways to improve."

"I guess I've thought that, too. I've always wanted my life to be better, so I've kept moving forward, making goals."

"Then you have no reason to be down or worry about next year. You're an amazing person. You've accomplished a lot."

"Thank you." She drifted back to the window because looking out was easier than looking in.

Jake slowed at a stop sign. "I'm not sure where you live."

"Cypress Drive."

He nodded and turned in the direction of the enclave where she lived. The homes were older bungalows built when Snow Falls first came into existence. In the past few years people were buying the houses to refurbish them. It was a nice neighborhood with mostly singles or retirees because the homes were small.

"The second house on the right," she said as he turned onto her dead-end street.

"This is nice." He pulled into the driveway.

She looked at the house and tried to see it through his eyes. She could only see it through her own. To her the small house with the covered porch and evergreen shrubs was perfect.

"It's mine." She grabbed her purse and stepped out of the SUV. He had opened the door, and Anna, already unbuckled, jumped into his arms.

"Do you want hot chocolate, Anna?" Jolie offered as she unlocked the front door.

Anna nodded against Jake's shoulder.

"What she probably needs is a nap before we have our big evening."

"It won't take me long to get the water heated." Jolie hung her coat on the hook next to the door.

Jake helped Anna out of hers and then shrugged out of his one arm at a time, switching Anna from side to side. Jolie took both coats and hung them up. It was strange, looking at the coatrack with a man's coat and a child's next to hers.

The longing began to build again, intensifying the way a fire catches hold of wood and comes to life. She looked away from the coats and led her guests into the living room. She loved this cozy room. It was shabby chic because that's what she could afford, decorated with used furniture she'd refinished and recovered to make the room comfortable and warm.

The fireplace had an insert and she bought wood from a man who lived outside of town. She crossed the room to open the door and shove in a few more pieces of wood from the box next to the fireplace. When she turned, Jake stood close behind her. Anna lay curled in her armchair with a blanket over her.

"Do you mind?" He nodded in the direction of his niece.

"Not at all." She wiped her hands down her jeans and took a deep breath. "Coffee?"

"Please."

She might have been able to breathe if he hadn't followed her. When she reached the kitchen, he stood, hip against the counter as she filled the water reservoir on her coffeemaker. He smelled good. He looked better. He was somewhere between *GQ* and Timberland, a crazy blend of urban and country.

She was shabby chic, like her furniture. She smiled at the thought. Together they created an eclectic style that really didn't seem to blend.

"You did all the remodeling yourself, didn't you?" His voice was smooth, like soft silk brushing against her arms.

"The painting, the shelves and the furniture, yes."

"Amazing. You have quite an eye."

"Thank you."

"I know that my buyer told you no local artists, but she was wrong. I wish you'd talked to Tansy. She's your biggest fan."

"Is she?" Jolie barely knew his cousin.

"Yes." He didn't say more and she wondered. She wanted to ask him questions.

She put a cup under the spout of the coffeemaker, inserted cocoa and pushed the button. The brown liquid poured into the cup.

"This will be hot. I have marshmallows." She rummaged through the cabinets as Jake stood there, watching. She reached for a cabinet door behind him. "You'll have to move. I think the marshmallows are in here."

He took one step out of the way. Her shoulder brushed his arm as she reached in for the bag of marshmallows. She closed her eyes and pretended that a handsome man stood in her kitchen every day of the week.

But they didn't. Ever. Jake took up all the oxygen. He turned her normally peaceful self into an unsettled mess. And he hadn't done anything. He was just standing there. Standing. A normal thing to do. It wasn't as if he'd touched her or said anything.

She closed her eyes, nearly groaning at the train wreck her thoughts were going to make of this moment. She'd invited him here for coffee. Because it was close. And warm. He'd accepted for the same reason.

For Anna's sake.

"Calm down." He took the marshmallows from her. "I'm not going to bite you."

"Aren't you?" She groaned and put a hand to her forehead. She raised her gaze to meet his. "I mean, of course you aren't. I'm fine. It's just…"

"History. We have a lot of history."

"Not really. Not real history. We have anger, betrayal, guilt and a couple of moments." Who could forget those moments?

"We also have forgiveness." He opened the bag and dropped marshmallows in the cup. He held one in his hand, his smile turning wickedly luscious. He leaned in and brushed his lips across hers. Then he rubbed the marshmallow across her lips and kissed her.

Oh, wow, how he kissed her. And it tasted like marshmallow and peppermint. His mouth claimed hers as he held her close, her back pressed against the counter. He tangled his hands in her hair and held on to her. Jolie sighed as he moved an inch from her mouth but then returned, brushing his lips across hers and then settling on the spot on her neck just below her ear.

"Jake," she whispered as he lowered his head and tasted her neck. Her hands moved to his hips. "Stop."

"Do I have to?" he whispered as his lips moved back to that sweet spot near her ear.

"Yes," she whispered into his kiss as his lips found hers again. She no longer wanted to stop.

"You're right." He brushed his lips across her cheek and she felt his breath, warm near her ear. "Time to stop."

He continued to hold her, though, his forehead touching hers. Jolie closed her eyes and waited for the world to return to normal. Normal. The real world. Jake owned Wildwood Lodge. She was Mac Godwin's daughter.

"Jolie." He kissed her again. "I'm not sure what to do."

"I think take a step back. Take a deep breath."

"Right, of course." He stepped back, but that smile returned, settling in his eyes. "I'm not sorry."

"We were sorry last year."

"We were?"

"Of course." She handed him the cup of hot chocolate. "Anna might be asleep."

"She might." He smiled and leaned in again, just a breath away from her mouth. But he didn't kiss her this time. "I'm not sorry."

He would be. She knew that, in a day or two when it stopped being fun or dangerous or whatever this was, then he would be sorry. He had a life so far removed from her simple existence that they didn't make sense. She'd seen him in town. She'd read magazine articles. She knew the type of woman he dated and it wasn't her. He dated Lamborghinis. She was a sedan. Maybe a van. Yes, a van, the 1960s version with peace signs and tie-dye.

After a long look, he turned and walked into the living room. She breathed a sigh of relief. And then it wasn't relief, it was something else, something that felt like disappointment.

THIRTY MINUTES AFTER hot chocolate and a kiss that should have sent warning sirens blasting through the entire community of Snow Falls, Jake carried a sleeping Anna from the garage at Wildwood Lodge into the elevator to his apartment. In an hour Jolie would be here to go skating.

Typically he worked on New Year's Eve. He made sure everything was set for the night. He made last-minute decisions. Because of Anna, he was learning to do what Tansy called *delegating*. Work days had never been as hectic as this day had proved to be, playing dad to Anna and…

Courting Jolie?

He shook his head as he placed Anna in her twin bed. She rolled over, reached for her stuffed doll and went back to sleep. He tiptoed out of the room. He had an hour to get his act together.

To decide what to do about Jolie Godwin and the insane emotions she'd managed to kick up.

As he changed into a flannel shirt, his phone rang. He answered it as he walked to the kitchen to make a cup of coffee. His head of security was on the other end to tell him last-minute details for the evening.

Jake might be taking a day off, but not really. He couldn't relax without having some control of his business. And he wanted security tight for a night like tonight. He had guests to think about. He had Anna to consider. She would be in this apartment with her nanny while he went to the ball.

The ball. A man couldn't say he was going to a ball without feeling a little itchy. Men went hunting or fishing. They didn't dress up in a suit, wear a mask and dance until the clock struck midnight. The idea made him more than a little antsy. There would be women down there lining up to dance, like he was the prince, and he planned on finding a bride before the clock struck twelve.

He blamed Tansy for this mess. He'd given her creative license a few years ago and this is what she'd come up with.

The phone rang again. Speak of the devil. He answered it, if only to give Tansy a piece of his mind for coming up with this ball idea and for insisting that he attend. Maybe next year she could come up with something new. Or not. The ball had become a favorite of visitors and locals alike.

"You back from town?" She sounded worried. He didn't like his ever-optimistic cousin to be worried. Her worry meant he should also worry.

"Yes, why? Where are you?"

"Outside your door. Can I come in?"

"Sure, you have a key."

A moment later she walked into the kitchen, her auburn hair in all directions and a stain on the front of her blouse. Not a good sign. Without speaking she made herself a cup of coffee. The silence caused him more concern. He should have stayed on top of things. He shouldn't have gotten distracted and left it all on her shoulders.

"Tansy, what's up?" He took another sip of coffee and wished he had something stronger. He didn't keep alcohol in his apartment. For Tansy's sake.

"Your mother called from the airport."

"Well, let's not beat around the bush." The news gave him the same sinking feeling Tansy probably had. His mother always brought some type of turbulence. Today meant too much to the resort to have the kind of problems Helena Wild-Langston could bring to the Wildwood.

"She asked me to send a car to pick her up."

"I wonder why she's decided to visit?"

"I asked. She said she wants to spend time with you." Tansy affected a snobbish voice to imitate his mother and finished with her hand on her brow.

"She needs money."

"I wasn't going to say it." Tansy sipped her coffee, closing her eyes and then taking another sip. "I wish this was…"

"No, you don't." He touched her back and she looked up at him. "Four years, Tans, don't let her mess you up. This is my battle, not yours."

"It always feels like my battle."

"It isn't. I don't want this night to be too much for you."

Tansy finished her coffee. "She'll ruin your night. She'll mess everything…"

"I think we're talking about two different things. I'm not sure what she'll mess up. I'll see her tomorrow, write her a check and she'll be gone again."

"Your dad left her enough money for a dozen families to live on. It isn't your fault she ran through it like a kid with a bag of candy." Tansy brushed a hand through her hair. "It isn't my business."

"I made it your business. Remember, you're the person who keeps me on track and keeps me from becoming like her." He set his cup in the sink and turned to look at his cousin. "With that in mind, why is it you seem to be trying to distract me?"

"I'm not."

"Yeah, you are. You're trying to distract me with Jolie Godwin."

"I'm not distracting you, just showing you that there's more to life than work. And there are women who can be trusted."

He leaned to kiss the top of her head. She was the closest thing he had to a little sister. Her mother had been his father's sister. "I trust you, so obviously I know that women can be trusted."

"You need to trust a woman to be in your life. Jolie is different. She makes you different."

"I hadn't realized I need to change, my matchmaking cousin. And what about you? Why don't you find someone to take you to the ball?"

"No, thank you. Been there, done that."

"So have I."

"But you didn't marry a mistake. You got out."

"And lost a lot of money along the way." He listened to the sound of Anna getting out of bed and moving around in her room. "Vivian managed to put it to me. I'm not going that route again."

"Jolie isn't Vivian."

"No, and I'm not the man I was seven years ago. Listen, I'm going to take Anna skating. Can you keep the hounds at bay for a while?"

"You mean keep your mother away?"

"I didn't say that."

Tansy smiled a wicked smile and he hoped she wouldn't go too far.

## CHAPTER SEVEN

JOLIE LOOKED UP at the wooden siding of Wildwood Lodge through the tinted windows of the luxury Escalade that picked her up at her house. Jake had sent the car for her because hers was still parked in town, and by now probably snowed in. When the Escalade had turned in her driveway she'd had to take a minute to pull herself together. She'd reminded herself the Cadillac wasn't a pumpkin drawn by mice. Or even a carriage drawn by horses.

It was New Year's Eve. She could celebrate and then tomorrow return to her real life. As she got out of the vehicle, leaving behind the heated seats and soothing music, she shivered.

She had time before meeting with Jake to go inside and take a look at her display. The sidewalks were shoveled but there were still slick spots. A doorman opened the front door as she approached.

"Good evening, ma'am. Do you have luggage?"

"No." She wouldn't be staying the night. She entered the luxurious lobby and the warmth hit her, taking her breath away. Her gaze settled on the massive stone fireplace on the far wall.

"Jolie, you're here early." Tansy crossed the room,

heels clicking on the stone floors, a welcoming smile on her face.

*Elegant,* that was the word for Tansy. She looked as if this had always been her life. Jolie felt like a child playing at being a grown-up.

"I thought I'd check my display."

"It looks beautiful." Tansy reached for her arm. "I'll walk with you and then show you to Jake's apartment when we're done."

"Thank you. I really wasn't sure if I should go to the front desk or call him." Jolie had a list of things she was unsure of.

"Either would have worked." Tansy led her down the corridor to the Aspen Room. Inside there were more than twenty exhibits. People milled around the room, some with cups of coffee, others with colorful drinks.

"This is amazing."

Jolie admired the other works of art. There were paintings, jewelry, sculptures and her copper wall hangings and light fixtures. Tansy introduced her to several people at her booth, discussing the pieces.

This was the part of being an artist she didn't enjoy. She enjoyed solitude and her workshop. After thirty minutes, Tansy led her toward the door.

"You're a hit." Tansy gave her arm a squeeze. "I've always known you would be."

"Really?" Jolie looked at the other woman. "Why would you think that?"

"I saw your work a few years ago at a show in Denver. What you do with copper is amazing." Tansy shrugged. "I happen to be a big fan and I'm glad Jake is going to put some of your art in the lodge."

"Thank you, Tansy." Jolie looked at her watch. "I should go."

She should go home. That's what she should do. An evening with Jake Wild was dangerous territory. Even if the evening was just about corn dogs with a young girl and ice skating. She wouldn't have been honest, and she was always honest, if she didn't admit she was more than a little attracted to the owner of Wildwood Lodge.

But every woman in a one-hundred-mile radius was attracted to Jake Wild, maybe a two-hundred-mile radius. Jake could have any woman he wanted. Tonight he would have his pick of any woman at the party. When that happened she would be the wallflower that slipped to the sidelines and watched everyone else fall in love.

"Hey, why the look?" Tansy led her down the hallway, away from the Aspen Room.

"Oh, nothing." Jolie did her best to smile.

"Worried about ice skating?"

"More than a little," she admitted, thankful that it was the truth.

Tansy led her down a quiet hall to an elevator marked Private. She slid a card into the slot and pushed a series of buttons. The door opened.

"We like security here," Tansy said as she stepped onto the elevator. "Anna really adores you. There aren't many people she trusts."

"She's a beautiful girl."

Tansy looked at her, a long look. "There aren't many people Jake trusts. Especially with Anna."

"Tansy—"

The doors opened and Tansy smiled. "Enjoy your night. Try not to question everything, Jolie."

"Thank you."

"No problem. Just ring the bell. They're waiting for you. And I'll see you later at the party."

"Maybe."

Tansy's brows shot up, but she didn't get a chance to comment. The doors of the elevator closed. Jolie turned to face the other door. The door that led to Jake Wild's private residence. Her heart thumped hard against her chest and she couldn't quite convince herself to move forward.

She could call and tell him something had come up. She wouldn't let Anna down that way, though. She took a few slow steps toward the door, thinking about years ago when she'd been a freshman in college and her dad had started to work here.

Jolie had been amazed by this world. It had been so far removed from her upbringing, she had been in awe. She had always been in awe of Jake.

Jake had kissed her that summer. On a quiet summer night at the pool, he'd brushed a whisper of a kiss across her lips. Jolie stood in front of the door remembering how she'd felt in that moment. And later, coming to terms with the reality that it had only been one kiss, nothing more. Not one to learn her lesson the first time, she'd repeated the kiss last year.

And then again just hours ago in her own kitchen. Jolie swallowed and let her hand drop to her side. What was that old saying? Fool me once, shame on you. Fool me twice, shame on me.

*Kiss me once, shame on you. Kiss me twice, shame on me.*

She wasn't a fool. But she'd always been a fool for Jake Wild.

The door opened.

Jake stood there, every inch the owner of Wildwood. He'd changed into a heavy, oatmeal sweater, but he still wore jeans and hiking boots. She remained motionless. What in the world had she thought, coming here.

"Are you coming in?" He opened the door wider. The insecure girl she'd been years ago resurfaced. It might be best to run.

"I think so."

His eyes narrowed. "Is everything okay?"

"Yes, fine." She cleared her throat. "I'm good, just…"

"We have corn dogs and French fries." He said it as if it should tempt her.

She smiled then. "Who could resist a corn dog?"

Did he remember that long-ago kiss? Or did he only remember the one from last year? She should have come up with a New Year's resolution last year that would have kept her from repeating the same mistakes this year.

"Come in." Jake took her hand and led her inside the apartment.

He led her through the living room with its many windows and gorgeous views of snow-covered mountains through to the dining room. The table sat in an alcove with a half circle of windows. A candle burned in the center of the table and the corn dogs were displayed on crystal dishes.

Anna appeared and reached for her hand, leading her to a chair. The little girl signed and Jake laughed dryly before interpreting.

"She said you have to sit next to me."

Jake held the chair out for Jolie. She looked at him, those dark eyes hiding something, maybe fear? He gave the chair a pointed look and she sat. He moved it close to the table and then stood behind her for just a moment, tempted by her long, dark hair that shimmered with hints of auburn when the light caught it just right.

She looked up at him and he let go and moved to his seat. Anna had already seated herself. She had her napkin in her lap and her hands folded patiently, waiting for him to say grace. He looked at the corn dogs, fries and green beans and he had to admit to feeling more thankful than he could have guessed he'd feel.

Tonight he reached for the hands of the two females at his table. Anna grinned up at him, taking his hand as he took Jolie's. He said grace and Jolie whispered a quiet "Amen."

He lifted his glass and clinked Anna's first and then Jolie's. "It's just water, but here's to the new year and all that it has in store for us."

"Cheers." Jolie smiled at him and then at his niece.

Jake reached for the serving tongs and picked up several of the miniature corn dogs, placing them on his niece's plate. And then he passed the plate to Jolie, meeting her gaze, her sweet smile. It should have embarrassed him, serving a woman a meal of corn dogs, but Jolie smiled and made it easy. He relaxed and he couldn't remember the last time he'd really relaxed. His physician had warned him that he'd be on blood pressure medication in the next year or two if he didn't learn to take it easy.

Sitting at that table with Anna and Jolie, he kind of thought maybe he'd found the cure. He hadn't enjoyed this apartment, his job or his life as much in the past ten years as he had in the past few hours.

Jolie had been right, something about New Year's Eve made a person look at their life in a way that forced them to make changes.

Anna signed and he had to look quickly to catch what she was saying. They were doing well with this sign language business, but they both had a lot to learn. She giggled as she repeated what she'd said.

"I agree." He grinned at Jolie.

"What?" Jolie wiped her mouth and waited.

"Anna says you'll have to hold my hand when we go skating."

"Did she really?"

"Yes, she did. She's worried that you'll fall and get hurt."

"I'm a little worried about that myself." She placed a hand on Anna's arm. "Thank you for letting me go skating with you tonight."

Anna signed, "You're welcome."

They were almost finished eating when Jake's phone rang. He excused himself from the table and answered it in the kitchen.

"Yes, Mother."

A long sigh that meant she wasn't happy. "I'm at the airport and your cousin Tansy says there isn't a car available at the moment to come and pick me up."

"That's probably true." But he smiled at Tansy's ability to handle problems. "We're having the masked ball tonight, so there's quite a crowd. And a snowstorm is hitting."

"Do you think you could send the next available one to get me? I don't want to have to stay in the city."

"I'll have one on the way as soon as I can. But with this storm I can't make promises. I won't put your safety at risk in this weather."

"Fine, I'll rent a room and wait. I'll call you when I know where I'm staying so you'll know where to find me."

She hung up. And the phone rang again. He was starting to think he should turn it off. "Tansy."

"You shouldn't sound so aggravated, not when you're with Jolie."

"My mother seems to be stuck at the airport without a car."

"Yes, I explained to her that we have quite a crowd coming and going and I'll get one down there as soon as possible. I didn't call about her. I called because there's a huge problem with the walk-in safe."

"A problem you can't handle?"

She sighed. "No, I can't. I'm sorry, I tried. I know you're busy and I don't want to pull you away."

He glanced over his shoulder to the two females at his table. "I can get away for a few minutes."

"It's the lock, Jake. I called security but I didn't want to take chances tonight."

He touched the cell phone to his brow. When Tansy said problem, he hadn't expected a major incident. "I'll be right down."

So much for his romantic night of courting Jolie. He shook his head. He had to stop calling it that. Even if that was exactly what he'd planned to do this evening.

He walked back into the dining room and neither

Anna nor Jolie was there. He heard the sound of dishes clinking and silverware rattling. He walked through the arched doorway into the kitchen. Jolie stood at the sink, rinsing their dishes. Anna stood next to her loading the dishwasher.

The scene did something crazy to him. It made him want to forget the ball, forget the breach of security and just stay in this kitchen with the two of them. Is that how it had happened to his mother? She'd gotten carried away chasing relationships and had forgotten to manage the business his father left behind.

Jake stood there for a long minute watching.

He wasn't his mother. That's all it came down to. He wasn't Helena. He could fall in love and still take care of Wildwood. He'd spent the past few months caring for Anna and the business hadn't suffered.

He had good people to help him.

Knowing that, what did he do about Jolie?

"Everything okay?" Jolie rinsed one last plate and handed it to his niece. Anna slid it into the dishwasher. "And I left your plate on the table."

"I need to run downstairs." He tilted his head at his niece. "You know I have a housekeeper who takes care of things like this?"

"I'm sure you do, but we were having fun. Anna taught me a few signs and I promised her I'd learn more." Jolie bit her bottom lip. "Maybe I shouldn't have."

"What, promised you'd see her again?" He tried to ease the moment with a smile. "Why wouldn't you see her again?"

He wondered what went through her mind at times

like this, when her eyelids lowered and she caught her bottom lip between her teeth. Was she thinking about the past, what her father had done, things Jake had said at the time?

"Jolie, I want the past behind us."

"Jake." She shook her head. "The past is never really behind us. It set us on a path. It made us who we are. My dad stole from you. That is always going to be between us, no matter what. Maybe you can overlook it, but it will never go away."

"I'm not going to let the past sway me."

"Of course you won't," she whispered and a faint smile turned her lips. "Go, I'll watch Anna while you take care of things downstairs. I saw checkers. We'll have fun while you're gone."

"Thank you. And don't think you're getting out of skating." He said the words but couldn't force himself to relax, to return to that sense of ease they'd shared thirty minutes earlier.

He was thinking of his mom and how many times he'd put her down for getting sidetracked by romance. Sidetracked seemed to be pretty easy to come by. Anger with his mother, just as easy.

Jolie touched Anna's shoulder and his niece looked up at her. "You get the checkers out. I'll walk your uncle Jake to the door."

Anna nodded and watched as Jolie followed him through the apartment to the front door. Jake glanced back at his niece and winked because he didn't want her to worry.

At the door, Jolie said, "I can make an excuse to leave after you get back. I know this isn't easy for you, having

me here, entertaining me. Anna is sweet and I appreciate the offer to ice-skate, but you don't have to do this."

Jake's cell phone rang. He hit the button to quiet the
ringtone. "Jolie, you're not here because Anna wanted
a playdate. I appreciate that my five-year-old niece has
taken a liking to you. But you're here because I wanted
to spend time with you."

"You don't act like a man who is crazy about spend-
ing time with a woman."

He let his fingers slide through her silky, dark hair.
Captivated, he leaned in to smell the hint of strawberry.

"I'm a man who has definitely gone crazy." He
turned his attention from her hair to her lips, but he
didn't kiss her. Anna was in the other room, or possibly
watching from a corner somewhere. And he had to get
control. He reminded himself that there was a problem
downstairs that needed his attention.

"Jake." Her voice was soft, shy, reaching out to him.

"Jolie, I can admit that I like to be in control. I don't
like to be distracted from business. You are definitely
a distraction. So let's just set the record straight. You
are here because I want you here, probably more than
Anna does and for completely different reasons."

"I don't know what to do." She licked her bottom lip
as she stared up at him.

"First of all, don't do that again or I'm liable to say
forget the jammed lock on the safe, forget the lodge,
and we'll just go live in a one-room cabin somewhere.
Let me take care of business and then we'll figure out
what this is between us."

She shrugged, still watching him intently with her

dark brown eyes. "I'm not looking for a one-night stand."

"I know. And I'm not sure what I'm looking for."

Reluctantly, slowly, he untangled his fingers from her hair and stepped back. "I'll be back as soon as I can."

As he walked to the elevator the door clicked shut behind him. He considered telling her not to let anyone in. She wouldn't, though. He knew Anna would be safe with Jolie.

As for himself and Jolie, nothing had ever felt quite as dangerous as this night with her. And nothing had ever felt quite as right, either.

## CHAPTER EIGHT

JOLIE WALKED BACK INTO the kitchen. Anna sat on a stool waiting with the book on sign language open in front of her. She held it out and Jolie took it with a smile. The child looked up at her, a look that Jolie couldn't ignore.

What would it be like to know only a few people in the world could speak your language? Her heart broke a little for the child, and broke more thinking of the years she'd spent in complete silence.

"I'll learn," Jolie said. "Thank you."

Anna nodded. Her signs were useless with Jolie at this point. Since she didn't have the ability to speak, their communication was limited.

"Is this what you're wearing skating or should we get you changed?" Jolie asked, because with the hearing aids, Anna could hear her somewhat.

Anna grinned and signed, but then she grabbed Jolie's hand and led her to a pretty bedroom, decorated for a child. Everything was clean and new. Anna opened a closet door and Jolie gaped at the amount of clothes.

"Wow."

Anna grinned and signed something else as she led Jolie inside the room-size closet. Anna grabbed boots, then found gloves and a stocking cap on a shelf.

"Looks like we'll be ready to go."

The doorbell rang. Jolie froze, unsure of what she should do. Jake hadn't said, but she kind of thought she shouldn't open the door to anyone.

"Someone's at the door. I'm going to go peek and see who it is."

Anna grabbed her hand and shook her head.

"You don't think I should?"

Anna again shook her head. She guessed that was the reason for the extra security, to give Anna peace of mind. A child should grow up feeling secure. Even if her fears were imaginary, Jake would make sure she knew no one could hurt her.

How would it feel to be protected by someone like Jake Wild?

"Okay, we won't open the door. We'll wait for Jake to get back."

They waited. And waited. Anna beat her twice at checkers. Jolie watched as the cloudy sky darkened and more snow fell. She could see the skating rink. There were a few people on the ice. Anna glanced that way, too. The child sighed and Jolie had to agree. But at least they weren't alone.

Jolie had spent more than one New Year's Eve alone.

The door finally opened. It had been an hour. Jake walked through, pulling at the collar of his shirt. He crossed the room immediately to Anna and hugged her.

"I'm sorry."

"Did you get it all taken care of?"

"I did. And now we can go skating." He sat in the chair next to the child. "We're going skating, right?"

"I'm ready. Anna has her boots waiting by the door."

"Then let's go. I have skates in the closet. There should be a pair downstairs that fits you."

"You have skates that fit me?"

He smiled, but from the tight worry lines around his mouth, she wondered how serious the problem downstairs had been.

"We keep several extra pairs for guests. When I was younger if we had friends over, we were prepared. So, are you ready?"

"I'm as ready as I'll ever be." Jolie winked at Anna and the child covered her mouth in a silent giggle. "Anna is sure I'm going to fall."

"I'll catch you."

He had to catch her twice.

The first time, she slid sideways the minute she stepped onto the ice. His arms went around her waist and he pulled her back up. Anna spun around fearlessly. Her cheeks and nose were red and her dark hair hung out from under her stocking cap, framing her sweet little face.

Jake held Jolie's arm. "You're doing great."

Her feet were going in all directions and her legs felt like overcooked spaghetti. "How do you figure?"

"Well, you haven't broken anything. Yet."

"I guess that's a positive. Now what do we do?"

He steadied her and then turned her loose. She instantly missed his hands on her arms. If she moved at all she'd go down. A person couldn't maneuver on two thin metal blades. It wasn't possible.

"Watch me." He kicked out and effortlessly glided in a circle, stopping in front of her.

"Of course, it's that easy."

His smile warmed her. And it wasn't right to be that warm on the ice. What if the ice under her feet melted?

"You're not going to fall."

"I was thinking of other things."

He grinned wickedly and skated up to her. "What?"

"Nothing."

"It was something. It made your cheeks pink."

"I was thinking that, the ice could melt."

"How would it melt? It's twenty degrees out here."

She gave him a meaningful look and then heat raced to her cheeks and she looked away.

He laughed and Jolie stood there, frozen to the spot, cold but warm. It was a strange situation she found herself in. Finally he said, "There would have to be a sudden heat wave for the ice to melt."

"I know." She didn't know what had come over her. She'd never been a flirt.

He leaned in close and blew on her neck.

"That the kind of heat wave?"

"Anna." Jolie tried to move away, but her left leg slid and her right leg went a little forward.

He grabbed Jolie's arm and held her. "Come on, I'll stop teasing you and teach you to skate."

"Thank you."

He placed a strong hand on her waist. "Watch me. It's really easy. Promise."

She watched his feet and she moved hers in what she thought was a similar motion. His hand tightened on her waist. She focused on her feet. She watched Anna just ahead of them. The child would skate forward, get a little ahead of them and turn to skate backward.

"Will I ever be as good as Anna?"

"She's only been skating for a couple of months." He moved her closer to his side. "Stick with me. I'll do all the work and you hold on."

Hold on. It sounded so easy.

He skated a little faster, pulling her along with him. She moved her feet, trying to keep up. Suddenly one of her feet slid in front of Jake's. And that was the second fall. Together, with Jake. The two of them went down. Legs, arms, bodies. Jolie hit the ice, Jake landed next to her.

Anna skated back to them, her mouth and eyes wide. Jake signed and must've told her they were okay. And then he looked at Jolie, a smile twitching at the corners of his mouth.

"*Are* you okay?"

She nodded, too embarrassed to tell him her rear end felt numb, but she thought it was from sitting on ice, not from injury. "I think I'm good."

"Does anything hurt?" He stood and held a hand out to her.

"Nothing but my pride." She took his hand and he pulled her to her feet.

Anna reached for her other hand.

"Are you going to teach me, Anna?"

The girl nodded and moved slowly, her feet taking easier steps than Jake's. Jolie turned to look at Jake, who stood behind them.

"She's a better teacher than you are."

"Yes, she is." He skated up beside her. "I should have gone slower."

Yes, slower. Slow is always a good way to start out.

"Don't be sorry." She reached and he held out his hand. "It's wrong that I've lived here my whole life without learning to skate."

"Or ski?"

"Yes."

"We're going to have to take care of that."

At almost thirty, it seemed to her as if it might too late. Anna let go of her hand and skated off. Together, Jolie and Jake stopped to watch her. Music played on speakers hidden inside the lampposts. In the ever-darkening sky, Christmas lights twinkled on the bushes and trees that surrounded the ice rink.

Magical. Romantic. Dangerous.

"I should go soon." She continued to watch Anna because looking at Jake seemed to be dangerous. She would want to study his lean, handsome features, his eyes, the way he smiled.

Focus on Anna. Easy. But the hand on hers was strong and eased her into Jake's side, his breath warm near her ear. She couldn't remember the hurt or the anger toward him the way she once had.

"You're coming to the ball, right?"

Maybe. If she didn't come to her senses. She looked up at him, because she needed to see in his eyes the reflection of his words.

"I'll be back. You'll have to find me. I'll have a mask on."

"I'll find you." He leaned in and kissed her cheek. "If you're leaving, I'm going to take Anna up and get her ready for bed before the nanny gets here."

"I'll see you in an hour." Jolie tottered to the edge of

the rink and dropped onto a bench. "And I am gladly returning your ice skates."

"I'll put them in the closet, but you're not getting out of this. You're going to learn to skate."

He took her by surprise, kneeling in front of her and quickly unlacing the skates. He pulled them off and replaced them with her boots. Jolie didn't know how a person could forget to breathe, or how a heart could stand still, but for a moment, both seemed to happen.

It wasn't until she was on her way home that she managed to catch her breath.

JAKE WATCHED JOLIE GO and then he skated out to Anna. He would take a few laps with his niece before going up to his apartment. He needed a chance to clear his head.

Anna didn't smile when he reached for her hand.

"What's up?"

Her shoulders drooped as she signed. She didn't feel good.

"Let's go upstairs. Maybe you'll feel better after some hot chocolate."

She shook her head. That worried him.

"Can I carry you?"

She nodded and raised her arms. He lifted her off the ice and carried her back to the bench. He sat her down while he changed into his boots and then he picked her up again and carried her across the lawn to the entrance that led to his apartment.

Anna had her arms around his neck and he felt warm tears trickle down her cheeks.

He carried her to the sofa. From the living room he could see the skating rink where couples skated arm in arm while children glided in circles and tried spins that put them on their bottoms. He turned back to Anna. Her bottom lip pouted out.

"Hey, kiddo, it's okay. I'll get something to make you feel better."

She wiped her nose with the back of her hand and then she signed with her little hands, "I don't ever want to leave."

He shook his head, confused by that because he'd been expecting tears.

"You're not going anywhere." It was a bold promise, but he made it anyway. He'd fight for her if he had to.

Anna sniffled. He pulled off her skates and helped her out of her coat and mittens.

"Do you want hot chocolate now?"

She shook her head and told him again that she didn't feel well. He didn't have a lot of experience with a child not feeling well. He touched her forehead because that seemed like the thing to do. Even with his lack of experience, she felt warm.

"Does anything hurt?"

She pointed to her throat and her belly.

"Then I think we should get you some medicine." The nanny had taken care of stocking supplies because he had no clue.

A minute later he had the right amount of children's aspirin and a glass of water. He got back to the living room just in time to see Anna race to the bathroom. He set the pills and glass on the table and followed, knowing only one thing he could do for her. He ran a washcloth under cold water and when she turned into his arms, he dabbed her face and neck.

"Time for bed, kiddo."

She clung to him as he carried her to her room.

## CHAPTER NINE

JOLIE STEPPED THROUGH the doors of the ballroom in the red dress Cassie had bought for her. It shimmered and clung…she never would have picked it for herself…but Cassie had been right. It was perfect. She felt as if she belonged in this world. Jake's world.

If only Jake had bothered to show up. She made her way through the ballroom, searching for Cassie in a sea of colorful gowns and masks. At least if she found her friend, she wouldn't feel alone.

Finally she spotted Cassie with Lance. Her friend turned, saw her and started through the crowd to her.

"It's about time you showed up." Cassie eyed the dress and smiled. "You look beautiful."

"I love it, Cass. But you shouldn't have."

"I wanted to. And seriously, every man in the room is looking at you. I'm jealous." Cassie looked over her right shoulder. "Except mine. He's smart and has eyes only for me."

"Because Lance loves you, completely. Every woman should be so blessed."

"Yes, and you will be, too." Cassie stepped away from her. "I'm going to dance with my man and you need to find Jake. I haven't seen him yet."

"I'm sure he's busy."

"He shouldn't be. He has Tansy in charge so that he can have a night off." Cassie pointed across the room. "That's our table."

Jolie made a sweep through the room, and then took a seat. Alone. She knew a few people in Cassie's party, but not well. She listened to their conversation, but they didn't include her other than a question from time to time. They were all paired up. Once again, she was the third wheel.

She didn't belong here after all. Nothing about this night was real. The connection with Jake wasn't real. The dress wasn't real. She was hiding behind a mask pretending she fit in.

She lifted her chin. Her art was being shown to visitors from all over the world. She belonged.

She watched Cassie, listened to the band and, more often than she should have, she looked toward the double doors wondering what had happened to Jake.

She reminded herself that he hadn't said anything about the two of them, just that he would see her down here. They'd had corn dogs, gone skating and he would see her later.

End of story. Obviously the end. She accepted a glass from a waiter and took a drink. Cassie returned and took the seat next to hers.

"I'm sure he's busy."

Jolie smiled at her friend and picked up the cracker with a thin slice of smoked salmon on top. "Cassie, don't make excuses for him. This is the way it goes in my life."

"Don't be silly. There's something between the two of you. I think there always has been, you've both just been too caught up in the drama of your lives to accept it."

"My drama was called surviving."

"His drama was called keeping this lodge in the black."

Jolie closed her eyes. "I know. Look, I'm going to the restroom. It's late and I might go home."

Cassie looked away. A guilty look, if Jolie had to guess.

"What?" Jolie stood.

"I kind of rented you a room."

"Oh, Cass."

Cassie half smiled and shrugged. "Sorry."

Jolie bent and kissed her friend's cheek. "Thank you. I'll go check out my room."

"Jo, don't go. He'll be here. I know he will. Until then, hang with us. I want my best friend with me tonight."

Jolie nodded in the direction of Lance. "You have the best and really, I need quiet time to get my thoughts together. I'll be back."

"Okay." Cassie touched her arm. "You're beautiful."

"Thanks. And he's the one missing out, right?"

"Definitely." Cassie reached for her hand and held it. "You're a successful artist who has done nothing but good her entire life. Stop living in your father's mistakes. They weren't yours."

Jolie closed her eyes and nodded. "Thanks, Cass. I'll be back down."

"Promise?"

Jolie nodded and Cassie let her go.

She eased through the crowded room and into the

corridor where it already felt easier to breathe. A quick glance in the direction of the lobby showed her there was no sign of Jake. She considered going to the desk and asking if there were any messages for her, but really, how desperate would that be?

Cassie had given her a key when she told her about the room she'd rented. Jolie would just go to her room and rethink everything a million times. What had she thought, really? Had she thought that Jake was interested in her? Had she thought that he really wanted to spend time with her?

Maybe a little.

But she'd also known that they'd been thrown together today by Anna and Cassie, both very determined. If the third time is the charm, then she would finally learn her lesson and forget Jake Wild.

Forget Jake. She walked into the bathroom of her room and stood there in the center of marble and stone opulence. She turned on the water and splashed her face, not caring that it would smear her mascara or wash away the makeup she had taken forever to apply.

She dried her face with one of the heavy, Egyptian-cotton towels and walked back to the main room of the suite. A suite. For one person. Cassie shouldn't have. But no one could tell Cassie she shouldn't.

Cassie just did.

Jolie walked to the glass doors that opened onto a balcony. She could see the lights of Snow Falls, the glimmering ice rink, the snowy mountains that glowed under the nearly full moon despite the clouds that threatened to cover it. The snow that had fallen earlier had stopped for a while. Wafting up from the banquet hall she could hear the band playing a song from the 1950s.

Happy New Year. She stared at her reflection in the glass door and felt sorry for herself. For the woman who had spent too many New Year's Eves alone. Even the miracle of a daring, red dress couldn't change history.

She closed her eyes and leaned her forehead against the cool glass. Soon it would be midnight. She would have to make a decision. Did she go downstairs and join the festivities, or stay up here, alone?

She preferred alone.

She whispered her resolution. Next year she would stop loving Jake Wild.


JAKE FOUND TANSY IN THE LOBBY. "Did you tell her?"

Tansy blinked a few times. "Tell her?"

"Jolie? I was supposed to meet her down here and I've been upstairs with a sick child."

The sick child now slept peacefully, with her nanny in a rocking chair next to her bed. Her fever had gone down. And she'd even smiled before she fell asleep.

Tansy closed her eyes briefly and shook her head. "Jake, I couldn't find her and then I had to take care of double-booked rooms. I'm sorry."

"It isn't your fault. This is the worst night of the year for me to take off."

"As if you've been off. You've taken care of the safe issue, you've taken care of Anna. And really, you deserve a day off."

"You don't deserve to have all this dumped on you. What can I do to help?"

Tansy pointed at him. "Don't try to take over. I'm in charge tonight. You have one mission, to find Jolie."

He headed for the ballroom, still trying to decide what he would do when he found Jolie. If he found her.

Music pounded from inside the ballroom. He opened the door and watched as couples danced. Once again the New Year's Eve ball was a success.

Except for one thing. He had thirty minutes to find Jolie, because he planned on kissing her at midnight. He had made a resolution while he sat with Anna. He wouldn't let this year be a replica of last. He was getting too old to keep letting the years go by without seeing what could be.

He found Cassie on the dance floor. She gave him the evil eye and he guessed he had it coming. He had thought Tansy would get the message to Jolie. He should have made sure, because from the look on Cassie's face, they must have thought he'd stood Jolie up.

The music ended and Cassie walked off the dance floor. Flounced, actually. Her lips were pursed and her eyes narrowed as she headed his way.

"You have a lot of nerve, Jake Wild."

"I do have a lot of nerve, Cassie. And before you lose your temper in front of everyone, Anna was sick and I had to stay with her until she fell asleep."

"Oh." Cassie touched a finger to her lip. "That's a problem."

"Yes, it is. So now, if you wouldn't mind telling me where Jolie is…"

"I wouldn't mind." Cassie eyed him again. "What are your intentions concerning my very best friend, whose heart you have been stomping on for a very long time?"

"Excuse me?" He really disliked games. He didn't have time for them. This reminded him why he rarely dated. He'd been duped more than once because he tended to trust people.

"Jake, you aren't clueless."

"No, Cassie, I'm not. But I'm also not going to have this conversation with you. Where is she?"

"Are you going to sweep her off her feet?"

"I might, Cass. If I can get you to tell me where to find her feet."

"She's in her room."

"Her room?"

"I rented her a room. She's upstairs."

Jake kissed Cassie's cheek as she told him the room number. "Thank you."

"Don't hurt her."

He was already walking away, but he turned. "I don't plan on it."

## CHAPTER TEN

Jake knocked on the door to Jolie's room. Maybe he should have called. Maybe she'd decided to go home. What would he say to her? Worse, what would she say to him? She thought he'd stood her up. Was she relieved or hurt?

He knocked again, this time louder. He heard the bolt slide, and the door opened a few inches. Her hair had come loose and dark tendrils curled around her face. Mascara was smudged beneath her eyes.

"I woke you up."

"Yes, you woke me up." She stood there, not moving to let him in.

"Jolie, Anna was sick." He rested his hand against the door frame. He'd put on his suit, even though he knew he'd be getting to the party late. He'd brought her a rose. He held it out.

"Is she okay?" She took the rose. It matched her dress. She looked amazing in that dress. It flowed and yet hugged her figure in all the right places. The shimmery cloth caught the light and sparkled like millions of stars on a clear night.

He cleared his throat. "Yes, she's going to be okay. The nanny took over when she went to sleep. Tansy meant to get a message to you but she got tied up. I should have come down."

"No, of course you had to stay with Anna." Her voice was husky with sleep. She still didn't move to invite him in.

"It's almost midnight. I wanted to spend New Year's Eve with you."

Her chin lifted. Her watery eyes met his. Had she been crying? Of course she had.

"Jake, what are we doing? Where are we going with this?"

"I don't know, but I want to find out."

"When you didn't show up tonight I had a lot of time to think."

"Okay..." He glanced at his watch.

"I'm good enough for you. My dad made mistakes. He suffered. But he was a decent man who couldn't cope with his loss."

"And he raised a strong, beautiful daughter—" he looked at his watch again "—who seems to think we need to talk when it's getting close to midnight. You don't have to convince me, Jolie. I'm not sure if I'm good enough for you."

"Jake—"

"Stop looking for a reason to send me away. We should at least enjoy the last dance and the fireworks." He took her by the hand and pushed the door closed behind them. "Will you be too cold on the balcony?"

She shook her head as he reached to open the doors. He shrugged out of his jacket and draped it around her shoulders.

"Will you dance with me, Jolie Godwin?"

She stepped into his arms as music drifted up from the ballroom. He wrapped his arms around her and after a minute she relaxed and leaned into his embrace. This had to be the most perfect moment ever with Jolie in his arms, her cheek resting against his chest.

Jolie shivered, or maybe trembled, as Jake held her. His right hand held her right hand. His left hand settled on her hip. She could smell the outdoorsy scent that seemed to be all his. Cologne and country air.

The song coming up from the ballroom played faintly, so faintly she could hear the tune but not the words. Jake pulled her closer, cradling her against him. She leaned her head against his chest and felt his lips touch the top of her head.

She could feel the rapid beat of Jake's heart. It matched her own.

"Jolie, this is perfect. I think we're perfect when we're together."

She looked up, because she needed to know that these were more than just words. She had to see it in his eyes, in his expression. And she did. She saw everything, maybe even her future, in the look on his face.

"It is perfect. But what happens tomorrow?"

"I think tomorrow we have another perfect day, together."

"And then?" She closed her eyes. "I'm sorry, I don't know what I want to hear."

He cradled her close again. "Jolie, whatever is between us is good. I don't want another year without you in my life. I want to do more than kiss you at midnight. I want to spend time with you. I want to get to know you."

"I...I want that, too."

Downstairs they could hear the countdown to midnight.

Jake held her loosely in his arms. They counted along. Ten, nine, eight, seven, six, five, four, three, two, one.

"Happy New Year, Jolie Godwin."

"Happy New Year, Jake Wild."

He bent over her and as she closed her eyes his lips touched hers, warm on her cold skin. His mouth covered hers, and she heard him moan deep in his chest as her arms circled his neck. Below, people shouted and blew horns. Jake continued to kiss her, his mouth inching from her lips to her neck, tasting her, teasing her.

"Jake," she whispered, and he must have heard it as an invitation to kiss her again.

As his lips touched hers, fireworks exploded into the night.

Jake pulled her close and her head rested on his shoulder as they watched the display of lights streak across the sky.

Jolie knew that next year they would be here together again. But she also knew that next year would be special in a different way.

*One New Year's Eve Later*

JOLIE COULDN'T BELIEVE this was her life. A New Year's Eve wedding at Wildwood Lodge, complete with several hundred guests and a few members of the media.

The ceremony would take place at seven, not on the ice rink, but next to it. Anna stood beside her, dressed in a white wool cape over a red velvet dress. She signed and Jolie answered, telling her they would walk outside in just a minute.

Cassie stood on her other side in a long, dark burgundy dress. She wiped at her eyes and shook her head.

"You are the most beautiful bride ever."

"No, you were the most beautiful bride."

"That was so six months ago. We're talking now, this moment, this wedding. Jolie, you're gorgeous."

"Thank you. And obviously, I couldn't have done it without your help."

Cassie kissed her cheek. "Of course you couldn't have. You have that red dress to thank."

The one she'd worn for New Year's Eve the previous year. Jolie laughed with her friend. "So you think it's all because of a dress you made me wear."

"You did look beautiful in it."

"Thank you, Cass. Thank you for being my friend, thank you for helping me put this wedding together. Thank you for helping me believe in myself."

"Thank me after you're married. They're playing your song."

Jolie took a deep breath as the wedding march started to play. She signed for Anna, the flower girl, and the child happily started down the candle-lined path that led to the rink. Jolie waited for Cassie to follow. She watched as her soon-to-be stepdaughter tossed rose petals. She watched as Cassie fairly waltzed down the snow-scraped walk. Christmas lights twinkled from every nearby bush and leafless tree.

She looked ahead, to the fires that would warm them, to Jake standing near a lamppost at the edge of the rink. Finally she took her first steps down the makeshift aisle toward her soon-to-be husband.

It seemed to take forever to make that walk. When

she reached him, they stood side by side facing the minister, who had red cheeks from the cold. People had warned her not to hold the ceremony outside, not on New Year's Eve. But she had been determined. Which explained the many fire pits.

Jake took her hand at the appropriate time and the minister read through the vows, a shortened version, in deference to the weather. As he finished reading, snow began to fall, beautiful, big white flakes. Jolie looked up at Jake as the minister pronounced them husband and wife.

She stood on tiptoe as he said those magic words, "You may kiss the bride."

Jake's arms went around her and, the crowd cheering, he kissed her. He kissed her as the horse-drawn carriage came up the driveway. He kissed her as fireworks, a few hours before midnight, lit the night sky.

"Happy New Year, Jolie Wild."

"Happy New Year, Jake Wild."

He kissed her again and then picked her up and carried her to the carriage that would take them to the restaurant for the reception.

Later they would make an appearance at the Wildwood New Year's Eve celebration.

And in the morning they would leave for a surprise location, somewhere warm, Jake had promised.

She snuggled in next to him in the carriage and she thought that there couldn't be any better place than by his side.

\* \* \* \* \*

*DEA agent Mia Cooper returns home to heal
her body, but her heart might need
a little help, as well.*

*Read on for a preview of
THE COWBOY LAWMAN
by Brenda Minton,
coming from Love Inspired Books
in April 2013.*

# CHAPTER ONE

How could it be a beautiful September day when nothing felt beautiful or bright? Mia Cooper stood on her porch surveying the quiet landscape of Dawson, Oklahoma. Leaves were turning, the grass had long since dried from lack of rain, and the neighborhood kids had gone back to school weeks ago. She felt alone in the world.

That shouldn't bother her. She knew how to handle loneliness. Even as a Cooper, surrounded by family, she had sometimes felt alone. She also knew how to adjust. She'd been told recently that her ability to readjust or reinvent herself were probably her strongest skills.

And her biggest weakness.

She just had to decide who she would be, now that she was back in Dawson at her mom's insistence. Okay, she admitted she had been easy to convince. She'd been ready to come home. Her apartment in Tulsa had been too quiet, too private.

She adjusted the sling that kept her right arm close to her chest, swallowed another gulp of water and jogged down the steps. She could run. She could take to the streets of Dawson, smile and wave to neighbors who might be out. She could pretend that everything would be okay.

Butch Walker was dead.

That would never change. Butch's wife, Tina, would raise two children alone. Mia would forever remember his face as he went down. She would always live with shooting too late and not being able to save him.

Her arm might ache. The possibility of not being able to go back to work hurt. But Butch gone, that hurt worse. She could take the pain of running.

She hit the pavement, taking it slow, breathing deep and easy as she lengthened her strides. She swallowed past the tightness in her throat and ignored the pain in her arm and shoulder.

*Don't ignore the pain,* her doctor had warned her after surgery a month ago. How could she ignore it? It was a constant reminder.

A car came up behind her, and she stepped to the side of the road. Her heart jumped as she glanced back to make sure it was someone she knew. In Dawson it was rare to see a stranger. Even people you didn't know well weren't considered strangers, they were just people you should get to know better.

Her brother, Jackson, pulled alongside her, the truck window slid down. She kept running. The truck idled along next to her.

"Jogging? Really?" He glanced at the empty country road ahead of them and then looked her way again.

"Yeah, I needed to get out. Alone." She smiled, but it took effort.

"Right, of course. You've never liked too many people in your business. But you have family. Mom has been trying to call you."

She slowed to a fast walk. "I'll call her."

"Today. You can't outrun this."

His big-brother voice shook her. She remembered a time when she'd been the older sister taking care of her biological siblings, making sure they ate, got dressed each day, survived. Her name then had been Mia Jimenez. And then her mother had died, and she'd become the little sister with people taking care of her. Mia Cooper. Reinvented at age seven.

She and her siblings had been separated.

"Mia, stop running."

"I'll call her." She stopped and closed her eyes, his words sinking in. She'd always been running. Always running from life, from the past, from pain.

The truck stopped next to her. "Mia, you're strong. You're going to survive this."

"I know." She blinked quickly, surprised by the sting of tears. She should have stayed in Tulsa. But as much as her family suffocated her at times, she needed them. Her mom had brought her home on Monday.

"Want a ride home?"

She shook her head and somehow looked at him, smiling as if everything was good. "No, I can make it."

"Okay, but be safe."

"I'm safe."

He smiled, nodded and shifted to drive away. Mia stood on the side of the road in a world with nothing but fields, trees and the occasional cluster of grazing cattle. A light wind blew, the way wind blew in Oklahoma, and the air smelled of drying grass and blacktop.

Jackson's truck turned a short distance ahead, but his words had opened the wound. Tears blurred her vision and her throat burned. She kept jogging. She kept pushing.

She brushed at the tears that continued to flow. It ached. It ached every minute of every day. Even in her dreams it hurt. She stopped running and looked up at the clear blue sky, at birds flying overhead.

"It hurts!" she yelled as loudly as she could. And then, more quietly, "Make it stop. Make it all go away."

There was no answer. Of course there wasn't. God had stopped listening. For some reason, He had ignored her when she pleaded for help, holding her hand on Butch's chest, trying to stop the flow of blood, crying as she told him to hold on.

She closed her eyes and slowly sank to her knees in the grass on the shoulder of the road, not caring who came by, what people said about her. It didn't matter. Why should it matter when she hadn't been able to save her partner—her friend's—life?

A car pulled up behind her. She didn't turn. She didn't want to know who had found her like this.

A door shut. Footsteps crunched on the gravel shoulder. She wiped a hand across her face and looked up at the person now standing in front of her, blocking the sun, leaving his face in shadows. He smiled a little, but his familiar dark gray eyes mirrored her sorrow. He held out a hand.

"It gets easier." His voice was gruff but soft.

"Does it?" She didn't think it would. Today it felt as if it would always hurt like this.

She took his hand.

"Yeah, it does. Is this the first cry?"

She nodded and the tears started again. He clasped

her left hand. She stood and he pulled her close in an awkward embrace. He patted her back and then stepped away, cleared his throat and looked past her.

"Let me give you a ride home."

She noticed then that he was in his uniform. He'd been a county deputy for ten years. He'd been the second officer on the scene the night his wife had died in a car accident.

"Thanks." She walked back to his car. He opened the passenger-side door for her. Before getting in she stared up at him, at the face she knew so well. She knew his gray eyes, the way his mouth was strong but turned often in an easy smile. She also knew his pain. "It feels like it might hurt forever."

"I know."

She got in and he closed the door.

THEY MADE THE TRIP BACK to Mia's in silence. Slade McKennon glanced Mia's way from time to time, but he didn't push her to talk. Their situations were different, but he knew how hard it was to talk when the grief hit, when your throat felt so tight it hurt to take a breath. He knew how hard it was to make sense of it all.

He knew how angry a person could get and how every time they opened their mouth they wanted to yell at God or cry until they couldn't cry anymore.

He pulled into her driveway and they sat there a long time, just sitting, staring at her garage in front of them. Finally, she turned to face him, her eyes still watery, rimmed with red from crying. Her dark brown hair framed her face, her normally dark skin looked a shade or two paler.

Tall and slim, athletic, she'd always been an over-achiever, the girl who thought she could do it all. And did. She'd been a star basketball player. She'd ridden barrels all the way to nationals, three times. She'd won the whole thing once.

Now she looked as broken as a person could get, but she still had *fighter* written all over her.

"Remember when Vicki used to tell you to just go ahead and cry." He smiled as he remembered his wife, her best friend. That was what time did for a person, it made the memories easier, made smiling easier.

"Yeah, she used to do that. When I broke my ankle, sprained my wrist, had a concussion. 'Cry,' she'd say." She rubbed her hand over her face. "But it didn't make sense to cry over it. Pain is an emotion."

Instead of crying Mia would just get mad. A defense mechanism he guessed from her pretty tough childhood, pre-Coopers. She reached for the door of his patrol car. He knew he wouldn't get much farther with her but he had to try.

"Mia, she would tell you to have faith."

"Don't." She opened the door and looked back at him, one foot on the paved driveway. "Don't give me the easy answers, the platitudes. It doesn't help. I can pray. I can have faith. I can believe in God to do all things. But there is one thing that won't happen."

"I know."

She closed her eyes and the tense lines of her face eased. She reached across the car for his hand and held it tight. "I know you do."

"But I promise you, those words are more than

platitudes. It doesn't feel like it right now, but it is going to get easier."

"Come in for a cup of coffee?"

Okay, she wanted to change subjects. He radioed in that he'd be out of his car but available on his cell phone. Dispatch responded, and he pulled the keys out of the ignition. Yeah, he did that every single time.

Mia saw the keys go in his pocket and she laughed. With watery eyes and red streaks where tears had made trails down her cheeks, she laughed. He smiled and shrugged; he'd take the humiliation if it made her feel better.

"A guy only makes that mistake once." He stepped out of his car.

"You know that Gage and Dylan did that to you."

"Yeah, I know."

She meant her brothers had hidden his patrol car. He'd been a deputy for two months and those two brothers of hers had spotted his car at the Convenience Counts convenience store, keys in the ignition. He'd been inside grabbing a corndog, and when he walked out, his car was gone. After fifteen minutes of searching on foot, he'd had to radio it in to dispatch. A BOLO, be on the lookout, for a police car.

Reese Cooper had come along a short time later and told Slade his car was parked at the rodeo grounds. Slade and Reese found the car just as three patrol cars zoomed in.

For several years the other deputies had called him BOLO. They still liked to bring it up from time to time.

Mia met him on the sidewalk, her smile still in evidence.

"Nighttime is the worst," she admitted as she walked up the steps to her front porch.

"I know." He had to tell her why he'd come looking for her. And he wasn't looking forward to it.

"I don't drink coffee," she said as she unlocked the door to her house.

He followed her through the living room to the kitchen. He hadn't been inside her house before today. He didn't know why. He guessed because Vicki and Mia had been best friends. But he and Mia had been friends, too. They'd grown up together. They'd trailered to rodeos together, a bunch of kids sleeping in the backs of trucks and trailers during those two-day events.

After Vicki's death, he'd been wrapped up in making his life work, in being a dad to his infant son, and Mia had taken a job on a drug task force that required undercover work.

He had to tell her why he was here.

In the kitchen, she bent to pull a coffeepot out of the cabinet. He reached to help her. She smiled a little and backed up, letting him put it on the counter.

"What are they saying about your arm?"

She ran the coffeepot under warm water and then filled it with cold water. He plugged in the machine and stepped back as she did a decent job, left-handed, of pouring water into the reservoir and then fitting a filter into the holder.

"Well, it's held together with a plate and screws. They did what they could for the damaged nerves." She looked down at her splinted wrist and shrugged. "I can start physical therapy pretty soon."

"What about your job?" He measured coffee into the filter and hit the power button.

She walked away, to the window that overlooked her small yard and the two acres of field. He'd always wondered why this place. She had her own land. Each of the Cooper kids had their hundred acres.

"I don't know about my job, Slade. The doctors say my right hand will suffer weakness because of the nerve damage." She sighed and didn't turn to face him. "I don't know who I am without that job."

"You're still Mia Cooper."

He moved a few steps and almost, *almost* put his hand on her shoulder, but he couldn't. She was a friend. She'd been Vicki's friend. She turned, smiling a sad smile.

"Slade, that's the problem. Who is Mia Cooper? For the past few years I've been everyone but the person I thought I was. I've had to pretend to be people that I never wanted to be. I've had to forget myself."

He watched the emotions play across her face, and even in that moment when she seemed to be looking for herself, she was still Mia. She was still the little sister of Reese, Travis, Jackson, the list went on. They were all friends of his. She'd been the kid sister who didn't want to stay at home with the girls. She'd wanted to do the overnight trail rides with the guys. She'd beaten them at basketball, caught bigger fish, ridden harder, played longer.

"You're still Mia. You're stronger than anyone I know. You'll find yourself."

"Stronger than you?" She smiled then, a real smile,

a flash of white in a suntanned face. "I don't think so. How's Caleb?"

"He's five now and going to preschool a few days a week. He's a chip off the old block."

"I bet he is. I haven't seen him in so long."

"Stop by sometime." He let the words slip out, easy because she was a friend.

"Yeah, I will." She walked back to the coffeepot and saw that he'd already put coffee into the filter.

"You've said that before. It would be good for him, to know you."

"I want to know him."

"I have to go pretty soon." He continued to watch her, slim shoulders straight. She nodded but didn't turn around.

"I'm good." She answered the question he hadn't yet asked.

"No, you aren't. But I'll let you pretend you are." Now he had to tell her the real reason he'd come looking for her. "Mia, Nolan Jacobs was released from jail last night.

"Mia?"

"I heard you." She faced him, anger flashing in her dark eyes. "What does that mean? He bonded out?"

"I guess so. And the charges have been reduced."

"No. Butch and I covered all of our bases. We spent six months living that filthy life, away from our families, pretending to be people we weren't. He had a way out the whole time. That's how he made us, through an inside source."

"They aren't going to drop this. They won't let you guys down that way."

She leaned against the counter, nearly as tall as he was. She held her right arm and turned to stare out the window for a long minute. Finally, she looked at him.

"What about Butch's wife? Does she know?"

"They're going to tell her." He considered letting it go, but he couldn't. "Mia, it would be best if you went out and stayed with your folks for a while. At least until they find a way to bring this guy down."

"That could take a year. It could take two years. I'm not going to live in fear of him, Slade. I'm staying right here in my house. I'm not going to let him win."

She turned and poured coffee into a thermal mug. She handed it to him.

"Thanks." Coffee. It made it seem as if nothing had happened, they weren't talking life and death. They were friends catching up on the news.

"You're welcome."

"And you know I'm going to be out here on patrol. Wherever the money is that went missing, someone is going to be looking for it."

"You're going to be watching my house? Please don't. I'll feel compelled to feed you and you know I can only cook enchiladas and boxed hamburger meals." She looked down at her arm. "And I can't even cook those right now."

"Maybe I can cook for you." The words slipped out and then hung there between them.

"Slade..."

He raised a hand to stop her objections. "Friends, Mia, that's what we've always been."

She gave him a curt nod. "Be safe out there, Slade."

"I'm always safe."

She walked with him to the front door. "Yes, I know you are. But Slade, I thought we were safe, too. I thought Butch and I would have each other's backs. I thought we'd always be able to save each other."

"You couldn't have known that you'd been made."

"I know." She stood in the front door as he got ready to leave. "Slade, what if I should have known? I keep going over it again and again in my mind, wondering if I saw something that should have given it away."

"Don't. I know that it's easy to second-guess, but it won't change anything."

He'd done it, too. He'd thought about it over and over, if he should have known what would happen that night to Vicki. He couldn't have known. He'd never seen it coming. But for a couple of years he'd beaten himself up, thinking he should have told her not to drive. He should have known there were storms coming.

He should have done something.

For a long minute he stood on Mia's front porch, thinking back. Yes, he knew how Mia felt. He knew the questions she'd been asking herself since the shooting. It took him by surprise when Mia leaned over and kissed his cheek.

"It was an accident."

He touched her arm and smiled down at her. "I know. And I'm asking you to be careful."

"I will."

"Will you be in church Sunday?"

She sighed and shook her head. "So I can yell at God in public? No, I think yelling at Him on the side of the road is enough for one week."

He nodded because he got it. "If you need anything, call me."

"I'm sure you won't be far away."

"No, I won't."

He walked down the sidewalk to his car, pulling the keys out of his pocket as he walked. He glanced back one last time before getting behind the wheel. Mia still stood in the doorway. She wouldn't cry again. He knew Mia. She would walk it off. Or jog it off. And unless people who cared pushed, she wouldn't talk about how much it hurt.

Her family would do that for her. They would push her to talk. He'd patrol and make sure she stayed safe.

*When bodyguard Arianna Jackson's life
is in danger, can she learn to let
U.S. Marshal Brody Callahan call the shots
to keep her safe?*

*Read on for a preview of
GUARDING THE WITNESS
by Margaret Daley,
coming from Love Inspired Suspense
in June 2013.*

# CHAPTER ONE

A HELICOPTER BANKED to the left and descended toward the clearing where Deputy U.S. Marshal Brody Callahan's new assignment, Arianna Jackson, was being guarded by the three marshals his team would relieve. He used his vantage point above the forest to check the area out. The cabin backed up against a medium-size mountain range on the north and west, while the south and east were bounded by a wall of spruces and other varieties of trees that stretched out for miles. A rugged land—manageable as long as the weather cooperated. It was the end of July, and it had been known to snow at that time in Alaska near the Arctic Circle. He had to be prepared for everything.

As they dropped down toward the clearing, Deputy U.S. Marshal Ted Banks came out of the cabin, staying by the door, his hand hovering near the gun in his holster. Alert. Ted was a good marshal whom he'd worked with before.

The helicopter's landing skids connected with the ground, jolting Brody slightly. Over the whirring noise of the rotors, he yelled to the pilot, "This shouldn't take long."

With duffel bags in hand, Brody jumped to the rocky earth from the door closest to the cabin, while his two partners exited from the other side. Brody ran toward Ted, still on the porch, as the wind created by the rotating blades stirred up dust.

Ted held out his hand and said in a booming voice, "Glad to see you."

"Ready to see your wife, are you?"

"Yep. I hope you've honed your Scrabble skills. This one is ruthless when it comes to the game. I'm going to brush up on my vocabulary with a dictionary before I play her again."

"I've read her file." Arianna Jackson was the star witness for the trial of Joseph Rainwater, the head of a large crime syndicate in Alaska after witnessing Rainwater killing Thomas Perkins. The man had bled out before the EMTs arrived.

"Doesn't do her justice. I don't have anything to add to my earlier phone report this morning. C'mon. I'll introduce you two." Ted nodded toward Kevin Laird and Mark Baylor, who were carrying a bag and three boxes of provisions, before Ted turned to open the door.

Brody scanned the rustic interior, noting where the few windows were located, the large fireplace against the back wall, the hallway that led to the two bedrooms and the kitchen area off the living room. His gaze connected with the witness he was to protect.

Arianna Jackson.

Tall, with white-blond hair and cool gray eyes, she looked as though she were a Nordic princess, very capable of taking care of herself from the way she carried herself, right down to the sharp perusal she gave him. From what he'd read, Ms. Jackson had been a good bodyguard caught in a bad situation. Her life would never be the same after this.

She tossed the dishtowel she held on to the kitchen counter, never taking her gaze off him. She assessed him, never indicating what she had decided about him. That piqued his interest.

"These three are our replacements—Brody Callahan, Kevin Laird and Mark Baylor. This is Arianna Jackson," Ted said, then he headed toward the door. "It's been quiet this past week except for a mama bear and her cubs."

"Good. Have you seen anyone in the area?"

"Nope, just the wildlife. We are, even in Alaska, out in the boonies," Ted said, giving him a salute. "Hope the next time I see you is in Anchorage."

Brody swung his attention to Arianna, who watched the first team leave. These assignments were intense and never easy on anyone involved. And with Ms. Jackson, the situation was even more so, because Joseph Rainwater was determined to find her and take her out. And the man had the resources and money to carry out that threat.

Her gaze linked with his. "The bedroom on the right is where you all can bunk," Ms. Jackson said in a no-nonsense voice as she rotated back to finish drying the few dishes in the drain board.

*Patience, Lord. I'm pretty sure I'm going to need every ounce of it this next week.* He was guarding a woman who was used to guarding others. He doubted she would like to follow orders when she was used to giving them.

Brody nodded to Kevin and Mark to go ahead and take their duffel bags into the room assigned to them. Then Brody covered the distance between him and Ms. Jackson. "We need to talk."

She turned her head and tilted it. "We do? Am I

going to get the lecture about not going outside, to follow all your directions?"

"No, because you guard people for a living and you know what to do. But I do have some news I thought you deserved to know."

Her body stiffening, she fully faced him, her shoulders thrust back as though she were at attention. "What?"

"Esther Perkins is missing."

ARIANNA CLENCHED HER HANDS. "No one would tell me anything about Esther other than she was being taken care of. She didn't witness the murder. She couldn't testify about it. What happened?"

"True, but Rainwater thought she might know something concerning the ledger that he interrogated Thomas about and went after her. Or rather, a couple of his men did, since Rainwater is sitting in jail. We moved her out of state while she tried to help us find that ledger long-distance."

"So the police never could locate it?"

"No. They figured it has to be important, since Rainwater killed a man over it. Usually others do his dirty work. The ledger probably details his contacts and operation. Thomas Perkins was in a position to know that."

"So how did Esther go missing? Maybe she left the program." She knew that was wishful thinking. When she'd stressed the importance of staying put, the woman always did. She'd been scared of her husband and now, knowing who the man worked for, Arianna could understand why.

"No, the Deputy U.S. Marshal running the case said it didn't look like she had. It was obvious there had been a fight. There was blood found on the carpet. It was her type."

Anger tangled with sadness and won. "She didn't have a security detail on her?"

"She was relocated thousands of miles away with a new identity."

"Then maybe you have a leak." She pivoted back to the sink, her stomach roiling with rage that a good woman was probably dead. This wouldn't have happened if they had stayed at Esther's lawyer's office for another hour or so. *Why, God?* It had tested her faith, and now with the situation with Rainwater, her doubts concerning the Lord had multiplied. Maybe it was a good time for her to change jobs.

The continued silence from Brody made her slant a look over her shoulder. A frown slashed across his face, the first sign of an emotion from him.

His gaze roped hers. "It's more likely Esther contacted someone when she shouldn't. Let it slip where she was. We've never lost a witness *if* they followed the rules."

"Take it from me. This isn't easy to do. Walk away from everyone you know and start a new life. I can't even call my mother or anyone else in my past." She'd always called her mom at least once a week to make sure everything was going all right, wishing and hoping that one of those times her father would talk with her. He never had, which broke her heart each time. Not being able to at least talk with her mom added heartache on top of everything else.

"All I can tell you is that the U.S. Marshal's Service is doing everything they can to locate Mrs. Perkins."

*Dead or alive.* She closed her eyes, weariness attacking

her from all sides. Since coming to the cabin, she hadn't slept much except for a few hours here and there. The marshals had moved her from Anchorage because they'd worried the safe house had been compromised. If that place had been, why not this one?

That question plagued her every waking moment. It was hard to rest when she didn't know the people involved in her protection. When she did lie down, she managed to catch some sleep because she had her gun with her. She'd brought extra money, a switchblade and her gun without the marshals' knowledge. In case something went down, she wanted to be prepared. That was the only way she would agree to all of this. She would see to her own protection. She didn't trust anyone but herself to keep her alive.

She turned toward the marshal, appreciating what her clients must have felt when she'd guarded them and told them what to do. "Promise me you'll let me know if you all find Esther. She was my client. I feel responsible for her."

"You did everything you could. If you hadn't been there, she would have been dead next to her husband."

"And now she may be dead, her body somewhere no one has found yet. May never find."

"Yes," Callahan said over the sound of the helicopter taking off.

The blunt reality of what might have happened to Esther, and could still happen to her, hung in the air. Arianna went back to drying the lunch dishes; anything to keep her occupied. If this inactivity didn't end soon, she might go screaming through the woods.

Mark Baylor, the oldest of the three marshals, strode to the door. "I'm gonna take a stroll around the perimeter."

"Do you need any help?" The deep, husky voice of the marshal who seemed to be in charge, Brody Callahan, broke into her thoughts.

"With cleaning up?" she asked, surprised by the question.

"Yes."

She glanced back at him. He was taller by six inches—and she was five feet eleven. Callahan carried himself with confidence, which did, in its own way, ease her anxiety about her situation. His appearance, his broad, muscular chest, and not an ounce of fat on him, spoke of a man who kept himself in shape. "I've got it under control." *About the only thing in my life that is.*

"We share the duties equally while we're here."

"That's good to know. I don't cook."

"You don't?"

She finished drying the last plate. "Never had a reason to learn. I went from living at home with my family to the army. Then, when I started working for Guardians, Inc., I found myself on assignment most of the time with wealthy clients who had cooks." She shrugged. "The short amount of time I was in Dallas I ate out or ate frozen dinners."

"That's okay. I love to cook." Kevin Laird, a young deputy probably not long in the U.S. Marshals Service, came into the living room.

Callahan chuckled. "That's why I like to team up with Kevin when I can. He can make the most boring food taste decent."

"Good." Arianna moved out of the kitchen area,

trying to decide what she should do next. A crossword puzzle or solitaire? She still had at least fifty varieties to work her way through. Just the thought heightened her boredom level to critical.

She began to pace from one of the few windows to the cold hearth. She counted her steps, mentally mapping out an escape route if she needed it. "This is a park ranger's cabin. Where's the guy that usually stays here?"

"On an extended vacation." Callahan prowled the living room in a different direction from her.

"Does he know we're using it?" She peeked out the window.

"No, the cabin belongs to the park service. No one knows you're here or that the U.S. Marshals Service is using it to protect a witness. They think we're here on vacation." Brody parted the drapes and looked out the only other window in the room.

"That would kinda defeat the purpose, if we let the park service know we're using it. A bogus agency has rented it while the park ranger is gone." Laird, the youngest deputy, tall and gangly, checked out the kitchen supplies.

"When's he due back?" Arianna spied a bull moose in the thick of the trees. Seeing the beautiful animals was the one thrill in being where she was. She loved animals, but because of her job she didn't have any—not even a goldfish.

"Not for two more weeks. Do you see it?" Callahan's gaze captured hers.

"He's beautiful. I wish I could go outside and take a picture of the moose. I took the Perkins assignment because it was in Alaska. After I finished guarding Esther, I was going to do some touring of the countryside up here. The most exciting thing that's happened to me this week was the helicopter ride to this cabin. Breathtaking scenery."

"Don't even think about going outside to snap a picture."

She held up her hands, palms outward. "I thought you said I knew the drill and didn't need to hear your spiel."

"I've changed my mind. You sound like a bored witness. That kind can do things to get themselves killed."

"I am bored. How in the world do you do this, job after job?"

"I'm on an assignment to keep you safe. I can't let down my guard ever. You should know what that means."

His intense, dark brown eyes drilling into her exemplified a person she should be able to identify with if she stopped feeling sorry for herself—something she rarely did. But she hated change more than she realized. She now had to get to know her three new guards, and she still couldn't shake the thought that her safe house in Anchorage might have been compromised. She'd feel better if two of the female bodyguards from Guardians, Inc. were here with her, instead.

"How about chess?" Kevin asked from the kitchen area.

"I don't play it. Where are you going?" she asked Callahan as he opened the door.

"Outside. I'm relieving Mark."

"But he just left."

"Yeah, I know."

"Can I come with you?" she asked.

He frowned and left, the door slamming shut.

"Ms. Jackson, I can teach you the game. It'll take your mind off what's going on." Kevin moved into the main part of the room.

"Nothing is going on. That's the problem." She strode toward the table and took a chair. "Sure. I might as well learn how to play chess." It was going to be another long day.

FINISHING HIS LAST TRIP around the perimeter of the cabin, Brody took a deep breath of the fresh air then mounted the steps to the porch.

When he reached the door to the ranger's cabin, he scanned the small clearing. Nearing midnight, it was still light outside. The temperature began to drop as the sun finally started its descent.

Inside the cabin, he found Arianna sitting on the couch, staring at him. Her gray eyes with a hint of blue reminded him of the lake he'd flown over this morning.

"Did you see the mama bear that's been hanging around the cabin lately?" she asked.

"No. Where's Kevin?"

"Right here. Sorry. I figured I needed a jacket since the sun was going down." Kevin picked up the shotgun and exited the cabin.

"So it's just you and me, since Mark is taking his turn sleeping."

For a second he thought he saw a teasing gleam in her eyes before she averted her gaze to study the spread of cards on the coffee table in front of her. He sat in a chair across from her. "Have you won any games?"

"Two, probably, out of fifty." She raised her head. "Wanna play Scrabble?"

"I've been warned about you and Scrabble."

"I took you for a man who likes a good challenge." A full-fledged smile encompassed her whole face.

"You're on. Where's the game?"

Arianna gestured toward the bookcase behind him. "I don't know what I would have done without the games. I brought a deck of cards and some books, but I went through them in the first four days and I'm sick of playing solitaire. Do you have any idea when I'll get to testify and can move back to civilization?"

"No. Rainwater's attorney gets big bucks to delay the trial as along as he can."

"Because he's got people out there looking for me."

"Yes, you know the score. If you testify, he'll most likely go down for murder. Without finding the ledger Rainwater killed Perkins over, you're the main witness in his trial. Without you, no trial."

"Something very incriminating must be in the ledger Rainwater was looking for. He's gone to great lengths to find it. I'm even more determined to testify."

"And he's as determined to stop you." Brody retrieved the Scrabble game, then laid it out on the coffee table. Then he pulled his chair closer. "Ready to get trounced?"

Forty minutes later it was confirmed. She was *very good* at Scrabble.

"What do you do? Study the dictionary?"

"Don't have to. I have a photographic memory. Once I see it, I remember it."

"So that's why you could give such a detailed

description of what went down the day Thomas Perkins was murdered."

"The gift has helped me in my job. When I go on a new assignment, I case the house or wherever I'm staying with the client so I can pull up the layout in a hurry in my mind. It has helped me on more than one occasion, especially in the dark." She began putting the game back into the box.

"I do something similar although I don't have a photographic memory."

Arianna yawned. "I'd better call it a night and try to sleep."

"Are you having problems sleeping?"

"Yes. Wouldn't you, with all that's been going on?"

"We're guarding you. You don't have to be alert and on the job."

"Actually it's too quiet out."

"I grew up in New York City. The first few years after I left were hard. Now I love it here. My house is outside Anchorage where it's—"

A blast from a shotgun exploded in the air.

As Arianna dove over the back of the sofa, he moved toward the door. Another gunshot reverberated through the quiet.

Mark rushed out of the hallway, weapon drawn. "What's going on?"

"Stay with Ms. Jackson. I'm checking."

Suddenly a rattling at the window screen diverted Brody toward it. A roar split the air as he opened the blinds to find a grizzly bear attacking the window. The screen hung in metal shreds from its frame. The huge animal batted it away, only a pane of glass now between him and the bear.

"Stay put, Arianna." Brody signaled for Mark to keep an eye on the window where the bear was.

Brody charged toward the exit, knowing his Glock might not be enough to stop a bear coming at him or Kevin. In the gray light of an Alaskan night, he saw his partner backing around the corner of the cabin while squeezing off another shot into the air.

"I'm behind you, Kevin." Brody approached him.

The tense set to his partner's body relaxed. "She's leaving. Finally. When I was making my rounds, two cubs came out of the woods. Mama Bear followed not five seconds later. I tried not to show any fear and backed away. She came toward me—not charging, but making sure she was between her cubs and me. When I fired my first warning shot in the air, both of the cubs ran into the woods. She didn't."

Kevin kept his gaze fixed on the departing bear while Brody watched the front of the cabin. When the threat disappeared into the woods, they both headed for the porch.

"I'll be turning in soon. Mark will be on duty in the cabin. I'll relieve you in five hours." When Brody reentered the cabin, Arianna stood behind the couch. "What part of 'get down' do you not understand?"

"The last order you gave me was 'stay put.'" She pointed to the floor. "I stayed put. Besides, Mark was here."

Brody shook his head. "I guess I'll have to spell it out for you next time."

"There's gonna be a next time?"

"If she's hungry enough or we threaten her cubs."

Mark interjected, "I'm going back to bed for the time I have left. I'll leave you two to hash things out."

As Mark left, Arianna said, "After this job, I was going to take a vacation and see some of the wildlife. I don't think that's going to work out." Another yawn escaped her. "That's my cue to say good-night."

"Good night. Mark will be back in here—" he checked his watch "—in an hour."

"Sleep tight then."

"Don't you mean sleep light? After all, I am guarding you."

"Every bodyguard has to grab some good sleep if he or she is going to do a good job. And believe me, I want you to do a good job protecting me."

He studied her body language as she said those words. "I think you believe what you said, but you also believe you can take care of yourself."

She smirked. "I'm gonna have to work on fooling you better."

"No one, not even myself, is invincible and doesn't need help from time to time."

"And who do you turn to?"

"God and my partner on the job. In that order."

Her eyes widened for a second before she rotated toward the hallway and headed for her bedroom.

Brody watched her leave, flashes of his own questioning of God's intention going through his mind. It had been an assignment he'd been the lead marshal on when he'd been working in Los Angeles. The witness he had been guarding had been gunned down on the way to the courthouse because the man had a cell phone in his pocket that had been used to track his movements.

Brody shook the memory from his mind. That was the past. He couldn't change it, but he could learn from it. He wasn't going to lose another witness, even if that person did something to put his—or her—life in jeopardy.

When Mark relieved him later, Brody strode toward his bedroom. His glance strayed to Arianna's closed door. An interesting woman whose life would never be the same. How would *he* deal with giving up all he knew and starting over?

HER EARLIER ADRENALINE RUSH finally subsiding, Arianna removed her Glock from under the mattress and put it on the bedside table by her within easy reach. That was the only way she would be able to get any kind of sleep. When she lay down and closed her eyes, the image of Brody Callahan popped onto the screen of her mind.

Sleep faded the picture of her and Brody facing each other over the Scrabble board and whisked her into a dream world that evolved into a nightmare she hadn't had in a year—one where she was shoved into a jail cell. As she tried to rush out, the door slammed shut.

The noise jerked her awake. Her eyelids flew open. Silence greeted her and calmed her racing heart.

Until she heard a muffled thud—like a gun silencer being used.